HACHIMAN TARO

HACHIMAN TARO

FIRSTBORN OF THE GOD OF WAR

NED GREENWOOD

Tate Publishing & Enterprises

Published by Tate Publishing & Enterprises, LLC
127 E. Trade Center Terrace | Mustang, Oklahoma 73064 USA
1.888.361.9473 | www.tatepublishing.com

Tate Publishing is committed to excellence in the publishing industry. The company reflects the philosophy established by the founders, based on Psalm 68:11,
"The Lord gave the word and great was the company of those who published it."

Book design copyright © 2011 by Tate Publishing, LLC. All rights reserved.
Cover design by Leah LeFlore
Interior design by Sarah Kirchen

Published in the United States of America

ISBN: 978-1-61777-532-1
1. Fiction / Action & Adventure
2. Fiction / Historical
11.05.24

This book is dedicated to Alverta
who spent as many hours as I did in reaching this goal.

TABLE OF CONTENTS

ORDEAL IN
ROCK CANYON

Gungnir Ragnvold came to briefly, aroused by the sound of a starting motor. It echoed in the dark canyon. With considerable effort, he raised and turned his head. He could see a faint violet glow. *Was that from the lynx-eye tail lights on my '48 Ford coupe?* Then it was gone. The effort was too much.

The pre-dawn chill hung over the depths of Rock Canyon. High above, the first shaft of sunlight had only now impaled the turret of Squaw Peak with its golden ambience. The fogged mind of Gun Ragnvold reluctantly accepted the throbbing pain and stiffness in his neck and shoulder. Still, he was unable to ascertain his whereabouts.

All settlement along the front-range of the Wasatch Mountains was in the valleys below. Instinctively, he knew that the next move had to be downward, before loss of blood and unadulterated sunlight made him too weak to travel. The thirst that now parched his throat would only grow worse. A jagged laceration in his shoulder was bleeding profusely. Though his mind was seemingly numb, he sensed the need to stanch that flow. With painful effort, he ripped pieces from the tattered remnants of his shirt, crudely binding them to apply pressure on the wound. Even so, some bleeding continued. Now it was a question of finding help as quickly as possible.

He shivered from the shaded coolness, but his mind was beginning to clear. Even as he stumbled over the boulders and attempted to avoid the pitfalls of the dry torrent-bed, there was a realization that he needed to recall as much as possible about the assault. *Oriental strangers. Tall one with hooked nose and a heavy five o'clock shadow. He wore black and attacked from a martial art stance. Was he the leader? There was a smaller man, perhaps an assistant, who always seemed to be in my peripheral vision? Think! Focus on the front man. What did Ragnor say about a Brutal Bird? Was it he who forced my car off the road in Spanish Fork Canyon? Did I have one or both nippon-to in the car? Did the Japs find them? How much did I tell them?*

The effort was too much. Gungnir blacked out on Canyon Road, still not knowing where he was.

WATANABE

Watanabe Hattori was in a truculent mood. He kicked un-emptied bed pans and slop jars in every direction as he stomped through the invalid ward of the Shinagawa POW Hospital where he was the ranking noncom prison guard. The sight of such weaklings was infuriating. *These nyu-jakuna should have committed ritual suicide while they were still capable,* he thought. He kicked another waste jar. It was fuller than expected. Human waste slopped over the kicking foot, soiling boot and trouser bottom. He grabbed the nearest human target on which to vent his anger. It was an utterly helpless, ninety-seven pounder, suffering from the bloody flux, with chronic diarrhea and uncontrollable vomiting.

All too late he realized his mistake. Fetid vomit covered his hands and lower arms. He threw the helpless prisoner to the slatted floor. Stepping back, he delivered a brutal kick into the lower ribcage. The now unconscious POW moaned softly. He would not survive.

Δ

Watanabe reveled in the POW's fear of him. They even had a name for him—"Brutal Bird." He took it to mean, "Eagle." They probably thought more in terms of "Vulture." His beak-like nose may well have applied to either bird.

The Bird also thought of himself as nascent Samurai, though the officer corps of the Imperial Army would have been more apt to perceive a night-soil collecting peasant best suited to gathering the offal of the warrior class. This class snobbery deprived the Imperial Military of a dedicated warrior and relegated Watanabe to onerous service in the Home Force and ultimately POW guard duty. Completely ignored were some highly useful characteristics. He was tenacious in a single-minded way. He was also totally fearless, wholly believing the Samurai aphorism, "Death will be light as a feather." He would have wholeheartedly laid his life on the line for the Divine Emperor of the Showa–Era of Bright Peace, Yamato Hirohito. Everyone who knew the Bird considered him a prime candidate for ritual suicide once Japan surrendered to Allied Forces.

It was exactly one week prior to imperial acceptance of "unconditional" surrender that an agent of a secret society approached Watanabe. "Are you the one the cowardly American POWs call the Brutal Bird?"

It had been a dismal week. B29s had continued to hammer south central Japan, particularly the cities surrounding Tokyo Wan, the bay. This morning's incident with the POW suffering from chronic dysentery had left him in a foul mood. The Bird had slipped out to a local *saki* house, hoping to bolster his spirit before returning to the guard quarters adjacent to the Shinagawa POW Hospital.

He was uncertain whether to take offense at the stranger or to show more circumspection. *These are perilous times*, he thought. *The man's speech seems indicative of a class better educated than my own, perhaps Samurai, that is if such a thing still exists in Japan. Best to answer with care.*

"Honorable Watanabe," the stranger continued, "I represent the Showa Brotherhood and would like to speak with you on a matter of importance. Our agents have checked out your background and are aware of the reprehensible way the Imperial Army has treated a loyal Son of Nippon. We are pleased to offer you membership in our brotherhood. I am confident that you will find fulfillment in its goals as well as sustenance from within its esoteric fraternity."

Watanabe silently flinched. The stilted advocacy made him uneasy, but he knew his reply would not be required immediately. He held his peace. He had heard of a secret society called "Showa," but knew next to nothing about it. At the same time the thought of believable goals and group acceptance in a tight brotherhood were seductive, especially in this present time of harsh uncertainty. Watanabe considered the ramifications of a positive answer, knowing that his acceptance or rejection would not be required or even accepted at this time.

The agent continued, "As you know, in one way or another Japan will soon surrender. The terms of that surrender will undoubtedly be unconditional. Showa leaders believe that the Americans will demand complete demobilization of the Imperial Military, including a purge of military officers from the government, disestablishment of State

Shinto, and total disarmament, possibly including Shinto Temple Swords. One of the prime objectives of Showa is to remove all National Treasure Swords from Japan for safe keeping.

"If you join us, you will be expected to attend instructions on the history of sword making, the role of art swords in Shinto Culture, and an intensive training in *Koryu*, the martial art of Fighting in the Spirit."

With the mention of martial arts, Watanabe's face grew hard, thinking of his demeaning experience at the hand of Hanare Masahiro. He thought, *I will be their star pupil.*

The Showa agent said, "The instructions mentioned are mandatory. Most likely, you will never know your instructors' real names or ever see them again following the completion of each line of study. Likewise, you will probably never know the identity of the national leaders. For now, our most important role is the acquisition of National Treasure Swords, to get them out of Japan and away from the demolition furnaces.

"You will have five days to consider our offer. On the evening of the fifth day, we will meet here. If your answer is negative, we shall not meet again. If positive, you will be required to swear a blood oath on your devotion to the Divine Emperor, and your willingness to advance the goals of Showa. With your acceptance, you will then receive your first assignment."

Watanabe already knew the answer, but the formality of acceptance into a secret brotherhood required a cooling off period, a time for reflection and reconsideration.

SHINAGAWA, JAPAN

9 August 1945

A second nuclear device was dropped at Hiroshima. One day later, Japan let it be known they planned to surrender, and Swiss Red Cross Workers were admitted into the Shinagawa POW Hospital and the adjacent Omori-ku POW Camp, now called the Tokyo Main Camp. They informed the prisoners that atomic bombs had been dropped on Nagasaki and Hiroshima, and they might expect surrender shortly. But the acceptance of the unconditional status did not come until the fourteenth. Only then was an Allied cease-fire ordered. The Island Nation was surely becoming Kuraitani—a Valley of Despair.

Initial occupation by Allied Forces required another eighteen days to accomplish. During that period, carrier planes continued to actively patrol Japanese air space, fully expecting a Japanese backlash. Meanwhile, American and Allied POWs were beginning to be evacuated from the brutal prisons and slave labor camps. The liberators were shocked at the condition of the evacuees. The sight of a six-foot man weighing as little as eighty pounds was most disheartening. Only later would they learn that mortality rates of POWs in Japan were twenty-seven percent compared to four percent in Germany. Many would blame this on *Bushido,* the warrior code of the *Samurai.*

The Supreme Commander of Allied Powers (SCAP) was becoming paranoid. With the Japanese surrender, he moved rapidly to demolish the principal supports of the militaristic state. Japanese armed forces were demobilized and military overlords theoretically purged from governing positions. State Shintoism was disenfranchised in an effort to wipe out the influence of Bushido.

Destruction of military arms was ordered. "Every weapon, every sword." Out went the jeeps; collecting every worn-out Arisaka Rifle and rusting Shin Gunto Blade the military police could scrounge up in the process of satisfying SCAP's demand. This resulted in the destruction of some three million swords. Forty-two documented National Treasure Swords, *Kokuho,* most made between the twelfth and fifteenth centuries, were included in that loss. Yet some 289,000 blades were brought to the United States by GIs following World War II. These were mostly *Shin Gunto,* New Army Swords manufactured during the 1930s and 1940s, but the roundup included many of the older, more valuable pieces.

KEPPEN

12 August 1945

Watanabe sipped his saki as he waited for Roku. But Number Six was in no apparent hurry. Even after Watanabe's affirmative answer, Roku took his time, "The organization of the Showa Brotherhood is built around small autonomous units, 'secret cells,' if you like. Each cell usually has no more than eight individuals plus their contact person. In your case I am that contact. In reality I am more than just a contact, I will be your cell's control person and at this point your soul contact with the brotherhood. I serve as control to other cells, but at this time I am not at liberty to say more. As you advance in the brotherhood, you will learn more, on a need to know basis. For any organization that gathers and utilizes classified intelligence, 'need to know' is the basis of compartmentalized security. For that very reason no general meeting will ever be held.

"As I mentioned in our previous meeting, you will receive instruction on various aspects of sword culture as well as training in the martial art of Koryu.

Watanabe yawned as he approached the edge of boredom. *Why doesn't he get on with the program?*

Rather abruptly Roku was all business. "Now Comrade Watanabe, it is important that you understand the gravity of a blood oath. It is a *keppen* that exerts the utmost control on your dealings within the brotherhood. If you harbor any reservations now is the time to cut and run." The Bird shook his head in firm denial.

Roku spoke softly but firmly, "As I administer the blood oath it is important that you grasp and assent to each point made therein. I will speak slowly and pause with each salient point for your repetition and a nod signifying that you agree and accept. If you cannot accept any provision, the oath will be nullified. You will repeat neither more nor less than that which is offered you. To initiate your familiarization, I will first repeat the oath without the acceptance breaks. 'I, Watanabe Hattori do fully pledge my life and my service to Showa, a brotherhood dedicated to the rightful succession of the Emperor Hirohito, Son of Heaven. Additionally I promise my unflagging efforts to the acquisition and preservation of Shinto Temple Swords to the greater honor and glory of the Showa Brotherhood. I further swear to maintain the secrets of Koryu, the Art of Fighting in the Spirit. Rather than reveal any of these secrets, I would suffer my life be taken from me or that I will commit seppuku. In testament of this and of my own free will, I hereby sign this keppen with my own blood, my oath of allegiance."

Roku was pleased that Watanabe scarcely hesitated during the swearing and when Roku offered him a lancet to draw the blood for his signature, he quickly pulled a tanto from his waistband jamming the point into his little finger. There was more than enough blood to form the complex figures of his name. In fact it would have satisfied the pigment requirements for an ornamental plaque done with broad brush calligraphy.

Acceptance of the keppen by Watanabe might well have been a retainer pledge with a wealthy lord of the ancient Kamakura Regime. The roots of Watanabe's peasant origins seemed to fall away. *I am Samurai,* he thought.

Number Six reinforced this heady conclusion. "From now on, among the Showa brothers you will no longer be Watanabe Hattori, but Watanabe SJ-1, for *Senguku-ji-1.* Even though I have already recruited other members for the Senguku-ji Cell, you will be the lead man—the Kazu Ichi—the big Number One—the SJ-1.

"Now for your first assignment and the source of the cell name just given to you, the Senguku-ji Temple in Shinagawa, has two of Japan's most important temple swords among its votive materials. First, a *Masamune Goro* blade of katana pattern—its name is "Fiery Blade of the Enduring Comet." It will be readily recognizable by the glowing structure in its *nie* temper line. Such luminous patterns are found only on Masamune blades.

Second is a blade named *Hachiman Taro*—"Firstborn of the God of War." It was the work of *Muramasa Sengo,* the wizard sword-smith, considered by some to be greater than Masamune. But in my opinion, this is doubtful."

Here, the mind of Watanabe SJ-1 wandered. *That's the blade my father took from the seppuku wound of Lieutenant Tokugawa Hattori, my namesake.* He was tempted to reveal the fact to Number Six. But life had taught him to keep his own council.

"Now Watanabe SJ-1, you have one overriding purpose—to find these nippon-to and deliver them to SJ-2, who will make himself known to you in due time. We believe that the *Johkai* Priest of Sengaku-ji with the help of Yoshida Nobu and Hanare Masahiro have already placed these swords in hiding."

The mention of this last name caused an involuntary tensing with SJ-1. But if Roku noticed, he chose to ignore it, continuing with his instructions. "You will leave your job as POW guard and devote your time to discovering the whereabouts of the Nippon-to. The Showa will provide for your sustenance."

Number Six handed him a beautifully decorated wallet of heavy rice paper lined with scarlet silk. "Here are six months of your pay. We will, from time to time, augment this with black-market goods like chocolate bars, American cigarettes, and even whiskey. These you will be able to trade at your own discretion.

"But be cautious. Both Yoshida and Hanare are potentially formidable adversaries. Make your moves with utmost caution and stealth."

THE SINKING SHIP

14 August 1945

Two days after the meeting with Roku, Japan agreed to unconditional surrender. Following a frugal lunch of rice, a sweet potato cake, and tea, Watanabe SJ-1 made up a small bundle in his best and only jacket. It contained a short tanto, a 9 mm Baby Nambu with six cartridges, his father's Russian Campaign Medal, still in the original case, plus rice crackers and dried fish in waxed wrappings.

Sergeant Blaz Carvajal saw him slip out of the POW hospital, but the orderly's only thought was, *Just another vicious rat deserting the floundering ship*.

In early August Japanese guards had detailed POWs to paint large "P W" on some of the more visible rooftops. This was the first direct hint the POWs had that the war might be drawing to a close. Then the ranking command officers, the doctors, and the more brutal non-com guards began disappearing from the POW Hospital.

By 14 August, only a few of the more humane guards remained with the POWs. Later that day, the intent to surrender was announced.

Δ

Meanwhile, the USS *Benevolence AH* 14 had been steaming north along the confluence of the Philippine Sea and the Western Pacific. They took care to maintain convoy with the fighting ships and carriers also bound for rendezvous off the south coast of central Japan. This was to have been it, the long-awaited invasion of the home islands, code name "Operation Downfall." However, the apparent intent of Japan to surrender had hopefully changed everything.

Still they had been doubly careful since a *Tokkotai*, a suicide pilot of the Divine Wind, had hurtled into a hospital ship, the USS *Comfort*, back in April, killing twenty-nine and wounding thirty-four, while doing great damage to the hull and superstructure. It would be a slow run, since final rendezvous was not scheduled until 20 August.

THE BRIEFING

14 August 1945

It was a surprise when Commander S. J. Hurlbert, XO and Ops Officer for the *Benevolence*, called a briefing session for the medical staff. "The Japanese high command has accepted the terms of 'unconditional' surrender as of today. This is certainly a welcome bit of serendipity and should save thousands of lives on both sides of the conflict. However, we are now faced with a difficult and immediate concern: the likelihood of reprisals against Allied prisoners under Japanese control.

To the man seated on his right, PO First Class Ragnor Ragnvold whispered, "I hope he isn't overly optimistic. Another killing field like we worked in on Iwo Jima might be more than I can accommodate. I saw too many young Marines shed their blood and body parts in that inferno. The youthful manhood of America was sorely wasted on that pile of rocks and cinders."

The other corpsman replied, "Not to worry my friend, I'm sure the blood and scattered young flesh will be overshadowed by the vomit, feculence and stench from the worn-out bodies and sour stomachs of our fellow country-men." Ragnor grimaced but remained silent in acquiescence.

Hurlbert stared right at them. Neither would dare converse again. The XO continued, "According to our best intelligence, some 9,000 POWs are held in the Tokyo area. However, our immediate concern is the Omori Main Camp and the adjacent Shinagawa Hospital. There are several reasons for this concern. First, Omori is the headquarters for the camp system, and we need to obtain the internment records kept there. Second, and most importantly, Omori is rumored to be the holding tank for the 'Bad Actor' POWs who have given their captors the most trouble. We had feared that reprisals on these men would result in thousands being slaughtered when the invasion began. Now we are concerned that the 'unconditional' surrender may stimulate the same kind of result." This reminded Ragnor of his brother who was a POW in the Philippines. He thought, *I'll just bet old Jubal was one of the "Bad Actors" at the Cabañatua Labor Camp.*

"A related problem, third point, the Shinagawa Hospital is the only medical facility for the 9,000 Allied prisoners in this area. The fear in this regard is *Bushido*, the code of the Samurai, as interpreted by Tojo and his cronies. This holds that all prisoners are weak in that they should have committed ritual suicide instead of surrendering. Furthermore, those needing medical attention are considered the weakest of the weak and should be eliminated for the benefit of the strong. Thus, we fear that the heaviest reprisals against Allied POWs is likely to occur in the Omori and Shinagawa areas.

"Our access to POW camps will be difficult because of the failed infrastructure of a nation now on its knees. This past week, B-29s with 'PW Supplies' painted on their under wings began dropping food, blankets, clothing, and medical supplies into many camps. These were low elevation flights, barely above 1,000 feet to maximize the accuracy of the drops.

Commander Hurlbert continued to pace the deck, knowing that these medics needed to be assembling gear and making final preparations to leave the ship, but there were tactical matters that needed to be dealt with. He said, "Even though the war is technically over, we still lack the ability to protect most POWs, so we are sending in an advance medical group, supported by four squads of Marines to provide immediate aid. We have four fast torpedo boats standing by to take you ashore, well in advance of the main battle fleet. These are seventy foot Higgins Boats, each powered by three 1,850 horsepower Packard V-12 engines. These boats have all been modified for high-speed missions. Six of the eight torpedo tubes have been removed from each boat. However the 20 mm Oerlikon Cannon and the two M2 .50 caliber machine guns have been retained for defensive action, if needed. All boats are equipped with Ratheon SO Radar, enabling them to operate at night.

"Operational crews of three officers and fourteen seamen have been reduced to a total of nine per boat. These streamlining measures will provide some additional space for evacuees, as well as increased operational speeds to above fifty knots. So depending upon weather and obstacles, they should get you on the dock in three or four hours from departure.

"Petty Officer, First Class Ragnor Ragnvold will be in charge of the medical contingent of eight corpsmen. The Swiss Red Cross Mission that visited Shinagawa on 10 August has reported that an army POW medic, Staff Sergeant Blaz Carvajal, is doing an excellent job of holding the hospital patients together. So Mr. Ragnvold, you will report to Carvajal and aid him in every way possible. Your first consideration, in consultation with Sargent Carvajal, will be to evaluate the patients to determine if any might benefit by immediate removal to the *Benevolence*. Keep in mind that the trip back on board the Higgins Boats is apt to be a tough one, so stabilizing on site may be a better option. I also want you and your crew to examine existing facilities to determine if it would be desirable or even feasible to upgrade them for our use in the coming occupation.

"Lastly, there is the pragmatic factor of movement once we anchor. The Tokyo infrastructure is chaotic. Most streets, canals, and coastal waters are largely impassable, so you might consider how best to move boats between the shattered dock areas and suitable anchorages in Shinagawa Bay. Even so, the movement of evacuees to the ships will require a complex lighterage between the docks and USS *Benevolence* or USS *Reeves*. Any questions?"

Ragnor raised his hand. "Sir, what are our orders regarding Japanese military personal? And if we should find it necessary to evacuate some POWs, what shelter can the Higgins Boats provide?"

"I abhor compound questions Mr. Ragnvold, but to answer the first part, the Jap medical officer, Tokuda Hisakichi, and Watanabe Hattori, the PO in charge of guards, as well as the more brutal staff personnel, began leaving the hospital a couple of days before the Red Cross team was allowed into the camp. Nevertheless, the Marine support group has been advised to arrest Tokuda and Watanabe for possible prosecution for war crimes, should opportunity provide. As for the second part of your question, almost all the shelter available for the evacuees will have to be provided by rigging canvas on the afterdecks of the PT boats. That in itself must be considered in your decision.

"The Marines have already been briefed and are now assembling arms, rations, and field gear for up to a week without resupply. Master Sergeant Bill Haynes is in charge of combat support under your directions. Sergeant Haynes and one squad will go with you and two medics on PT 309, the lead boat. The other boats will have similar compliments of medical and combat personnel.

"Each combat squad will be armed with .30 caliber M1 carbines, augmented with one Browning automatic rifle. Each medic will carry a .45 caliber 1911 A1 and an extra clip of ammo. The Marines will bring additional ammo. My concern here is that the medics must be free to carry as much medical gear as possible to cover anticipated contingencies. The squad on your boat will remain at the hospital with you for protection and to aid with the weak and injured. The remaining combat personnel will proceed with Sargent Haynes to secure the Omori Compound.

"We are uncertain what the Swiss Red Cross was able to leave, so take ample surgical gear, morphine, and sulfa drugs. Assemble your men and gear at the aft gang for a 2400 departure. That should put you on the Omori Dock before daylight.

"Shinagawa POW Hospital is almost a euphemism for holding tank where the moribund awaited their turn at the crematorium, while undergoing the surgical ineptitude and brutal experimentation with intravenous injections by Tokuda Hisakichi. These ranged from sulfuric acid to heavy castor oil. According to Swiss medics, the records seemed to show a hundred percent mortality rate for those patients. When Allied bombing destroyed the crematorium, other prisoners were forced to burn the cadavers on spits over open fires.

"Many POWs from here and the greater Tokyo area will be evacuated via the nearby Asano Docks. This is where the giant Mitsubishi Corporation once loaded their slave labor forces, obtained from Allied prisoners. Mitsubishi is a *zaibatsu,* a company that made handsome profits providing war goods and services with minimal labor costs. They even supplied ties for the Thai-Burma Railway with its Bridge over the River Kwai that proved so difficult for our bombers to take out. For such cause, SCAP has prohibited this company from doing business in occupied Japan."

OMORI DOCK

They had been cruising for over four hours. There was a definite chop in the *Izu Shichito*, but this had subsided to a murmur as they moved into the more protected waters of *Sagami Nada*. The PT 309 skipper was careful to avoid anything that might be a hazard to the wooded hulled boats. Here the Raytheon Radar proved invaluable.

There was no obvious traffic. The Asano Dock was deserted. The four Higgins Boats were able to tie up to a floating ramp, which gave access to the 200-meter long bridge connecting the manmade island of Omori to the Omori Station on the west shore.

Sergeant Haynes led Squad 1 up the ramp and onto the large dock. The automatic rifleman set-up on a high platform which provided some cover and a place for his bipod. Two infantrymen took up positions on either side of the automatic rifle, while the remainder of the squad began to off load ammo and other supplies.

Ragnor went back to PT 309 to consult with the Lieutenant Junior Grade in command. "I am taking all the medics, except two with me to the hospital. One squad of marines will also go to the hospital. We will take as much equipment and supplies as we can manage. The marines with me will have a two-way radio and will monitor channel five. If you need to put to sea, let us know. Otherwise, I would appreciate it if you can wait here until we have time to evaluate conditions at the hospital. I will call you as soon as I have had opportunity to consult with Sergeant Carvajal."

It was barely full daylight when they reached the hospital, but Sergeant Carvajal and some of the less fragile patients had already gathered at the entrance to honor them with a snappy salute.

Ragnor returned the salute. "Good morning, Sergeant Carvajal. My name is Ragnor Ragnvold, and we are here to assist you in any way possible."

He was shocked at the skeletal forms of Carvajal and the men who stood with him. Most looked like matchstick cartoons, held together by so many strips of flaccid skin totally lacking musculature. He tried to hide his shock.

"Boy, are we glad to see you." Tears clouded the eyes of the waiting men, and Ragnor found it difficult not to break down like a bawling baby. The scarecrow patients were clad in rags and makeshift loincloths. Yet the wounded sported fresh bandages.

Ragnor cast a questioning glance at Carvajal, who, sensing the question replied, "Compliments of the Swiss Red Cross. We are also indebted to Colonel; that is *Taisa* Hanare Masahiro and the guards brave enough to stay with us. They have done a fine job helping us through a difficult period. Taisa Hanare, please to come out."

Quietly, but with long practiced dignity and distinguished look, an emaciated ghost appeared. He was nearly as thin as the POWs. A patch covered his left eye but failed to hide the delicate scar tissue that surrounded the area once occupied by a cheekbone. His left hand was somewhat withered, and he walked with a distinct limp.

Carvajal spoke with obvious respect and friendship. "Colonel Hanare, this is Petty Officer Ragnor Ragnvold of the US Navy. Ragnor, meet Colonel Hanare Masahiro. He's been a godsend these last few months."

The Taisa returned Ragnvold's salute and accepted his handshake. "Colonel Hanare and four other guards, at grave personal risk, have remained at the hospital to help with our disabled patients. Without them, I fear our mortality rate would have been considerably higher.

"There is another whom I must also mention, though I have yet to meet him. He has always worked through Colonel Hanare, so I only know him by name; Yoshida Nobu. He is an assistant to the Johkai Priest of the Sengaku-ji Temple in Shinagawa. The colonel assures me that the Johkai firmly upholds the three sacred treasures of Shinto—wisdom, benevolence, and courage. At our expense, the treasure of benevolence has largely been discarded by the Tojo military regime.

"Yoshida is the Johkai's right arm, working behind scenes to carry out his purposes. Thus Yoshida, working through Colonel Hanare, was able to smuggle in food under the very noses of the brutal Watanabe and inhumane Doctor Tokuda. I believe at least twenty men are alive in these wards that would not be here without the risky work of such humanitarians. But, enough of my maudlin sentiment."

SHINAGAWA HOSPITAL

"Now Mr. Ragnvold, line-out your men, then you and I can tour the facility, and I will introduce you to our most needy patients, so we can make some decisions regarding the next few days. The hospital is divided into four wards, with beds for twenty to forty patients each. The over-riding problem is the lack of facilities to care for the needs of more than 9,000 POWs in the greater Tokyo area."

As he paused, Carvajal noticed his companion staring at the spaced decking. Ragnor said, "It would seem these wards would be very cold in winter. Wouldn't it be better to have tile floors placed directly on the ground to keep the cold air from circulating underneath?"

"Fortunately I am not a Jap architect," said Blaz, "but the concept of slotted floors raised above ground level makes for easier cleaning and summer ventilation. The down side is of course the winter cold. Ostensibly they install tightly woven tatami mats to ward off the circulation of cold air. Unfortunately we have yet to see enough tatamis and summer ventilation remains problematic. Sanitation is poorly facilitated by pit latrines outside the north end of the main building. The stench from these is often unbearable, especially in summer."

"Even now it doesn't exactly smell like a French perfumery," Ragnor said. What kind of bath facilities do you have?"

Blaz replied, "The stench you smell may be from the pit latrines. Or it could be because we were lucky if we got a weekly turn in the dirty communal tub. We weren't allowed to change or heat the water often enough for a truly sanitary experience. However, it was the bedridden with chronic diarrhea who suffered the most.

They walked in silence for a time with Ragnor trying to maintain a positive demeanor in the fetid atmosphere. Ragnvold thought, *This is worse than caring for the seriously wounded while under fire on Iwo Jima.* Finally, he turned to Blaz and asked, "What can we do to alleviate this smell?"

Blaz replied, "Since the most brutal of the Jap guards left, we have made a start. Warm water is kept round the clock. But fuel is so scarce that this is apt to be a short-lived benefit. We also try to have enough people on each shift to help the very weakest with their personal hygiene. You must remember that the odor has been building up for years. It has permeated everything: the walls, the floors, and the little bedding we have. Now we need to sterilize and deodorize everything, a job for good old fashioned Lysol. Did you bring any?"

Ragnor started to respond to the obvious, but decided the lighthearted banter was beneficial in this somber hellhole. "No, but it will be on my first requisition. Sorry, but the smell has really nauseated me, and I should be able to handle it. It will be extra hard on these spit and polish Marines who seem to handle blood all right, but the odor of other body fluids and the necessity of their cleanup is apt to spoil a number of watches."

Blaz smiled and sadly remembered the death and stench along the eighty miles of the Bataan March of Attrition. But the death march itself had paled in comparison to the misery on the Hell Ships on which they were transported from the Philippines to Japan. There had been standing room only in most of the stifling hold of the *Haruna Maru*, which they tagged the "Horror Mara." Therein were a very few buckets for urine and excreta and they were seldom drawn up by their guards to be emptied over the side. And when the buckets were drawn up, it was with much sloshing to further humiliate the POWs and amuse the guards. It took more than thirty days to bring them from Bilibid to the home islands, the so-called "Mainland." It was a month of little food or water, no cleaning up, and a constant fight for space to sit or lay. Thinking back, Blaz realized it was only the strong companionship of his personal friends from Bataan, with their massive hatred of the Japs and the drive for revenge that had made their survival possible.

Starvation on the Hell Ships was precursor to years of undernourishment in the prison camps that sapped their health and trampled their vitality. Blaz seldom thought of noxious environments without correlating them with the evil sister, malnutrition. Little wonder the kindness of Yoshida and the Johkai Priest were prominent in his mind. How many POWs were still alive because of the efforts of Yoshida and the Johkai Priest to augment their food intake? The answer could never be known.

As they left the last ward, Ragnvold turned to Carvajal and asked, "What is your opinion about trying to transport the worst-off of these back to the *Benevolence* immediately?"

Carvajal's response left no doubt about his opinion. "I think such a move would do far more damage than good. With the added help, medical supplies and fuel, it will be less risky to attempt stabilization here. Sending the boats back for additional supplies would do far more good than a long bumpy ride. My vote would be to further the stabilization already under way right here."

Ragnvold sat down with pencil and paper to carefully prepare a requisition list before contacting the P T skipper. Then he motioned for the radioman to go over the list with him to economize wherever possible on what was going to be a long transmission.

Meanwhile, Sergeant Haynes had taken three squads of marines to help straighten out matters in the Omori Camp. Most of this complex was built on manmade sand islands near the Shinagawa Station at the western edge of Tokyo Wan. The complex was joined to Honshu at the Omori Station on the rail line connecting Tokyo and Yokohama. Once the POWs were secure, the next objective would be to confiscate all the internment records they could find.

EVACUATION

27 August 1945

Selected ships of the American and British fleets moved northward through the Izu Strait into Sagami Wan and Tokyo Wan. The USS *Benevolence AH*-13 and her escort, the USS *Reeves*, anchored in the narrow Shinagawa Wan, which is an extension of Tokyo Wan on the west. This gave ready access for the evacuation of the Omori complex. Lighter transfer would be required, but the runs would be short, less than two nautical miles over usually calm water. Evacuation began at 1300 hours and proceeded from dawn until twilight for several days.

Ragnor had set up three teams of two to move the weakest POWs to the gigs and liberty boats being used as lighters to the *Benevolence*. He cautioned them to limit the stretcher cases to three on the whaleboat gigs. The liberty boats could carry six or more.

Over the next several days following the hospital evacuation, some of Ragnor's duty time was occupied with resetting bones and performing minor plastic surgery. But most of his time had to be devoted to correcting the damage of malnutrition and dysentery. These would be slower to respond and depend heavily upon good food, gradual exercise, and companionship for these gaunt shells of men to regain their normal strength and vigor. For some, it would never occur.

Fortunately, he was regaining a better outlook on life, as well as the grim situation here. Gradually, the impact of thirty-six days on Iwo's hell was coming under his control. The angst of night dreams still flowed blood red, but they were less continuous. The shattered bodies and minds of young marines were still scattered through his subconscious apprehension. But his work and an ability to focus his leisure on the surrounding culture helped him control both his waking thoughts and levels of dream angst.

Ragnor spent much of his off-duty time visiting cultural sights. He especially enjoyed Shinto shrines. He purchased what books he could find on Japanese history, religion, and art. He quickly learned that the currency of American occupation was measured in cigarettes, especially Lucky Strikes and Camels, rather than occupational script. His tobacco allotment provided a sure means of obtaining books, prints, and artwork. He soon had several native suppliers catering to his particular tastes.

With the final evacuation of Allied POWs from Shinagawa and the Omori Camp, Blaz Carvajal had been temporarily assigned to the USS *Benevolence*, now anchored off Yokosuka. So far, only the more healthy and ambulatory American prisoners had been evacuated to temporary facilities on Okinawa and other secure bases, where they would await transport to North America. Those suffering most severely were assigned to the hospital ship and like facilities mostly concentrated around Tokyo and southeastern Japan.

Care had to be taken to save enough of the 802 beds on the *Benevolence* for those with the gravest needs.

Beginning 29 August, all POW processing would be done on the *Benevolence*. Normally, Carvajal would have been sent to Okinawa for the trip home, but the onboard medical staff asked him for a voluntary extension. His mental and physical toughness astounded them, but most importantly, his years as a POW and his work with the injured and malnourished had given him an empathy they considered invaluable.

DAVY JONES, THE SAILOR'S DEVIL

30 August 1945

Sargent Blaz Carvajal e Mendizaval rapped lightly on the metal door bearing the imposing information, "Capt. David Jones, Medical Chief of Staff, AH-13." Even though Captain Jones was basically a nice guy, the sailors would always refer to him as "Davy Jones the Sailor's Devil," and his office would always be "Davy Jones' Locker, graveyard for those who perished at sea."

A quiet voice from within commanded, "Enter." The sound, if not the volume, was engendered to produce certain awe, if not fear, to anyone approaching.

While Blaz was somewhat surprised to be summoned by the chief medical officer, his years in Japanese prison camps had nearly purged fear from his repertoire of emotions. Nonetheless, curiosity remained. He opened the door, stepped inside, and came to attention. A snappy salute worthy of his new uniform and master sergeant stripes was returned in the sloppy fashion of an officer more surgeon than line.

"Stand at ease, Sergeant, and take a seat. I have sent for you to ask a favor. My staff has observed your work with the POWs. We want you to remain with us until we have finished processing these poor devils and get them on their way home.

"You were praised by the patients who suffered under the brutal medical experiments of Tokuda Hisakichi. We badly need help at this time. As you know, I am the medical chief of staff for this floating hospital. My specialty is orthopedic surgery, but I am also trained in psychiatry. Believe me, for most of these POWs now assigned to the *Benevolence*, it will be much easier to mend their broken bones than cure their brutalized spirits.

Blaz turned on his chair, uncomfortable in the spotlight of praise by others for actions he considered no more than the fulfillment of duty. He started to speak, but the Captain plowed right on.

"It is obvious that you are tough mentally as well as physically. It is also your right to go home immediately if you so wish, but we are in great need of your help. I can offer you an alternative that might be of interest. We would like you to develop a patient humanitarian program to maximize their response to medical care until we can get them home and into the best treatment programs available. In return, I am prepared to offer you an immediate promotion to chief warrant officer in the US Navy and an option to go to a medical school of your choice if you make the navy your career."

Carvajal sat in stunned silence.

Captain Jones slowly intruded upon that silence. "If you need more time ..."

"No, no. It's just…"

"Take your time."

"I came out of the New Mexico National Guard, 200th Coast Artillery, which was inducted into the US Army in 1941. If it is possible to take the warrant officer commission in the regular army, I would be more than happy to accept," said Blaz.

"Well, I can't guarantee the Army's response to these conditions. However, since most of your patients will be soldiers, they should be amenable to such an arrangement. Give me a few days. But if you would proceed with processing ex-POWs, it would be greatly appreciated."

Carvajal arose, snapped a salute, and left.

Blaz went directly from Captain Jones's office to the line of POWs waiting processing. Fortunately, the MPs were doing a good job keeping the waiting line manageable. This was comparatively easy, since the nearby mess hall was open, serving food and beverages. So it had become a matter of balance between the rambunctiousness of the relatively healthy ones and the fatigue and suffering of those badly abused, malnourished, and ailing.

Carvajal and Ragnvold had already devised a proto-triage screening system that separated them by needs. The more healthy ones were sent to one group of processors and were soon on their way to Okinawa or other secure transport points. The rest were separated into those who had severe medical conditions and those who had severe emotional trauma. Most of these were assigned to the *Benevolence* for thorough evaluation and immediate help. Between August and November 1945, Carvajal, Ragnvold, and their team of screeners processed an additional 1,500 POWs.

BACK TO DAVY JONES' LOCKER

6 September 1945

When Carvajal was summoned again to the office of the Chief Medical Officer, Captain Jones, it was in the company of Petty Officer Ragnvold. The Captain waved his hand at the chairs in front of his desk.

"I am pleased to convey good news to each of you. Mr. Ragnvold, you have passed the exams that qualify you for advancement to Chief Medical Corpsman. Your scores were higher than I have previously seen. Your promotion is immediate. You will now move to chief's quarters and dine in their mess. Now as senior NCO of all enlisted medical personnel onboard the *Benevolence*, you will change to chief's uniform as soon as practicable. You will see to these things immediately after you hear the good news awaiting Sergeant Carvajal.

"Sergeant Carvajal, for you, I have even better news. The Army has accepted my proposal that you be commissioned in the regular army, but attached to the USS *Benevolence* or other occupational hospitals here in Japan until all ex-POWs are transported to North America. We anticipate that four or five months will be required. After that, you will be given home leave for one month. Then you will be transferred to the University of New Mexico to finish a bachelor's degree before entering medical school. During that period, you will be attached to the Santa Fe Army Hospital, where you will be expected to work with ex-POWs, as time allows.

"For both of you who have worked so hard at repatriation, I have granted three days of leave beginning 10 September and every Monday following that, as long as you are attached to the *Benevolence*. You are now dismissed."

TEA HOT WATER

10 September 1945

Chief Petty Officer Ragnor Ragnvold and Warrant Officer Blaz Carvajal made their way around bomb craters and jumbles of bomb-created rubble, from the Omori Station into Shinagawa. Traffic was virtually impossible in most areas. The work of clearing was making progress, but it had yet to reach as far west as Sengaku-ji, the Spring Hill Buddha Temple which was the city's most historic site. They had dressed in civilian clothing, hoping to mitigate their obvious role in the developing occupation.

A few blocks from the *torii* ceremonial gate, they paused and Blaz explained a few points of Shinto and Buddha ritual. As they drew closer to the shrine, there was a sharp contrast between the manicured grounds beyond the torri and the ruined buildings and rubble-littered streets of their immediate environs. Ragnor had never before seen a Japanese formal garden. His eyes widened at the subtle splendor. "Look at those boulders with the coarse white sand raked into wave patterns. It's like a sea with white water surrounding black islands."

Blaz explained, "This is a *kare-san-sui,* a dry landscape. They're found in many formal gardens of Japan. Your characterization of the 'sea with islands' is probably close to the gardener's intent. He undoubtedly rakes it every day to keep out leaves and trash, as well as to maintain the wave-like texture. But also the shrubs and trees at the periphery, look how healthy and neatly pruned they appear. In spite of orders to disfranchise State Shintoism, someone is obviously caring for this sacred site."

Before they reached the torii, Blaz laid a hand on Ragnor's arm. "A few days before you arrived at the hospital, Hanare brought me here. He explained many things and demonstrated the more simple rituals. It might be easier if we take these step by step as we proceed."

Past the gate, they found the ablution bowl. Ragnor watched as Blaz rinsed his hands then took a dipper of water from the trickle emanating from a small pipe. Then he carefully lifted the dipper, letting water pour over his other hand, some of which he caught in his mouth, taking care not to touch the dipper rim, which would have contaminated it for further use. Ragnor followed the example carefully. They each deposited a coin into the nearby offering box. Approaching the oratory, the place of prayer, Blaz bowed to the inner sanctum and clapped his hands. He then took the small padded stick attached to the base and lightly tapped the gong. It gave a surprisingly resonant sound, but no one appeared.

They walked on into the garden, being careful to stay on the stepping stones, meanwhile conversing in whispers. They soon found a bench on which to rest. Blaz continued to explain Shinto rituals, even as Ragnor looked furtively for a priest or keeper. Then they attempted meditation. This was a totally foreign experience for Ragnor; however, Blaz seemed more relaxed, more fulfilled. Perhaps his years as a POW had taught him about the deeper aspects of the human spirit. They lingered in the cool calmness. Not a soul marred their solitude.

Possibly an hour passed. Blaz suggested they find a place to buy some soup. The all American appetite of Ragnor hoped it would be a hearty, rich blend. They found a narrow, standing-only bar with a makeshift charcoal brazier, on which sat an ancient cast-iron kettle that had somehow escaped the medieval swordsmiths' search for the purist iron to forge into the steel for the renown nippon-to of the thirteenth and fourteenth centuries. The soup cooking therein had a devilishly tempting odor. Native patrons were using chopsticks to lift thick noodles within slurping distance of their mouths, then smacking vigorously as they downed the scalding soup. Blaz handled the maneuver adequately.

As Ragnor was contemplating the scalding aftermath, a slight, middle-aged man lightly touched his sleeve. With a total lack of ostentation and speaking softly, he asked, "Please to take tea?" Then, still softly, he offered a formal invitation in Japanese. Ragnor cast a questioning glance at Carvajal.

"He has just honored us with an invitation to participate with him in *chanoyu*, literally 'tea hot water,' the tea ceremony. More than that, we will have *tenshin*, light snacks most likely sweetened rice cakes. Apparently, there is a *chashitsu*, a tea hut nearby."

Ragnor *was* surprised by the use of the term "tea hut" rather than "tea house" or "tea room." Then he realized the intent was to downplay all thoughts of pride or ostentation. "Please accept for us."

Blaz spoke a few phrases of simple Japanese, to which the would-be host smiled.

Ragnor swallowed the last of the hot soup, and they followed the genial stranger. The tea hut appeared to be just that, but it was neatly kept and very clean. The host entered first through the traditional host's entrance. The opening was so low that even he had to bend to clear the *kamoi,* the upper guide-rail called the "duck's place." This feature hung from a transom and served to hold the sliding *fusuma* in its vertical position. He indicated to his guests that they should enter through the entrance around the corner. At the guest entrance, Blaz and Ragnor both struggled with the low overhead, bending nearly double to clear the duck's place.

Inside, the host was already kneeling on the tatami mat of rice straw covered with woven rushes. He had just taken fresh water from the *mizuya* the so-called "water room," where the initial tea preparation occurred. Ragnor watched as Blaz squatted cross-legged on the tatami, facing the host. He followed suit, also facing the host who was now fanning the live coals in the *ro* to hasten boiling.

A low table, scarcely a foot high, stood to the side of the ro and in front of the host. On it were three *chai* bowls, the implements for serving the tea, a plate of rice crackers, and to one side, an incense stick from which a thin line of blue smoke wafted toward the ceiling. As Ragnor watched the dark iron teapot nearing a boil on the ro, he thought, *Tea has probably prolonged more lives than any other cultural inovation throughout history. It's amazing what boiling water can do for health.*

The host now placed a chai bowl in front of each participant. The bowls were immaculately clean but so old the blue designs were nearly worn away by years of handling and washing.

Ragnor watched both the host and Blaz trying to make the best of his ignorance. The host poured a small amount of tea into the bowl in front of Blaz who lifted it and felt the warmth with both hands. He then turned the bowl so that the main design, or what was left of it, was facing away from him. Ragnor glanced at his bowl, which was now receiving tea. He looked at Blaz, but his friend seemed to be enjoying the ritual. Ragnor rotated his bowl, and the host smiled. He relaxed somewhat. *So far, so good.* Then he noticed the others watching the hypnotic spiral of smoke. The warmth of the tea bowl in his hands, the mesmeric waft of color, and the subtle fragrance of sandalwood finalized the seduction away from his discomfort. Ragnor was learning a fundamental virtue of *Zen*, patience. He thought, *Perhaps I am even enjoying it. Perhaps there is something to this thing called meditation.*

Slowly the host lifted his chai bowl again, enjoying the warmth on his hands and the fragrance in his nostrils. The Americans followed suit. The host then took a sip with care not to burn his lips or mouth. By this time, the tea was only scalding. The host took two more sips. He then sat the bowl back on the table. The novices followed his moves. The host bowed his head and closed his eyes. Ragnor copied the master, but kept his eyelids slightly parted, ready for any unexpected action. Meanwhile he was considering, *This is like keeping your eyes open when someone is praying.* Minutes passed; the host again poured and offered dainty sweetmeats; there was more silent relaxation. To Ragnor, it seemed intolerable. Finally, the host nodded to each guest and slowly arose. *Thank God it's over.*

YOSHIDA NOBU

A short way from the tea hut, where they seemed almost alone their host stopped. He glanced around then bowed slightly. In hesitant English, he said, "My name is Yoshida Nobu." His tone and emphasis indicated the name order was Oriental, the surname given first. He then drew two small cards from his kimono. On each, he had hand lettered his name using the Roman alphabet but with a calligraphic flourish that made them objects of art carefully printed on quality rice paper. Ragnor scarcely knew how to respond, so he thrust out his hand and said, "Ragnor Ragnvold."

Blaz was a bit more enterprising. From his pocket, he extracted a note card and carefully printed, "Blaz Carvajal, US Army and Ragnor Ragnvold, US Navy," and handed it to Mr. Yoshida, who accepted it with a smile. When Blaz spoke his name, he emphasized the Hispanic pronunciation of "Carvajal," which seemed to please his host.

"Please to call me Nobu." He went on to explain in a mix of Japanese and English, "I watched you at the Sengaku-ji Temple. The Johkai Priest and I were honored by your reverence for sacred things and the time you spent in meditation. As you know, the American High Command has taken drastic measures against Shinto. Were I a priest, especially a Johkai, there would be grave risk even in this conversation. But I am a simple groundskeeper who serves the *Kami* of Shinto and the Great Lord Buddha in my poor way."

At the mention of groundskeeper, Ragnor thought to compliment him on the beauty of the formal garden, but before he could formulate his expression, Nobu forged ahead.

"But time catches me. I must make report to the Johkai. Would it be possible to meet one week from today? If you can; enter the shrine as before through the torii, make ablutions, and bow toward the *honden*, the sanctuary. If you still feel secure, tap the gong, then clap three times. Afterwards go to the same bench for meditation. We will observe and make sure no danger follows. This may take some time.

At that point Nobu seemed to focus his communication on Ragnor. The younger man glanced at Blaz seeking his guidance. The urbane warrant officer nodded his head. Ragnor said, "As things now stand, a week from today should be fine. We will catch the earliest launch and should be at Sengaku-ji by mid-morning. Is there anything we can bring?

Nobu thought a bit. "Some chocolate bars for the Johkai's charity slush fund would be nice." Then he returned to the subject of the next visit. "Should one week prove inopportune, we will wait and watch for at least four additional days. If you haven't appeared by then we will assume that you have decided the risk is too great, or that Shinto is simply an extension of Bushido."

Here an agitated Blaz broke in. "Forgive me, Yoshidasan, but it is my understanding that Bushido is the Samurai

Code of Conduct that provides prisoner protection similar to the Geneva Convention of 1880."

Nobu replied, "I wish that was the case. But unfortunately the guards, for the most part, were simply extending their understanding of the Tojo Hideki edict found in the Japanese Army Field Service Code, which holds that becoming and remaining a prisoner of war is the ultimate disgrace. And from that I quote the admonition to the Japanese Army, "Do not receive humiliation by being captured alive as prisoners of war."

Blaz acquiesced, "Sometimes it seems that further enlightenment carries a burden of sorrow."

Nobu nodded his agreement and then added a disclaimer. "For the common man in Japan, such extreme interpretation of Bushido would have been tempered by Buddhist humanism. It is often said that, 'Eighty percent of Japanese are Shinto and eighty percent are Buddhist.' The irony is simple. Forgive the near use of an American metaphor, 'We keep our eggs in more than one basket.' Even *Zen* is apt to transcend the basket walls.

Blaz again spoke pointedly to his host. "I can not accept that as justification for the actions of either Tokuda or Watanabe."

Nobu replied, "This is neither apology nor justification, but a statement of unfortunate fact. Shinto and Bushido have both been badly manipulated by Japanese militarists, especially in their treatment of Allied POWs, but we have not all indulged in such inquisitional barbarism. My Johkai is a humble, good man who sought to help the POWs, as well as the downtrodden in Japan long before the surrender. From you, Mr. Carvajal, I especially beg forgiveness. If you can, erase the memories of the incompetent surgeries and inhumane experimental injections of Doctor Tokuda Hisakichi, and the brutal treatment by Watanabe Hattori. For the sake of our friendship, please focus your memories on the actions of Hanare Masahiro, and those guards who remained with you through the process of liberation." Yoshida shook each American's hand and quietly slipped away.

HANARE MASAHIRO

Making their way back across Shinagawa provided time to think. Finally Ragnor asked, "What did Yoshida mean about, 'remember Hanare Masahiro?'"

Carvajal thought for a while on just how to answer. Finally he said, "During my years as a POW, I have been fortunate. My health has been reasonably adequate and my medical training extremely useful. But perhaps most beneficially, I have been able to overcome the deep hatred that had built up during the death march and the inhumane treatment on board the hell ship which transported me here. At one point, my faith became so weak that I vowed to the Holy Mother, 'If you will give me strength to survive and return home, I will make the sacred pilgrimage to *El Sanctuario del Chimayo.*'

"That *promesa* turned my life around. I never regained my normal strength, but my bouts with dysentery and malaria were milder than before. I was able to help my less fortunate companions, including those of the New Mexico 200th Coast Artillery. You would be surprised how many of these tough guardsmen also made the promesa."

"Promesa? Are you saying promise in Spanish? Ragnor asked.

"Well, yes and no. It is a cognate for promise; but Mag-witch Russell, my bruiser friend from the death march and hell ships, told me it really means a 'corban,' an offering to God, or in my case, it was an offering to the Mother of God. Incidentally, Mag is quite an intellectual, but he would never admit it."

"Oh Sorry for interrupting," said Ragnor. "Please go on."

Blaz continued, "But for my own peace of mind, there came a realization that my captors were also human. As we were marched from Asano Docks through the crowded streets toward the holding center, a small lady in a ragged kimono slipped a persimmon into my hand. In the crush of people, I furtively ate that luscious fruit. There had been no fresh fruit or vegetables for weeks. Oh, how it filled my needs.

"Now, I have never tasted manna, but if it is comparable to that *fuji* persimmon, I plan to move to Sinai and live on manna, dates, and camel beef for the rest of my life. Just kidding, but that little Japanese lady gave me more than fruit; she provided me with the ability to look at a larger picture, to see beyond the brutal guards, to feel beyond starvation and rations, to have the will to live again."

"Yes," said Ragnor. "But I was a little concerned about your move to the Sinai; knowing how you feel about the Rio Arriba and the Sangre de Christos. Thanks for the clarification. You're now free to become an MD and go back to the Land of Enchantment. I firmly believe it might be possible to get the adobe out of the muchacho, but it is impossible to get the muchacho out of the adobe, at least for the long haul."

Blaz laughed then continued, "As months became years, there were few such incidents to remind me of that trip from Asano. Then one day, a Japanese guard died. His place was taken by Hanare Masahiro, who had been a former Imperial Army officer. Badly wounded in Burma, he lost his left eye and much of the bone structure of cheek and eyebrow. My immediate reaction was, 'How did he ever survive?' He was slight of build but wiry as a bandy rooster and apparently a master of martial arts. The other guards gave him a wide birth."

"I was checking patients in the first ward the morning he arrived. He stepped inside and just watched. His stern countenance looked almost brutal, with the scar tissue covering what had once been his brow and cheekbone. A patch covered the empty eye-socket. But his voice was even, almost restrained. His English was hesitant but solid. He said to me, "Your patients are very thin. But food is so scarce. Even my countrymen suffer, but not like this.

"Hanare left immediately, allowing me no opportunity to respond. But the following morning, a bag of fruit, mostly shriveled plums and apples, sat next to the workstation where I kept meager, coded records of patient treatment. I immediately realized the source. Then trying to emulate that generosity, I cut the fruit into as equitable portions as possible, making sure each starving man would have a tiny taste. Similar gifts appeared from time to time. Seemingly, the watery gruel became a little thicker and I feared the brutal Watanabe might take vengeance upon either the benefactor or the beneficiaries.

"Then one morning as I approached the closest ward, there stood Watanabe at rigid attention, a livid red mark across his face, nose spurting blood. Masahiro was dressing him down in Japanese so rapidly, I scarcely caught a word. In his shriveled left hand was a tattered cloth bag that I knew contained bits of food for hungry POWs. I was thrilled by this show of valor and martial skill. This was a display of true *bushido–bushi-no-nasake*, a warrior's compassion that reflected the high principles of Buddhism and Confucianism."

"Didn't you ever wonder why the Imperial Army would dump a seemingly capable officer into such an ignominious slot as a POW guard when major holding actions on Formosa and the Ryukyus were crying for good officers?" asked Ragnor.

"Absolutely, but the Taisa was a singularly private person. He was a very considerate individual, but his personal life was kept to himself, never hinting as to why he was buried in this blind alley," replied Blaz. "Only one thing ever really tweaked my imagination. Hanare seldom talked to the other guards, but one morning as I made the hospital rounds I caught snatches of his conversation with one of the younger guards, 'By the time Prince Chichibu reached the Home Islands he was spitting up blood. Even so he was still the Kuromake of the Golden Lily."

"And what in the world does that mean?" asked Ragnor.

"I looked up 'kuromake.' It is some kind of stage manager. I never learned the significance of Golden Lily. So keep your ears open. Perhaps we should have a wager on who solves the conundrum first. What would you say to the loser buying the winner the art print 'Fuji from Tagonoura that we saw this morning?" asked Blaz.

Ragnor replied, "I accept, knowing full-well you are taking advantage of my ignorance. By the way, how did you gain so much knowledge of Japanese culture? "

"That I largely attribute to the little lady with the persimmon and Hanare Masahiro with his bags of shriveled fruit. Of a sudden, I wanted to learn more about Japanese culture, especially the Samurai. But the more I pondered the situation and the vindictiveness of the Brutal Bird, the more I worried about the Taisa. Even-so Hanare became my mentor in Japanese language and culture.

WAY OF THE KAMI

Exactly one week following the tea ceremony with Yoshida Nobu, Chief Petty Officer Ragnor Ragnvold went alone to the Sengaku-ji. Blaz Carvajal was so busy with debriefing by military intelligence and striving to obtain proper care for his "patients" that he was unable to leave. So Ragnvold, with trepidation, approached the torii of the temple. His greatest fear was that he would make mistakes in the ritual. Fortunately, the ablution went smoothly. He approached the oratory with a bit more confidence. He bowed to the honden; then straightened, clapping his hands three times; then tapped the gong. Slowly he turned, making his way to the bench where he seated himself, trying hard to relax and meditate. His mind was definitely not geared to Zen, so he just sat quietly. The minutes seemed like hours. He had no real concept of how long he waited,

Finally, he heard a soft bird-like call from an obscure part of the garden masked by *sugi*, Japanese cedars, which he had not previously noticed. Carefully, he peered into the somber shadows, finally realizing a hand was beckoning from this spot. He quietly made his way into the leafy solitude ready to greet his host, but Nobu in a silent motion raised a cautionary finger to his lips.

Through the thick foliage, they made their way past a small structure that might have been a potting shed or tool storage. From there, an obtuse route brought them to a narrow alley that gave access to a busy street of public shops and small food and liquid refreshment stands. Even now, they followed a devious route before reaching a tiny shop where Nobu quickly entered. It might well have been the Japanese equivalent of a poorly stocked American mom and pop market. They passed through the shop and into the room beyond. It was obviously the living quarters.

Nobu motioned for his guest to be seated. Cushions and backrests made it more comfortable than the tea-hut. Nevertheless, a pot of water simmered on the coals, ready for tea preparation. On the short table was a tray of *hashipan*; light refreshments like English tea biscuits had been placed on a blue willowware plate. Ragnor was now happy that Blaz had suggested bringing a small bag of sugar cubes. Sugar was so very difficult to obtain in old Edo and most expensive on the black market.

Paper-thin walls did little for sound insulation, making Ragnor cautious. Sensing this, Nobu smiled and said, "Please relax. What we discuss today will be largely innocuous. After all, even the Supreme Commander of Allied Powers shouldn't care if I instruct you concerning the Japanese language and history, even if it deals with Shinto religion and Samurai culture. Indeed, the absence of Mr. Carvajal may be a fortunate thing. It will allow us to delve into the facets of culture in which you are most interested."

Ragnor was surprised at the breadth of his host's usage of English grammar and syntax. No more Pidgin English of their first meeting. "So where shall we begin?"

Ragnor thought a bit before replying. "How did *Shinto-ism* start in Japan, and how does it fit into Samurai traditions and Bushido?"

"A big order, my friend; somewhat like eating an elephant." Nobu poured two cups of boiling tea and smiled when Ragnor handed him a small bag of cubed sugar. "One or two cubes?" he asked.

"Just one, please."

"Biscuit?"

Ragnor took the largest he could see.

"Perhaps it is well that we begin with the *Devine Edict of Amaterasu Omikami,* the Sun Goddess, the greatest of all 800 *myriad* (sometimes rendered as 10,000) Kami, to her grandson Ninigi." Nobu picked up a small book and turned to a previously marked place. "It is better that I read it. It is stilted, even in Japanese, so I can only guess of its difficulty in English translation.

"This Reed-Plain—1,800-Autums-Fair-Rice-Ear Land is the region which my descendants shall be lords of. Do thou my August Grandchild, proceed thither and govern it. Go! And may prosperity attend thy dynasty, and may it like heaven and earth endure for ever."

Stilted was right. Ragnor thought about what he had heard. Then he asked, "Would you please translate it again?" The obliging Nobu read it again, pausing with each phrase, so his guest could chew smaller bites of the elephant. Ragnor thought, *Past the description of the land; it wasn't so bad. It has similarities with other ethno-origin myths I have heard, a chosen people taking possession of their promised land.*

Nobu paused, either to let Ragnor absorb or respond.

"Sounds like Joshua leading the Children of Israel into the Land of Cana, but with a far eastern twist," said Ragnor.

"Fair enough." Nobu took another book and from another pre-marked place read. "The Japanese people were created on the Islands of Japan and are a superior race, supporting an unbroken dynasty for all ages and have no racial origins outside the Japanese Islands."

Ragnor flinched and asked, "Source?"

"The Tokyo Anthropological Society 1936."

Nobu expanded the thought a bit further with a hint of emperor worship. "Now Hirohito, as Emperor, claims direct decent from Jimmu Tenno, the first emperor and founder of the dynasty—the Imperial Household. Jimmu was the grandson of Ninigi who had first pacified the islands and was grandson of Amaterasu Omikami the Sun Goddess. Since the time of the first emperor there has always been one of the Imperial Household on the throne.

"The economy of ancient Japan was based on rice cultivation. Political control was poorly consolidated and often shifted to feudal lords, leaving the emperor to dangle puppet-like from the controlling strings of a warlord puppeteer.

"In the fight for control, the emperor sometimes employed professional warriors called Bushi. Hence Bushido is the code of warriors. The Bushi themselves evolved into the Samurai class. Samurai means 'one who serves.' A retainer if you like"

Ragnor asked, "Yoshidasan you have considered emperors and bushi, but what about shoguns who seemed to have played an unprecedented part in the direction of Japan's political development?"

"Point well taken," replied Nobu. "Unfortunately their impact was often more negative than positive. All too often their rise to power was through hereditary, military command. Plunder was apt to be more important than fostering good for the common man. Battle capture of the sword and armor of a military adversary was more important than the development of a thousand hectares of patty rice land. Some how the dictatorial bent of these powerful men were seldom devoted to the good of society."

"That's interesting," said Ragnvold. "I have heard a number of army reservists, some rather intellectually inclined, refer to Douglas MacArthur, the present SCAP, as 'Shogun.' I had assumed it was merely a reflection of his military command style. Now I'm beginning to suspect self-interest and an underlying tie to military-industrialism. Why else would he remove the steel fist from the velvet glove in dealing with certain zaibatsu corporations which are again conducting business in occupied Japan?"

"I can't answer that, my friend, but I'm sorely vexed by SCAP's arbitrary disarmament policies which will ultimate lead to the destruction of National Treasure Temple Swords."

Nobu went on to explain how over time larger and larger sectors of feudal Japan came under control of strong daimyo lords, often descended through both noble and Samurai bloodlines. From the twelfth to the fourteenth century two such aristocratic families held national power sequentially from the capital at Kamakura.

Nobu said, "I must take you and Blaz to Kamakura soon. It is less than thirty miles south. Besides being a historic capital, it is home to the great bronze Amida Buddha cast in 1252."

At this point, Ragnor's ears perked up. He interrupted his mentor, "The Amida Buddha?"

Nobu briefly altered the storyline. "Long ago in the western reaches of China, or perhaps it was in Tibet, a monk named Dharmakara took the forty-eight requisite vows to establish a *Buddhaak-setra*, a purified land around the Buddha of Immeasurable and Everlasting Light. We in Japan usually refer to it as the 'Western Paradise.'"

Before Nobu could get back into the trivia of Japanese dynastic foibles, Ragnor said, "Time grows short, so would you tell me the significance of the Hideyoshi Edict?"

.

Nobu attempted to hide his irritation. He answered, "From a Samurai point of view, the 1588 proclamation was a most significant occurrence. It strictly prohibited people below the Samurai class from owning swords, bows, or other arms."

Here Ragnor cut in. "Sounds like the mighty protecting the mighty. Right out of English history, like the Crown forbidding Saxon peasants from owning crossbows in order to protect those poor defenseless Norman knights."

"Exactly," said Nobu. "The stage was set for the rise of the Tokugawa Shogunate, the Yedo *Bukufu*, since the capital was established in the ancient city of Yedo, now modern Tokyo. In many ways it epitomized the glory of Samurai culture. It would be the last Shogunate and would witness the demise of the Samurai.

Nobu paused to pour them a fresh cup of tea. They leaned back against the cushions to savor the aroma and flavor of the beverage. Nobu stood and stretched. Ragnor eagerly followed suit. Then Nobu asked, "Are you ready to chew on another chunk of the elephant?"

SHINTO

Ragnor nodded hesitantly. "Very well, would you be so good as to explain why *Shinto* is such a thorn in the side of SCAP."

Nobu replied, "In preface, Shinto is the way of the Kami. There are many gods and many aspects of their teachings. Within the great blanket of Shinto, there is ample room for a multitude of concepts. This allows one considerable latitude in which to formulate his own moral and spiritual development.

"The earliest roots of Shinto may have originated as primitive animism began to focus on specific Kami honored by ancient Jamon people who have always existed on the Islands of Japan. The only pure remnant of the Jamon is the *Ainu* of the North, who some believe to have been the source of the first Samurai."

Ragnor interrupted, "Sounds like you support Watanabe's claim to be Samurai. After all isn't he is as Ainu as Ainu can be?"

Nobu nodded but didn't allow Ragnor time to explore the new deviation. "The migration of Yayoi people from the west began about three hundred years before the advent of the Christian era, forming the basis for the modern Japanese race."

"Just where, did the Yayoi come from?" asked Ragnor.

"Northeast China and the Korean Peninsula for the most part," replied Nobu. But their religion, like that of the Ainu, seemed to have lacked focus. The Kami, *locus genii* of certain springs or mountains, provided at best a loose framework for belief. This loose structure has largely continued into the present, even though Zen Buddhism almost became the state religion near the end of the sixth century.

"Meanwhile, ferric metallurgy was making rapid advances. The art of steel fabrication was closely linked to Shinto ritual. By the tenth century, Japanese sword making led the world in steel methodology.

The mention of sword making snapped Ragnor out of a near somnolent state, which was just as abruptly smashed on the rock of Jinga Shinto.

"The broadest aspect of Shinto's teachings we call *Jinga Shinto*. Throughout our land are thousands of shrines. A few of these receive national recognition, but most serve the needs of a village or a small congregation of worshipers. These are often dedicated to a single Kami. You might liken these to patron saints, each being having distinct strengths and weaknesses to which individual worship is somewhat customized. The guardian gods, or genius loci of a particular place, called the *Ujigami*, becomes the principle focus and harmonizing element of powers that reside there."

Ragnor extended his hands in a questioning gesture. "And how do temple gifts fit into the scheme?"

"Votive gifts fall into three groups that are symbolic of Shinto values. These have derived from the Kami Amaterasu, Glorious Goddess of Heaven. The first class of gift is the mirror that reflects the image in which we behold ourselves. It is a reflection of our true nature. If we are pure that image will reflect the higher aspects of the Sun Kami.

"The second class of gift is the sword, which is symbolic of Shinto power also emanating from the Sun Goddess. It represents the sword with which Susano slew the eight-headed dragon. It holds the power of purification.

"The gift of the third class is the jewel that represents our power over others. It is said to signify the jewels hung in a tree to lure Amaterasu from her cave that we might fully bask in the effulgence of her warmth and fecundity."

Ragnor was again fighting to stay awake and remember pertinent details.

Nobu continued, "So Shinto is highly flexible. Even great religions such as that founded by Prince Siddhartha the Lord Gautama Buddha, who brought enlightenment to mankind, adapts readily to its comforting ambience. In fact, some Shinto Kami are viewed as protectors of Buddhism and Zen. Best known of these are the King of the Mountain Guardians of Tendai Buddhism. These guardians are prominently focused on the *Samreizan*, Japan's three holy mountains: Fujiyama, Tate, and Haky. Most important of these Kami are those guarding the Fuji summit crater shrine.

"*Kokka Shinto* is that aspect Shintoism considered most sinister by the American High Command. Within its precepts, the emperor is considered divine and exerts control over all aspects of government and religion. To the occupational government, it appeared as the major obstacle to constitutional democracy. For that reason, it was addressed directly within the terms of our unconditional surrender. It is the 'State Shintoism' abolished by SCAP only a few days ago, along with the Bureau of Shrines within the Ministry of Home Affairs.

"The Imperial Family was allowed to remain as a figurehead but was forced to give up its claims to divinity, along with any real political power. Hence, the statement from Hirohito and its acceptance by SCAP: 'The ties between us and our people have always stood upon mutual trust and affection. They do not depend upon legends and myths. They are not predicated upon the false conception that the emperor is divine and that the Japanese people are superior to other races and are fated to rule the world.'"

Here, Ragnor interrupted in a way he feared might be offensive to his genial host. He attempted to soften the impact. "Honorable mentor, please forgive the rudeness of my interruption, but as I read about the culture of the Samurai, I have been unable to effectively link it to the principles of either Shinto or Zen Buddhism. Perhaps you would be so kind as to point my thought processes in more succinct pathways? So far, my library has been geared to art and history rather than religion and ethics."

But Nobu did not feel the time was yet right to discuss his complicated problem with Ragnor.

"Mr. Ragnvold, would you have time to accompany me to Sengaku-ji? It may require some hours." Since Ragnor did not have duty until 1600 tomorrow, he nodded his agreement.

As they walked, Nobu iterated some of his feelings about the abuses of Japan's defunct military government. "Chief Ragnvold, you are already aware of my feelings against the Tojo Military Dictatorship. In almost every way, the Tojo Hideki regime was a Shogunate in its most brutal form. In some ways, it started with rescripting of school curricula, beginning in the 1930s. In many respects, it was propaganda built around the philosophy of Friedrich Nietzsche, especially as applied by Adolph Hitler—a super race and a resurgence of Divine Imperialism. This inspired, in our most recent generation, a belief they held the right to conquer the world and subdue it for the enhancement of Imperial Japan.

"Close upon the footsteps of rescripting came the rebirth of *Kempeitai,* our version of the German Gestapo. The secret police, seemingly with the approval of our young people, maintained a harsh discipline on our civilian population all through the Manchurian Campaign and World War II. The fall of the Tojo military government and the Kempeitai, plus a defunct state Shinto, seemed to stimulate a degree of anarchy accompanied by a rebirth of *yakuza,* the secret brotherhoods that SCAP appears unwilling or unable to control. So my list of grievances grows longer.

"However, my immediate concern is with SCAP's ordered destruction of all military arms, 'every weapon, every sword,' to be found and consigned to recycling smelters. I am amazed at MacArthur's shortsighted and narrow-minded edict. A man of his military finesse knows that twentieth century warfare is not conducted with swords, even though many Japanese military officers strutted through the last war carrying Samurai katana and tashi while dreaming of Bushi heroism. But more importantly, how can he consign to the smelting furnaces such priceless art that carry the sacred nature of Shinto temple gifts, many of which are Kokuho, national treasures?"

Ragnor walked on in silence trying to fathom the depth of Nobu's passion and his own feelings for the great art swords.

After a bit, Nobu returned to his gripe. "SCAP has quietly, but rapidly stepped up his campaign against Kokka, state Shinto, resulting in an administrative structure called '*Yaskuni*' that supports the more beneficial aspects of Shinto. However, it has been reluctant to broach the problem of National Treasure Swords. Minimal support for groups like Showa and the *Kanesuka* are failing. Both groups have become increasingly active and secretive. Unfortunately, they have also become more oriented toward profits and crime syndicates than the retention of Japanese history.

"Sadly, their work has already served to place some of our greatest national treasures in the secret collections of very rich people outside Japan. Many have vanished just as effectively, as though they had gone to the recycling furnaces."

By this time, they were at the Sengaku-ji Shrine.

GENROKU 14

A plaque with Japanese characters told Ragnor nothing about the place. But Nobu's voice took on a more reverent tone. "We now stand in the Graveyard of Honor. Here lie the most famous of Samurai, the Forty-seven Ronin, those warriors who had lost their leader, Lord Asano Naganon who had been ordered to commit seppuku by the Shogun. Their story is known to every Japanese child and is a choice theme of *Kabuki* Theater. You are familiar with the nearby Asano Docks, where the infamous Mitsubishi Company, until recently, marshaled their POW slave labor forces and from whence you evacuated many of those same POWs to the hospital ship *Benevolence*?"

Ragnor nodded.

"Well, those docks were named for Asano Naganon; daimyo of Ako. It is said that the perpetrator of the Shogun's order for the ritual suicide was Kira Yoshinako of Tsuwano. Now at that time, Asano had over three hundred retainers under his command, but only forty-seven chose to seek revenge for his death. For a year, they plotted. With the passage of time, Lord Kira became complacent and seemed to forget the fealty of Samurai warriors.

"Seizing a propitious moment, the Forty-seven Ronin, under the leadership of Tadawaki Kaneska, captured Lord Kira, severed his head, and brought it here to Sengaku-ji, where they placed it on the grave of Lord Asano then awaited the Shogun's order for their own ritual suicide that they accepted as the price for 'sweetest revenge.' The Forty-seven are buried here. You now stand upon the most hallowed ground of Samurai tradition, the Treasury of Honored Retainers."

At this point, Nobu broke into verse that in English translates roughly:

The savory food when left untasted

Remains apart its sweetness wasted

In peaceful lands the loyal courage

Of its warriors remain unnourished

As stars invisible by day

At night show off in bold display

"The Forty-seven Ronin committed *seppuku*, Thursday 21 April 1701. That was the year, *Genroku* 14."

BUSHIDO

Following their repast of red-rice, namely rice seasoned and colored with *adzuki* red beans, Nobu resumed the education of Ragnor Ragnvold. "Much of what you and I would conceive as Samurai tradition is of rather recent origin, having been formalized late in the Tokugawa Shogunate, which covered the period between 1603 and 1868. I am of course referring to the Tokugawa, 'Way of the Warriors.' Bushido is a code of conduct as much touted as maligned.

"It was the Tokugawa feudal regime that bonded Confucian morality, dating from the fifth century to Shinto deities and paved the way for *Satori*, the Enlightenment of Buddhism achieved through Zen meditation. Buddhism, becoming important from the sixth century on, was nearly adopted as the state religion in the seventeenth century, well before the Meiji restoration of 1868.

"Perhaps the low point of Bushido veracity was the Tojo interpretation that came as a result of their downplaying of bushi-no-nasake, 'a warrior's compassion,' a sense of mercy, benevolence, and tenderness based on Confucian teachings."

ART OF THE SWORD

Another week had gone. Ragnor and WO Blaz Carvajal returned to Sengaku-ji. In a sizeable brown paper bag, they carried four boxes of Hershey bars, three cartons of Lucky Strikes, and a carton of Camels. No Cools. It was a small fortune on the Japanese black market.

They handed these to Yoshida. "For your Johkai Priest's relief slush fund."

Nobu bowed and in turn handed each of them a roll of carefully tied rice paper. "Please do not open until you return to the ship."

"By your leave Blaz, I would like to continue with more facets of Samurai lore. When Ragnor and I ended last week, I had just finished telling him about the Forty-seven Ronin of which you are familiar."

Blaz nodded, and the Americans followed their host through the narrow, crooked streets of Shinagawa to a dilapidated park, where they could converse without unwanted listeners approaching too closely. However, they quickly realized it was only a pause to check on the security of their movement. Yet throughout, Nobu continued his discourse. He was perhaps the best-informed sword historian in Japan.

"It is often said that 'the sword is the soul of the Samurai.' Be that as it may, the roots of sword metallurgy extend so far back into the prehistoric past that we know little about its beginnings. By the tenth century of your Christian era, sword-smithing was already well established. Complex metallurgy was tied to detailed ritual and observable color changes that governed each step of forge welding. Meticulous control was required to achieve the proper layering of different steel properties, which would insure the sword's ability to take a fine edge, even as the blade retained great strength and resistance to shattering upon impact.

"The steel billet was heated in the forge, cut, pounded out, then folded and pounded out at least fifteen times to create over 30,000 layers in a single sword—a masterpiece of laminated flexibility and hardness. The curve of the two-handed cavalry tashi and similar blades is caused by different layers of steel formed in the forging process. The master smith, through observing color changes, is able to control the nature of the steel going into a given lamina of the blade.

"It was and is labor intensive in the extreme. A sword created under grand masters of the past often took up to sixteen workmen half a year to make a top quality tashi. Aesthetic elaborations for wealthy lords and temple gifts may well have required another six months. Even by a measure of the labor theory of value, so often used in capitalist economies like the United States, such weapons are essentially priceless. To the Japanese, the values are even greater, enhanced as they are by historic traditions and religious symbolism.

"Unfortunately, SCAP's thoughtless edict has instantly created an international black market in temple swords that attracted the attention of the yakuza, the secret societies, or brotherhoods that grew out of a need for protection against increasing numbers of Ronin after 1700 in the Tokugawa Shogunate. One such group, the 'Showa,' was a recent break-off from the Kanesuka Brotherhood maybe in August this year. Some of the brotherhoods are reasonably altruistic, attempting to find ways to sequester National Treasure Nippon-to until they can be brought back safely to Japan, where they rightly belong. But Showa and others seem to have been subverted by greed and the potential for large profits that can be made by acting as clearing houses for extremely rich international collectors."

This thought made Nobu's eyes narrow to mere slits.

FIERY BLADE OF THE ENDURING COMET

Nobu knew his time to act was drawing short, but he wanted the Americans to know as much as possible about Japanese swords, their development and ties to Shintoism before he broached the feasibility of their help. So as they made their way across the city, he continued his discourse as rapidly as possible without losing all continuity.

"The cult of the Samurai was evolving parallel to the development of the superb new weaponry. Without such weaponry, Japan might now be just the eastern extension of the Chinese Empire. Timing then favored the Japanese. For seven years, the great Kublai Khan, grandson of Genghis Khan, sought to conquer our home islands. Beginning in 1274, he sent various small fleets against our coastal defenses. These probes, seeking points of weakness, were readily repulsed by Samurai swordsmen and archers with their superior steel weapons. Then in 1281, Kublai sent what should have been an overwhelming invasion—a Spanish Armada of its day. Fortunately, the Kami came to our aid with a divine wind, a Kamikaze, which devastated the invasion fleet of the Khan, driving it upon the rocks and shoals of our homeland, where Samurai defenders made short work of the remnant.

"Many believe that the pressure exerted by Kublai Khan hastened the perfection of blade steel. If so, the superb work of our greatest sword smith, Goro Nyudo Masamune, between 1288 and 1328, was a brilliant anticlimax."

As he talked, Nobu altered their progress into a highly convoluted pattern designed to expose or confuse any covert observation. Shortly afterward, they were at the presumed residence of their guide at the back of a small shop. He slid the inner fusuma of bamboo and heavy rice straw paper along the lower *shiku* track. A small, elderly woman in blue *yukata* and *mompei* arose, bowed, and moved silently into another part of the building.

"The *mamasan* is our *rusaban,* the house guard. With food and fuel so difficult to obtain and income uncertain, people will steal almost anything. We are fortunate in one respect; so far, there has been little violence to homes. So any little grandmother usually makes an adequate rusaban."

Nobu opened the heaviest piece of furniture in the room, an ornately carved chest of camphor wood. Setting aside neatly folded articles of clothing and linens, he withdrew a beautifully sheathed two-handed sword. "This nippon-to is a katana blade of a popular fighting length but made specifically for the Sengaku-ji Temple here in Shinagawa, six and a half centuries ago."

Yoshida then drew the blade from its cover, taking great care not to touch the steel where body acids might etch the highly polished surface. He pointed to the graceful waves of pale steel along the cutting edge of the blade. "These were made when the smith painted a thin slurry of clay, iron filings, and probably charcoal along the edge before the final quenching."

Then he inserted the blade three-quarters of the way back into the *saya*, the scabbard. Holding the scabbard with blade horizontal so it wouldn't slip, he extracted the *mekugi* or bamboo pin to release the *tsuka*, the wooden handle covered with ray skin. The visitors were surprised at the length of the handle. It appeared to be more than nine inches. It would accommodate both hands of the largest Samurai.

With a square of clean silk, he removed the other sword furniture, including an iron *tsuba* hand guard beautifully inlaid with a gold pheasant. These he placed on a nearby cushion.

The now exposed tang revealed the sword's history. Nobu interpreted the markings. "The *katana-mei*, side closest to the body, assuming a right-handed swordsman, reads, 'First year in the reign of the Emperor Hanazona, Enkyo Era.' The latter phrase means 'Becoming Prolonged,' referring to the year of the Great Comet. That was 1308 of the Christian calendar.

"The other side of the tang, the *tachi-mei*—away from the body, bears the signature, 'Goro Nyudo, Masamune.' The last word indicates 'master sword-smith.' The name of this sword is 'Fiery Blade of the Enduring Comet.'"

"Soon after Japan's surrender, a Kokuho, National Treasure Sword created by the same great master, Goro Nyudo Masamune, was presented to your president, Harry Truman."

Taking care as Yoshida had demonstrated, Blaz and Ragnor each thoroughly examined the six-century-old blade that looked like it might have been made six months ago. With hushed awe, the Fiery Blade of the Enduring Comet was handed back to Nobu who wrapped sword and scabbard in a large square of silk and laid it back in the chest. The lid remained open.

WALKING STICKS

They stood in silence. No one seemed to know what to say. Finally, Blaz broke the impasse. "Aren't you afraid to keep this extremely valuable national treasure in such an insecure place, knowing that Showa or some other secret brotherhood is likely searching for it?"

"Joss has been with us so far. We know that Showa has been searching diligently, but we have kept just a little ahead. This hiding place will now have to change immediately. My inviting you here has already compromised this covert."

In the outer shop, they paused to examine a small assortment of walking sticks in various patterns. Some were finished in black lacquer with scarlet *tsuka-ito* handle wrapping. These reminded Ragnor of the sword scabbard he had just seen. He thought, *These would make nice souvenirs.* There was even a pair of elaborately carved crutches, finished with a combination of black lacquer and scarlet tsuka-ito. They were surprisingly elegant.

Nobu, noticing his interest, explained, "A handicapped artisan designed and carved these beautiful pieces. He has long used crutches like the ones displayed here. Not surprisingly, we have sold quite a number of these."

As they were preparing to leave, three men entered the shop. One carried a packing quilt. Nobu nodded his head toward the room where they had just viewed the Nippon-to and the little rusaban had so recently appeared to be the only security.

It was deep twilight as the Americans stepped into the street. Far down the adjacent alley, Blaz noticed a tall figure slink into a hidden doorway. *Are my eyes playing tricks? Perhaps it is the result of too many stories. Best not mention it to Ragnor, at least not yet.*

HACHIMAN TARO

Evening 24 September 1945

As they returned to the Sengaku-ji Temple, Shinagawa was transmogrifying from twilight into full darkness, but their outbound route was totally different from the path they now followed.

Once inside the temple, Nobu continued to elaborate on the subject of Nippon-to. "Our other national treasure, Temple Sword is hidden elsewhere. We no longer dare risk the luxury of having our two Nippon-to at the shrine or even hidden together at the same place.

"The second sword is named 'The Firstborn of the God of War.' Its story is even more compelling, if possible, than that of the Masamune blade.

"In 1905, a young officer in the Imperial Japanese Army named Tokugawa Hattori carried an ancient tashi into battle against the Russians near Port Arthur. The tang inscriptions on its katana mei side read, *roku, nen, hachi, gatsu*. This means sixth year, eight month of the Bun-gi Era. That would place it in the sixteenth century. On the Tachi-mei side, most of the signature has been filed away. Only 'Sengo' remained faintly visible near the sword name, 'Hachiman

Taro,' which means 'Firstborn of the God of War.' With the era and partial signature, Lieutenant Tokugawa was certain his blade was a Sengo Muramasa.

"He purchased a replacement *kashiae,* a set of sword furniture from the thirteenth century that included an iron lace *tsuba*, or hand-guard, that probably cost him more than the Muramasa blade. The tsuba was of the Kamakura Period. I should mention that tsuba style periods differ from sword periods.

"A gold *menuki* in the form of a chrysanthemum was affixed to the *same* of giant ray skin that covered the handle. Tsuka-ito, the handle wrappings or bindings, were of heavy silk cording, dyed teal green. The nearly ten-inch, two-handed *tsuka* terminated in a rich gold *kashira* butt-cap, cast in the form of an open-mouthed dragon. Indeed, Tokugawa was on his way to fight the Russians with a national treasure Sword.

"Still, there was a nagging doubt from a different vector. Some said that Sengo Muramasa was the most skillful sword smith in all Japanese history. But like Faust, to gain his greatest wish he made a pact with Oni, the devil. From thence came such skill as no other smith could match.

"The sorcery of his mad mind tended to impart animated passions to his blades. They became bloodthirsty, often driving their owners to murder or suicide. Once drawn, some blades could not be sheathed without tasting blood. These curses had caused such losses to the Tokugawa Shogunate and their Samurai retainers that Shogun Tokagawa Iemitsu, in a 1501 edict, ordered all Muramasa blades destroyed. But warriors and traders alike were reluctant. The chiseled signatures on the tachi-mei were often filed away. Thus, the few remaining Muramasa are largely identified by the era marks, the name type, to wit 'war gods, epic battles etcetera,' the filed tachi-mei, and the superb workmanship of that master smith.

"So Tokugawa Hattori prided himself on his Nippon-to and worried about the validity of his sixteenth century ancestor's edict against the blade he now carried. To reassure himself, he brought it to a Shinto priest here at the Shinagawa Sengaku-ji. The priest took the sheathed sword from Tokugawa at the torii. Holding it above his head, he carried it into the temple to the ablution basin. Still holding the weapon aloft with his left hand, he dipped the fingers of his right hand into the water, and then lifting them upward, let a few drops fall on the sheath. Facing the honden sanctuary, he tapped the gong to summon the Genii Loci, the Guardian Kami of the Spring.

"In a low voice, the priest then spoke to the sword, 'O Hachiman Taro—thou Firstborn of the God of War, I will now unsheathe thee. As I draw thee forth, the curse placed upon you by the great smith Sengo Muramasa centuries ago will no longer be in force. Henceforth, the warrior Tokugawa Hattori will be your master. Like the warrior who carries you into battle, you are now subject to the Bushi-no-nasake, the warrior's code of mercy and benevolence. Nonetheless, you will retain your superior edge and strength of impact, imparted to you through the peerless forging and esoteric ritual of Sengo, Muramasa.'"

ORE SANJOU

6 May 1905

"Just four weeks after the ritual at Sengaku-ji, Lieutenant Tokugawa was at war on the Liaotung Peninsula of Manchuria not far from Port Arthur. Three days of bloody fighting had already made a legend of him, but it was his famous sword that engendered the greater interest. He was simply known as the 'Furious Lieutenant with the Cursed Muramasa Blade.'

"More weeks passed, but fame did not rest easy with him. It was annoying to have perfect strangers asking to view the 'Firstborn.' Behind his back, some were beginning to call him 'The God of War.' No one was sure whether this would have pleased or angered him. His own fame was soon to catch up with that of his tashi.

"The Japanese Imperial Army had landed on Liaotung Peninsula in a drive to cut off Port Arthur from Mukden and the other Russian military concentrations to the north. For days, a gray drizzle enveloped the contested territory. Russian machine gun placements guarded the ridge on which a large encampment had been set up.

"Lieutenant Tokugawa held back his vanguard platoon, waiting for the advancing Imperial Army to optimize its position. He then sent four troopers up a spur of the ridge, two on either side of the forward gun position. The remainder of the squad concentrated their rifle fire on the machine-gunners, but the Russians were well protected and maintained a steady barrage. The four Japanese advance men were annihilated.

"Tokugawa then sent four men up the uneven terrain further along the ridge, hoping they could find enough cover from which to establish a harassing fire against the Russians. It seemed to be working. Then as the firefight intensified, he holstered his Model 26, 9 mm revolver."

Realizing his American listeners were unlikely to be familiar with that weapon, Nobu paused to clarify. "The Model 26 was the martial sidearm of the Japanese Army adopted in the twenty-sixth year of the reign of the Emperor Meiji. That would be 1893 of the Christian calendar. Now the 26 was a strong serviceable weapon, but its quasi double-action required a long pull on the trigger to fire the first round. Many thought it was less than adequate for combat. So in 1914, it was replaced by the Nambu semiautomatic Type 14 handgun. Nevertheless, many 26s saw service even as late as World War II.

"But back to Tokugawa Hattori. Bushido was ingrained in his soul. Samurai and Imperial bloodlines flowed heavily in his veins. Traditions were deeply embodied in his mentality. He drew the Firstborn from its scabbard and slipped up the right side of the spur to a level with the gun emplacement. From the top of the protective embankment, with the tachi in both hands he charged, screaming like an Oni, 'Ore Sanjou'—I Have Arrived.

"The machine gun was firing at his troops on the other side of the spur, so his was a flanking attack. With tachi held above his head in both hands, he struck. With exquisite timing and strength of passion, he swung. The peerless steel of the Muramasa defined a perfect arc downward, severing the water jacket and the enclosed barrel of the machinegun in one fell swoop.

"Tokugawa did not even feel the jar of impact in his hands, arms, or shoulders. He stood in dumb amazement; The Firstborn was still quivering in his hands. This piece of laminated fury had severed the pride of twentieth century technology. His thirteenth century blade endowed with incantations and superb craftsmanship had become the symbol of Meiji resurgence.

"The remnant of his platoon broke through the Russian placements, followed by a battalion of the Imperial Japanese Army on its way to glorious victory. From above, the Sun Disk of Amaterasu shown down on them and in the front it waved from their battle standards. The Imperial Battle Flag with Rising Sun followed the defeated Tsarist army in full retreat. The usually ebullient Cossacks were nowhere to be seen. What the world thought to be a second-rate military power had manhandled the Tsarist forces. It seems there might have been a lesson there from the annals of one Kublai Khan.

"Little did the Russians know that they were witnessing the rise of military-industrialism in Imperial Japan. Nor could they have foreseen the role of Samurai traditions, thought broken by the Meiji Restoration, or the subversion of Shintoism in the rapid rise of a powerful new military state that would dominate East Asia for the next half century."

ORDER OF THE RISING SUN

"In 1875, Emperor Meiji established Japan's first national medal—Order of the Rising Sun. The order came in several classes, but few have received the first class with its Paulownia Blossom Cluster and Grand Cordon. Lieutenant Tokugawa Hattori was among the few recipients, and that receipt was posthumously.

"Some days following the victory over the Russians, the commander of his battalion came in person to visit Tokugawa. He asked for the *Chusa* (Lieutenant) by the now widely used sobriquet, 'May I speak with Tokugawa-san, whom they call the God of War?'

"He was answered by Tokugawa's sergeant, Watanabe Tose, a sturdy peasant of a man who had once cultivated rice near Shiraio in the Hidaka District of Hokkaido, known as Yezo to his people. That was before his conscription into the imperial army to fight the Russian hoards in 1904. With due obsequiousness, this survivor of the machine gun incident went to find his *Chusa*."

By now Blaz, Ragnor, and their Japanese mentor were at the temple grounds. The Johkai Priest had arranged for a mamason to serve them a meal in a sheltered overhang, where they could still converse freely. In addition to rice balls, they were served sliced onions served in saki. So as not to be impolite or render offense during the repast, Nobu was silent as they ate. When the story continued, they understood why.

"The body of Tokugawa was discovered in a small, wooded copse slumped over the Muramasa blade— 'Firstborn of the God of War.' Lacking a short dagger like tanto, most often used to initiate a ritual suicide, Hattori had used his tachi to perform seppuku. The blade was so long, he had to grasp the cutting edge with both hands to make the initial thrust into the left side of his abdomen. Even more pressure was required to draw the blade from left to right through his intestines. The ritual death of Tokugawa Hattori was complicated by his lack of a *kaishaku-nin*, the seppuku assistant, who would have normally stood at his left with drawn sword in both hands ready to decapitate the doer at the propitious moment. So gripping the ultra sharp Muramasa with enough force to pull it through the abdominal cavity had cut the flesh and tendons, all the way to the bones of each hand. The blade had fallen forward across the sheath and onto a sizeable piece of black silk meticulously laid out before the ritual."

"As the colonel watched, Watanabe carefully, almost reverently, laid the body back. Taking the black silk, he removed the blood and offal from the polished blade. He turned to look at the colonel, who was obviously having trouble sorting his feelings about having to deal with this peasant, yet he was impressed by the way he was handling the ordeal. He could not but realize the competence of this less than handsome peasant of obvious Jamon descent.

"The colonel swallowed his pride and spoke directly to Watanabe. 'I carry two documents with me that pertain to your Chusa. First is a battlefield promotion to Brevet Taisa colonel. That would have placed him in command of my battalion, as I have been moved to general staff. Obviously, other arrangements will now have to be made. Second, I carry a recommendation that Chusa Tokugawa be recipient of the Order of the Rising Sun, first class with Paulownia Blossom Cluster and Grand Cordon.'

The colonel paused then firmed up his decision. 'With this change of circumstance, I have decided to send you with a small escort to return the body and sword to the Sengaku-ji at Shinagawa. There he will be buried as near the forty-seven Ronin as possible and the sword, 'Firstborn of the God of War' shall be a temple gift to Sengaku-ji in perpetuity. Because of the heat and condition of the body, we will place it in a box of lightweight tinned steel, soldered closed.

"'To facilitate your orders, I will promote you to *Socho* (Sergeant Major). So Socho Watanabe, select three men from those left of your platoon, and we will make arrangements for your trip to Shinagawa.'"

RUSSIAN CAMPAIGN MEDAL

March 1906

The Emperor Meiji commissioned a service medal for the Russian Campaign, years thirty-seven and thirty-eight of the Meiji Era. It carried the crossed flags of the Japanese Imperial Army and the Japanese Imperial Navy, with a Chrysanthemum crest above and Paulownia crest below.

"Later that year, two packages were delivered to the Johkai Priest of the Shinagawa Sengaku-ji. The priest opened the small package first. It contained a general citation of service and a Meiji 37–38 medal. Below, there was another citation, 'To the honored Taisa Tokugawa Hattori the Emperor Meiji presents the first-struck medal for the Russian Campaign.' It was signed by a functionary in the 'Bureau of Medals and Decorations.'

"The larger package contained an elaborate, rolled scroll of rice paper, hand-painted and inscribed." Here, Nobu pulled from his pocket a paper, from which he read. "By the Grace of Heaven, Meiji Emperor of Japan, seated on the Throne occupied by the heirs of the Sun Goddess, Amaterasu from time immemorial do bequeath on Taisa Tokugawa, Hattori the Order of the Rising Sun, First Class.

"The Johkai Priest paused to open the heavy, embossed case. Light striking the burnished rays of that metallic sun combined with the tears welling around his eyelids was enough to momentarily blind him. He paused to let his eyes adjust then slowly resumed reading."

Nobu returned to his notes and read, "Let energy as powerful as the Rising Sun reflect the services you have rendered. Let the peace of your sleep next to the Forty-seven Ronin be always fulfilling. Know that this medal in the First Class represents the highest honor that falls within my power to confer. Meiji, Emperor of Heaven, year 39."

"A short note of instructions lay beneath the citations: 'Please display the medal and citations with the Muramasa blade—Hachiman Taro.' The package also contained a note from an imperial scribe.

The emperor is pleased that these medals honoring the great warrior Taisa Tokugawa will remain in perpetuity with the mirrors, jewels, and swords given to the Kami of Sengaku-ji. May I suggest that they be displayed behind secure glass, along with the votive offerings from the faithful of Shinto? Do not be surprised if the emperor himself should make pilgrimage to the Shinagawa Sengaku-ji.

Δ

Carvajal and Ragnvold had become enthralled by the traditions of the Samurai and the evolution of Japanese swords. They could hardly wait for the next session with Yoshida. Meanwhile, they made detailed notes on everything he brought up, but they knew they would need many review sessions to flesh out the details. But most of all, they speculated on where Nobu's time and friendship might be leading them.

WATANABE TOSE

When Blaz and Ragnor next met with their mentor, they were so anxious for the story's continuation that they shunned the preliminary niceties, forcing Nobu into story mode. "In 1906, Sergeant-Major Watanabe Tose also received a Russian campaign medal and a small stipend upon his release from the JIA. He returned briefly to Shiraio, but he was dissatisfied. The army had made him deeply conscious of his peasant status, even more his Ainu peasant status.

"He drifted south to Honshu in an effort to modify his cultural constrictions. There, the soils were deeper and more fertile, the weather warmer, and the rice more productive. Frugality and native intelligence paid off. He became a reasonable economic force. Late in life, he married a Yayoi woman, hoping to meld his family into the mainstream culture. But the advent of his firstborn in 1917 came as a shock. The son was pale of skin and long of limb. Even so, Tose bestowed the honored name of 'Hattori' upon the infant.

"As the lad grew, his Jamon features intensified. He grew tall, soon overshadowing his village cohorts. His heavy beard came in early, and worst of all, his hawk-like nose could not have been more unlike the dainty appendages of his schoolmates. He became 'The Bird,' shunned by his contemporaries and relegated to a lonely existence within his own inferiority complex.

"Still, Tose worked with the lad. The best education available to a peasant was provided. It was assumed that his career would be in the military. Watanabe Hattori was conscripted into the Japanese Imperial Army in 1937.

"His duty tour in Manchuria was anything but glorious. He in no way participated in the success of the Golden Lily Saga that so enriched the Yamato Dynasty. The army sent him back to home guard duty, and he eventually became the brutal enforcer that you, Blaz Carvajal, knew at the Shinagawa POW camp."

"What's the Golden Lilly?" In his excitement Ragnor literally shouted the question.

Nobu's jaw dropped in puzzlement.

"Sorry Nobu San. It's just that Blaz and I have a wager on who could first learn the underlying meaning of the term Golden Lily. Since I asked you first, it would appear that when you answer the question, Blaz will need to buy the block print of Shinsei's, *Fuji from Tagonoura* that he owes me."

Nobu said, "Far be it from me to deprive Blaz of the privilege of buying the print, if my small understanding of Golden Lily will answer your question. Golden Lily was a poem written by Hirohito which seems to be related to Japanese plunder of China, Southeast Asia and the Philippines during the Manchurian and Pacific wars. Golden Lilly seems to have become the code name for the looting operation. Apparently Prince Chichibu was on Luzon sequestering loot when the Americans invaded. The prince and one companion made a difficult escape through the jungles to the north end of the island where they were picked up by submarine for the trip home. The ordeal aggravated his chronic tuberculosis, and he was coughing up blood when they arrived. That's about all I know."

Blaz asked, "Did Hanare Masahiro have any connection to Golden Lily?"

Nobu looked puzzled. "You know, there were rumors that his stint as a POW guard was precipitated by his opposition to the whole operation. Apparently some of his superior officers, who were involved, had him sent to Omori Camp to get him out of their hair."

Both Blaz and Ragnor looked relieved. Blaz said, "Well Ragnor you shall have your wood block print with my blessing."

THE SHOE FALLS

22 October 1945

Between more distant excursions and constricted schedules, Ragnvold and Carvajal had not been together with Yoshida Nobu for some time. Even so, they were a little overwhelmed by his profuse welcome. The tension was almost palatable. Then he drew back and apologized. "Please forgive me, my friends. I have great need of your help, but obviously I have overplayed my hand. But somehow, I hope you will understand. Now as you Americans might say, 'I lay my hand on the table, face up.'"

"Sergeant Carvajal, I have known who you were for a long time. The Johkai Priest and I were aware of your efforts at the Shinagawa Hospital well before the surrender. Now, the Johkai is a magnanimous man of great intelligence and broad understanding. As early as 1943, he realized the waves of war would eventually overwhelm us, but he was always one who could hold panic at arm's length. He reorganized the resources at his disposal. Working through his many friends and associates, he attempted to make urban gardens more productive. He set up an informal network to maximize efficiency of production and distribution. This even extended into rural areas, where rice and red beans were produced."

"Out of the Kuraitani, the Valley of Death, as we call the period which extended across the Great Depression and World War II, he lifted so many. His network of help and exchange would have been considered a black market by the Tojo government, were it not rendered invisible by the efficiency and thinness of its dispersion. No one grew fat, but it is likely that more survived than would otherwise have done so. We had, on occasion, been able to smuggle small amounts of fruit and vegetables into the prison hospital, even before Colonel Hanare Masahiro was assigned there. Then with his assistance, we were able to augment more routinely, even though still thinly, the food parcels going to those undernourished men."

Yoshida knew his little speech sounded self-serving, and it was, but he continued anyway. "With increased pressure of MacArthur's disarmament squads and the Showa Brotherhood trying to obtain the Sengaku-ji Nippon-to, we have become increasingly desperate. Unfortunately, we have no contacts outside Japan where we can safely cache these national treasures until the attitudes and policies of the occupying forces change. Furthermore, the actions of Showa and even the Kanesuke Brotherhood show more greed than a propensity for the preservation of cultural resources. Is there any way you might help us get these two historical blades to America and care for them there until it is safe to bring them back to the Sengaku-ji Temple? Consider that it might require years, but at this point, we have no alternative. Too many national treasures have already been lost. For your help, we would be eternally grateful.'"

Ragnvold looked at Carvajal. Their faces registered total shock and amazement, yet deep down they each had expected something like this. Neither could have refused. Then Blaz spoke in a very personal way, using Yoshida's given name. "Nobu, both Ragnor and I have been expecting something of this nature, yet we were taken totally by surprise. However, now that you have focused the precise problem, we need time to consider its full ramifications and potential alternatives."

To which Ragnor added, "I am aware of Carvajal's gratitude and deep feelings for the Taisa. But I am indebted to you personally for the hours of instruction and fellowship you have so generously provided for both of us. I no longer feel the hatred for your people that I came here with, even though I still hate the inquisitional barbarism incurred by Tojo militarism. Both Blaz and I have become so immersed in your culture that we will do anything we can to help preserve its long held traditions. Give us a few days to explore the possibilities."

They shook hands with the overwrought Yoshida and left.

MAGWITCH

31 October 1945

Back aboard the *Benevolence*, Blaz proceeded along the line of POWs awaiting processing, he saw a hand come up as if to shade the eyes of a gaunt man. *It can't be.* Blaz quickly pulled an assistant from the closest table to fill in.

The hand came up again, the head turning back and forth, as though looking for something on the horizon. "Perhaps a band of sheep?"

Blaz sprinted the five yards or so to the gaunt, burley fellow standing with the aid of crutches. Throwing arms around the man, crutches and all, they fell to the deck. "Mag, you damned old Mexican hater, I had assumed the Japs had tired of your thievery and killed you long ago." They laughed like schoolboys, as the more able-bodied POWs attempted to get them on their feet again.

Magwitch said, "Looks to me like you're still herding sheep."

Blaz shouted to Ragnor, who was interviewing at a nearby table. "Come here and meet the meanest son-of-a-gun from Lino County. He would have been practically your neighbor in his illegal hoss trading days. Ragnor, meet

Magwitch Russell, and be warned that last name should have been spelled R-U-S-T-L-E"

"Mag, this is Ragnor Ragnvold from Bluewater, New Mexico."

Mag grinned and held out a big, gnarled paw. "Yeah, I once knew a Ragnvold from over in the Ramah area somewhere. Not quite sure. Hell, he wasn't much of a bulldogger, but he was pretty good with a skinning knife once we had a critter drowned."

"What the hell are you talking about, Mag?" asked Blaz.

"You remember the bunch that came to Cabañatua Camp from Corregidor? It was after the Bataan troops were already there. That would have been sometime in July of '42. Well, when Yates and I drowned our first water buffalo and convinced the Japs that it died of natural causes so they wouldn't eat it, Jubal Ragnvold was there with his handy skinning knife to help butcher it properly. But I always called him the Skinner, so you might not have remembered him by name."

Ragnor grinned, remembering how fast his brother could skin out and cut up a poached deer.

In the first excitement of realizing that his friend from the death march and hell ship was still alive Blaz had failed to see the crutches. As he realized the seriousness of Mag's condition he ordered a medic with a wheelchair and hustled him into the line of those requiring immediate medical attention. It was gratifying to see Captain Jones himself examining the mangled leg and foot of that tough, old puncher.

By this time, the staff was processing an average of more than fifty POWs each day. For most, it began with a preliminary separation as to medical need, mental condition, and those fit for an immediate transfer to Okinawa or another secure base for a hurried trip home.

Unfortunately, movements out of these bases were not always without glitch. Military transport planes were getting old and less reliable. Makeshift conversions of heavy bombers were not much better. But when the rumor mill began circulating a story about cargo doors tearing off a C47 and sucking out six returning POWs high above the Pacific Ocean never to be seen again, the popularity of flying home suddenly plummeted. Those who had requested such transport were strangely absent when their flights were called.

Meanwhile, back on the *Benevolence*, the MPs controlling the liberated warriors had developed their own categories. They rushed the worst-off to the processing lines first. The less critical ones they kept busy eating, drinking, sleeping, and enjoying an unusual leisure.

Later that day, Ragnor received an airmail letter, postmarked San Francisco, California, 20 October 1945.

Dear Rag,

Just got your address, so will try to catch you up on a few things. American troops retook Manila, 4 March this year and within two weeks liberated us from the hellhole at Cabañatua. But with all the intestinal parasites, malaria, and a positive TB test, they kept me in Manila longer than expected. Finally in June, they shipped me to the military hospital here in San Francisco. The doctor says I'm stable enough to do pretty much what I please but must stick around until they have the parasites whipped. Right now, their best esti-mate is six to eight months, with maybe an occasional long weekend to visit home.

The folks just left to go back to Bluewater. Guess they need to get the stock out of the high country before the snow flies.

They said you were now processing liberated POWs in the Tokyo area. I was hoping you might have run across an old mate of mine, name of Magwitch Russell. He saved my life and many others in the brutal days of the Japanese takeover of the Philippines. He's a mean son-of-a-gun externally, but internally, he's a pussycat with a heart of gold. Last I heard he was moved to Bili-bid for shipment to Japan. That was in '43, and I've heard nothing of him since. Let me know if you find out anything. I'd sure like to get in touch. If chance arises, ask Mag to tell you about Bataan and the butcher shop operation.

Thanks, Jube.

Two days later, Ragnor and Blaz set out to find Mag some-where among the 802 patient beds of the *Benevolence*. To their surprise, the clerks had an up-to-date bed assignment and an almost readable flow diagram. That surprise was compounded when they found Mag sitting propped up with pillows and the shattered leg heavily cast to the knee.

They pulled up chairs, prepared for a session of encouragement and psychotherapy, only to find Mag already in good spirits.

"Looks like I have at last, completely beaten these Japs."

"How's that, Mag?" Blaz cautiously interjected.

"Just before the death march, I had decided to join the Philippine Resistance. Fortunately, or unfortunately, I watched from the jungle as that progression of hopelessness passed by. It was unbearable. Seeing my comrades, most of them ill with dysentery, malaria, or TB, or all three, and all of them totally disheartened by the surrender that should not have happened, I could not walk out on them. I said to myself, 'Mag you gotta help these poor bastards. If you are unwilling, who's going to do it? You must beat these damned Japs at the most brutal level of this conflict.'

"I gave my Springfield, my Colt, and what ammo I had to a Philippine family and told them to 'give these to the Resistencia por Martar Japos.' I rejoined my buddies and for the first time, I knew I could survive anything these little rice-heads could hand out. We talked over our problems and realized we had to organize our efforts. We must stick together. I didn't know what was ahead of us at the end of the line, but it was obviously a march of attrition. The Japs did not know what to do with so many prisoners. They were hoping we would all die along the way, and they were perfectly willing to give the Grim Reaper a helping hand. We reasoned that our best chance was to get to the head of the line as quickly as possible. Anything would be better than dying of dysentery while puking in an already completely contaminated water hole.

"Funny thing, I can never remember my own birth date, but I can never forget the date we started the death March, 9 April 1942. It was less than a hundred miles from Bataan to San Fernando, where the death march ended. All survivors made it in eight days, but in that time, we had bypassed the entire column and were first to board the narrow gauge train that would take us to Cupas before the final eight-mile walk into Cabañatua Labor Camp 1. You know, Blaz, I truly believe that getting on that train first saved all the lives in our group.

"It was probably a month later that I ran into Ragnor's brother. He had been at Corregidor, where a gutsy commander held out another twenty-eight days and delayed the Jap occupation, allowing the evacuation of more of our military brass. It seems the Japs were so single-minded about controlling every rock that happened to interfere with their objectives that they would concentrate the entire force at their disposal upon that obstruction, rather than isolating it in order to gain the greater objective. Had they isolated the resistance at Corregidor and applied their efforts toward the greater objective, they would have captured the entire high command of American Forces in the Western Pacific. As it was, your brother Jubal and his buddies on Corregidor became the thorn in the Jap's side that tied up so many troops in the effort to eliminate the rock that MacArthur and the entire American command structure had time to be evacuated by PT boats.

"Anyway, old Jube and I were in the group assigned to work the paddies after rice harvest. We were using water buffalo to plow the soil above the clay pan that seals the bottom, so as to retain water during the growing season. There was just enough water remaining in a couple of paddies that we might be able to drown one of the beasts. It would have been simple enough to slit its throat, but we had to make it look like the caribou died of natural causes."

"Caribou?" quizzed Carvajal.

"Yeh, some New Mexican sheepherder, maybe it was you, never heard of a water buffalo and started calling them 'caribou.' Who knows where you might have heard of caribou. Seriously, the Tagalog name is 'caraboas.' Anyway, back to my story that you so rudely interrupted; there was another bulldogger from the Socorro country named Yates. He and I decided we would try drowning one. That was worse than dogging a Brahma bull."

He grinned at his old friend Blaz and continued, "One day, the Jap guards had gone to a meeting of some kind without leaving anyone to watch the henhouse. Now my friend Yates was a big dude and had to use a Clydesdale for a cutting horse. Well, we put the old cow buffalo in the drowning pool, and the pair of us tried twisting the head to throw her. She would kinda lift her head playing with us then shake us off like a pair of rag dolls.

"When bulldogging a two-year-old steer in a rodeo, you use the momentum of your horse and the steer as leverage in the throw. As the horse carries you along the left side of the steer, you lean out over the head and grab the horns. Then, lifting out of the saddle, you lower your feet, gradually digging in the heels of your boots to slow the speed of the animal while twisting its head back across your legs and body to take it off balance. Once down with its head twisted back, the animal is virtually helpless until you release it.

"Unfortunately, the water buffalo was not moving or cooperating in any fashion. So we brought over the bigger bull I was driving. We tied a heavy rope around the right horn of the cow, took a half hitch on the nose, and brought the length of rope up along the left side of the neck and over her back. This we tied into the tugs of the bigger buffalo's harness, leaving no slack. With a heavy jerk on the rope, the big caribou easily accomplished that which Yates and I together were unable to do. Yates jumped on the left horn, while hanging onto the right to keep her head under water I whipped the other caribou just enough to keep pressure on the rope. The ensuing struggle may have lasted ten minutes, but it seamed like the longest fight of my life. I expected the Jap guards to reappear at any moment.

"I still wonder what kind of meeting those Japs were having. Perhaps a little saki was involved. But before they returned, we had pulled the old cow out of the water hole, hooked her back to the plow, and were playing the concerned drivers wondering at the death of a beloved *gamusa*.

"After some difficult explaining, a few crocodile tears, and the suggestion of a possible profit, we convinced the guards that we could tan the hide for a variety of uses, and we would dispose of the probably tainted carcass. Here was where Jubal the Skinner and his dandy skinning knife came in. Somewhere, Jube had obtained a butcher knife that looked like an early American Green River skinner used by mountain men and Ashley beaver trappers. Where he hid it and how he kept it sharp, we never knew. He did a masterful job skinning that old cow and butchering her out. We worked all night, carrying meat to the various POW labor camps. Trouble was we had no refrigeration. In the tropics, preventing meat from spoiling is most difficult. But the cooks managed to keep it safe by constantly simmering the stew to keep the bacteria at bay.

"The next day, the Jap guards had half the farm crew gathering ashes and scrounged up a large open barrel from somewhere to let the lye form in. Jube had done such a job of skinning that there was little extra work necessary to remove remaining chunks of fat and meat from the hide. The honcho guard did find a meat saw, so we could remove the huge horns for trade with some Philippine craftsman for a small profit.

"Our remaining obstacle was convincing the guard to accompany me into the jungle to find a tree with suitable tanbark for the final curing of our leather. Once I communicated that he should bring another guard, he agreed, becoming an avid tanbark hunter. It was easy enough. Rainforest trees have a very thin bark; so even with a small knife, you simply cut out a piece of the cambium layer and taste. Tannin is highly astringent. Did you ever whittle on a cottonwood branch and put the end in your mouth? That's the taste." His listeners looked bewildered. Mag continued, "Even my Jap guards were more adventurous than you turkeys. They ran through that forest like kids on an Easter egg hunt and old Tojo, that's what I called the honcho, discovered the best kind of tree. We striped several gunnysacks full of bark and brought them back to dry before preparing the tanning solution. The leather tanned beautifully, and we turned a small profit with the aid of the enemy, but more importantly, scores of starved POWs had several meals of water buffalo protein.

"Old Tojo must have done quite well trading the leather. He stopped hounding me about liberating Red Cross packages he kept for his own use. And it was seemingly easier to fill the *quam* pot with scraps left over from their kitchens, as well as from stray cats, rats, and crickets. Our cups ranneth over."

Δ

Eventually, the conversation drifted away from prisoner economics into more subtle avenues. In a quiet tone, Blaz asked, "Now Mag, I have a question. Are you still planning to fulfill the *promesa* to the Holy Mother and me to make the pilgrimage to the holy shrine at Chimayo? As my memory serves, you are the one who told me that a promesa is really a *corban,* an offering made to God in fulfillment of a vow. According to my best accounting, all but two of the 198 survivors of the 200th Coast Artillery plan to go when we get back and can all go together."

Mag displayed one of his fiendish grins. "Yeah I should probably need some new saddle blankets by the time we can all get there. Those Chimayo weavers make good heavy ones that are less money than the Navajo jobs."

This was scarcely the answer Blaz was seeking, but he knew that in Mag's own blasphemous way, it meant yes. He let it drop.

A WILLING ACCOMPLICE

Blaz then changed course. "Now Mag, we've a favor to ask of you. Knowing how you hate Tojo's militarism and scarce have more love for MacArthur's dictatorial occupational government, we have a project that might go against both of these and could certainly use your devious capabilities."

Without giving Mag time to object or acknowledge Blaz plowed right on. "Soon after becoming SCAP, MacArthur ordered all Japanese weapons confiscated and destroyed. This order includes swords, even Shinto temple swords of great beauty and value. Some of these art swords, called nippon-to, are documented national treasures as well.

"At the same time, Japanese secret societies, such as Showa and the Kanesuka Brotherhood, are trying to sell them to big time foreign collectors for the lucrative profit they will bring.

"The Johkai Priest of the nearby Sengaku-ji Temple and his assistant, Yoshida Nobu, has asked us to smuggle two extremely valuable swords out of Japan and keep them hidden until political conditions are favorable for their return. The Johkai and Yoshida, like Colonel Hanare, have long tried to mitigate conditions of hospitalized POWs by surreptitiously slipping extra rice, soy, and fresh fruits into the hospital whenever they could. This was at grave personal risk. We came to realize that Shinto and Buddhism, in spite of Jap militarism and SCAP paranoia, still contained much humanity of the common man. Both Ragnor and I feel an obligation to help their efforts."

Mag said nothing, but Blaz knew that beneath that rough exterior, he was remembering his own humanity. Finally, he looked up for awhile at the heavy cast on his leg and foot and asked, "What could I do?"

Blaz smiled. "Without knowing it, you are looking at the answer to your own question."

Mag held out his hands in a questioning manner.

Blaz smiled again and said, "In the shop at the front of the house where one of the swords was hidden, a number of hand-carved walking sticks, crutches, and the like are offered for sale. Some of these have black lacquer finishes with hand-painted scenes and scarlet silk ito bindings that would make them ideal mementos for American veterans.

"What Ragnor and I had in mind was to have a set of these beautiful crutches custom made for you. The right crutch would just happen to have the sword named, 'Fiery Blade of the Enduring Comet' hidden inside. The second sword, 'Hachiman Taro, Firstborn of the God of War,' would accidentally be concealed within the left crutch. The First Born was created by the wizard smith, Sengo Muramasa, circa 1501. He was the creator of the accursed blades of the Tokugawa Shogunate. The two Sengaku-ji blades together with their furniture, which you will carry separately, would probably bring over a million dollars on the international black market for temple swords." Mag whistled. "Looks like I'll be able to buy the Dan Thornton spread sooner than I had anticipated."

Ragnor smiled, remembering the money asked for the White Mountain Hereford Ranch when Dan Thornton left Arizona and shortly became governor of Colorado. That was before the outbreak of the war.

"Avarice aside," said Blaz. "Could you or would you be willing to help us?"

Mag's face grew somber. "For you, my sheep herding friend, I would do most anything. Go ahead and make your arrangements, then clue me in about my role."

Both Blaz and Ragnor breathed a sigh of relief. Then Ragnor asked, "Do you prefer the traditional black lacquer finish with red silk cord wrappings and traditional landscapes, or does your flamboyant nature crave a brighter finish, perhaps a yellow-orange background with pink wrapping and geishas painted in between?"

Fortunately, Ragnor's quick reflexes saved him from the coffee mug hurled by Mag.

"I take it you are a traditionalist after all," said the smiling Ragnor.

"Now you remind me of your ornery brother, Jubal the smart mouth," replied Mag.

"Speaking of Jubal, I have a letter in my pocket; I'll let you read in a few minutes. But first, we do need to discuss crutch design and measure the size of the army-issue ones you are now using; that is, if they fit okay. For lacquer color, you might consider the deep cherry with the black silk wrappings, which is highly traditional. Otherwise, the black lacquer with teal wrappings might be the most conventional. Either combination is found on sword saya, the scabbards, of the Koto, or Old Sword Period. Either would be quite appropriate, considering the contents of the crutches. Between the wrappings on the right crutch, I would suggest miniature paintings of Mount Fuji and the Torii, the ceremonial gate of Sengaku-ji Temple, both identified by Japanese characters.

"On the left crutch, I would suggest an Oni, the devil, to suggest the character of the wizard smith, Sengo Muramasa, and the evil enchantments associated with his blades. Then on the area in front of the hand grips where wear will not be a problem, we can have a *netsuke* carver execute in ivory small dragons in a Japanese style."

Mag sat in silent contemplation, his mind obviously reconstructing the patterns Ragnor had carefully outlined. "What's a netsuke?"

Ragnor replied, "These are the miniature carvings of which Japanese artisans are so fond and expert at creating."

"Do you reckon they would carve a small bull on one crutch and a horse head on the other? I would gladly pay extra."

"I'm sure there would be no problem," Ragnor replied.

Ragnor pulled Jubal's letter from his pocket and handed it to Mag. The latter read it slowly and thoughtfully. It was obvious when he read the part about Bataan and Corregidor. Mag's face was still somber as he folded the letter and handed it back.

Slowly, Ragnor broached another problem. "If we are successful in getting these swords to the States, we are still faced with the problem of safe coverts for what could be a rather extended time period. As a matter of policy, we should sequester the swords separately with different care-takers." He let his voice trail off.

Mag knew they were waiting for his response. Mag considered, *In point of fact, this is extending my commitment well beyond just being a smuggler of illicit arms.* He took his time in answering. "My family and I have ranch properties scattered over the high country of eastern Arizona. I could probably find a secure place for one nippon-to."

He turned to Ragnvold and added, "Perhaps old Jubal could take care of the other. There must be secret spots known only to the Ragnvold clan somewhere on the slopes of the Ashiwi Mountains south of Bluewater. Back in my horse-trading days, I occasionally hid out in a mine head-frame that was well concealed from casual traffic. Surely old Jube could stash one of them swords somewhere up there, where even the Jap Ronin can't find it."

Ragnor pondered the last revelation, *Who would have thought that Magwitch knew so much about our stomping ground?* But seeing the logic in what Magwitch had intimated, he said, "All right, I'll get in touch with Jubal."

BACK TO SENGAKU-JI

4 November 1945

Blaz and Ragnor caught the gig from the Yokosuka Anchorage. The thirty-two nautical miles had required nearly an hour. With the new anchorage, *Benevolence* had reduced the number of Omori runs to a couple each day. The first run departed the ship about 0715 each morning, and the last run departed Omori at 2200 hours. It was a far cry from the convenience of the gig and liberty boat runs from Shinagawa Wan to Omori that occurred about every fifteen minutes and took less than ten minutes to dockside.

To accommodate the lengthy and inconvenient commute, Blaz and Ragnor had started to schedule their liberty in three-day blocks. They would leave the ship on the early morning run of the first day, spend two nights in Shinagawa, and then return the evening of the third day.

That morning in Shinagawa, they found a very anxious Yoshida. "Where have you been for so long? The Johkai and I have been worried."

"Our apologies my friend. Since the *Benevolence* moved to Yokosuka, commuting has been a problem. But for the last few days, we have been considering the greater problem of getting the nippon-to out of Japan and safely sequestered in America," Blaz replied.

"And?"

"We have worked through various options. Most had to be abandoned because of insurmountable dead-ends. Then a few days ago, an old friend of mine from the death march and hell ships showed up at the processing center. He had suffered severe reprisals by Japanese guards at the Fukuoka Coal Mine, where he worked as slave labor since May 1943. The prompt action of his mates and immediate removal to the *Benevolence* appears to have saved the limb."

Blaz continued, "I believed we have convinced him to help us. So here is our proposal. On the day you showed the Goro Nyudo nippon-to to us, there were some beautifully made walking sticks and crutches displayed in the outer shop. If you could have a pair of crutches made in such a way as to conceal the blades, it might be possible to slip them out, right under the noses of the Showa. Once they are ready, we could bring Magwitch into the shop to buy the crutches as representative art to take back home with him. He could leave his old crutches behind and walk right out of the shop with the Sengaku-ji Temple Swords concealed in his new sticks. Ragnor and I would carry the sword furniture separately in small packages.

"Once onboard ship, it would be quite difficult for Showa or Kanesuka ronin to get hands on them. Once in the States, Ragnor or I would have to coordinate transport and sequestering. It would be unwise for either you or the Johkai to know the details of our actions. You would have to rely completely on our judgment and veracity until it becomes opportune to return the swords to Shinagawa. Are you willing to take such risks?"

Nobu suddenly looked startled. The blunt question made him realize the greater ramifications of their actions. He wished the Johkai were here to take or share the burden. He swallowed hard and bit the nail. "I hadn't realized the weight of the burden we have asked you to carry. Indeed, I am humbled even by your in-depth consideration. Now it seems that in addition to putting the two of you in harm's way, we may have extended the danger to a maimed wartime prisoner of Imperial Japan."

Blaz laid a hand on his shoulder. "I believe the dangers to us are minimal. Perhaps the gravest concern is, do you trust us to handle everything once the nippon-to leave your hands?"

Nobu almost looked relieved.

Ragnor then continued, "The *Benevolence* is scheduled to leave for San Francisco on 27 November. The crutch pickup would need to be three or four days before that. Do you think your carvers and painters could have them finished by then? After all, it is only two weeks away."

Ragnor had spoken rapidly, not wanting to give Yoshida an opportunity to question anything before hearing the whole proposal.

The usually voluble Yoshida seemed speechless.

Ragnor pulled out some rough sketches showing how he and Blaz envisioned the final production. They discussed size, contours, carvings, colors, lacquers, wrappings, and even menuki and netsuke. Then he asked, "How many artisans would you have working on these? And are they reliable?"

Nobu scanned the drawings and said, "Two weeks is a very short time for such an involved project. The final carving, base painting, lacquer drying, scene painting, and intricate cord wrapping are sequential and time consuming processes that cannot be overlapped. Fortunately, only two artisans will be involved and so far, I have been able to trust them. Unfortunately, secret societies are highly adept at infiltration and information extraction. My carver is a close associate of the Johkai Priest's efforts to save the nippon-to. The painter is less certain. The problem here is the hollow sections that will hold the blades are a dead give away. It seems the best option is to take him into our full confidence."

Yoshida continued, "Now we must decide upon an exact date for the transfer and work to that end. But we must not risk an inauspicious time. Please give me pause to consult my almanac of meteorological and astrological forecasts. Can you give me the year of your friend's birth?"

"It's Magwitch," Blaz responded. "Now let me think. He joined the Guard in 1941, and it seems like he said he was twenty-seven at the time. He had to have been born in 1913. I hadn't realized he was such an old codger for all these war games."

"Ah, that would make him *ushi*, born in the Year of the Ox. Let us check the astrological almanac for ushi that would be within our time constraints. Thursday, 22 November. It advises, 'Unusual foods, travel and swords must be avoided at any cost.' Most unsuitable. Let me try Friday 23 November. It advises, 'Avoid embarking on any new enterprise.' Not good at all. Well how about Saturday 24

November? 'A good day to trust new friends.'" Yoshida fairly beamed at the auspicious reading. "Let us attempt that day."

Blaz was astonished that such an erudite person would place deep faith in these astrological almanacs. He thought, *What the heck, it can't hurt?*

THE TRANSFER

More than once during the long commute from Yokosuka Anchorage to Omori Dock, Ragnor had thought, *How convenient it would have been from our previous anchorage in Shinagawa Bay*. Then he thought again, *Mag is a tough old codger and even now, he seems to be enjoying the salt spray and the signs of a defeated Japan all about him*.

The coxswain pulled the liberty launch alongside the Omori Dock. Ragnor and two sailors lifted the wheelchair, Mag and all, onto the planking. Blaz followed with aluminum, military issue crutches. On the dock, Ragnor spoke briefly with two shore patrolmen with truncheons and side arms. "Follow us, but keep a little behind. Try to make it appear as though you are on routine patrol or just checking us out. We will be playing the gawk-eyed sailors looking for embroidered jackets and war souvenirs. I don't believe it will fool the Showa or Kanesuka any more than your patrol routine will, but it may create enough distraction that we can get Mag into a certain shop to buy special-made crutches and back to the launch before the brotherhoods realize what we are doing or decide how to respond. Your side arms may be just enough to deter or slow down their response."

He left the patrol more confused than before, but that was probably for the better. Fortunately, there were enough American military types on the street that morning to make them a little less conspicuous. Many of the shops sold souvenirs and war relics, so shopping should be viewed as normal. But Mag was not much of a shopper. Before the war, he bought his Levi's at Barth's, but his boots, shirts, and horse tack were mail-order from Sears' or Monkey Ward's. There really wasn't much here to his liking. Finally, he bought two prints on beautifully textured rice paper, one for his mother, one for the sister. Each print depicted Samurai vengeance as portrayed on the Kabuki stage and illustrated by Hirosada Konishi. These were obviously starving artist copies, since Hirosada had been dead for over a century. Still they were good ones; even so, the wheelchair was less than loaded down.

Before the next shop, Blaz whispered, "This is the pickup point, Mag, so act like there is something inside that interests you." He looked at various items and pointed at something in the window, so they went inside. Still it was hard for the old puncher to spend that back pay on dry goods when it should be saved to purchase breeding stock when he got home, or at present on those more liquid goods—the kind that would have been appreciated by the poet Omar Khayyam,

I often wonder what the vintners buy
One half so precious as the goods they sell
The Rubaiyat

No one dared guess what Mag's reaction to the ornate crutches might be. He took one and examined it carefully. A luminous, deep-hued cherry lacquer had been applied as the background. Around this were wrappings of heavy black silk cord set off with cast bronze fittings, and a gold chrysanthemum menuki adorned each crutch. An extension of the upper wooden crosspiece on the right crutch was carved as the face of the Sun Goddess, Amaterasu. On the left crutch, it was the Firstborn of the God of War, Hachiman Taro. In a protected spot near the lower crosspiece was a miniature ivory bull, one of Mag's suggested netsuke. On the left crutch was a horse head netsuke. Blaz and Ragnor were jumping inside themselves with delight. Then they watched as Mag slowly examined the details. His face showed no emotion as his eyes passed over the miniature paintings of Mount Fuji and the Sengaku-ji Torii or even the gold menuki, but they both caught the flicker of prideful ownership, as the hard eyes of Mag passed over the netsuke bull and horse head. It was worth the whole effort. Even Nobu felt a pride of accomplishment. Mag smiled and pulled out a roll of bills, making a show of payment. Yoshida gracefully accepted the proffered money.

Slowly, Mag took both sticks and laboriously rose to his good foot, swung the heavy cast toward the door. As a second thought he expressed the need to use a water closet. Both Blaz and Ragnor hurried to assist, but Mag pushed them aside with his new right crutch. "Can't a man make a little water without the accompaniment of two nursemaids?" Here Nobu came to his aid, opening the back screen and pointing to a high board fence and shrubs enclosing and lending some privacy to an outdoor comfort station. Mag grunted then carefully placed the new sticks against the wheelchair, before reaching for the army issue metal jobs.

"No need of messing up these beauties in a cesspit." Further assistance was not offered.

As the crippled ex-POW pushed through the bushes, he detected movement on his right. As he turned to check it out, someone behind him threw a hammer-lock on his right arm and a choke hold on his neck. The aluminum crutches fell into the pit. To an experienced bar-room brawler like Mag, this was scarcely a setback. Standing on the heavy leg cast he leaned as far forward as possible while kicking backward and upward into the attacker's groin. The man fell forward, following the crutches into the cesspit. Round one went to the cripple. He shouted for help.

A swarthy face with an eagle beak leered at him and growled, "Where are the crutches containing the nippon-to?" Realizing his second failed attempt at the Sengaku-ji National Treasure Swords, the brutal Watanabe crazed with anger, plunged a tanto into Mag's chest. Searing pain accompanied the severance of tissue. Muscle, tendons, skin and nerves each felt the sundering as the tanto was turned in the deep wound. Mag fell in the entry way. The one with the dark face jerked the tanto from the wound, wiped it on Mag's shirt and was gone before those in the shop realized what was going on.

Blaz immediately took charge. He was already blaming himself for implicating his best friend in this deplorable affair. "Ragnor get the sterile surgical dressing and sulfa powder out of my medial kit. We must get the bleeding stopped immediately then apply the antibiotic. So you are in charge of pressure point application. Nobu if you would, put water on the ro to boil, it will help with sterilization and we are going to need a lot of strong tea as well." Between shouting orders, he placed his ear on the other side of Mag's chest. "His vital signs appear to be good. I don't believe any of the critical organs were injured so the main factor now seems to be shock." By then Nobu was back and Blaz asked him for mats and blankets to keep the wounded man warm.

Until this moment no one seemed to have thought of the swords. Ragnor said, "Nobu have you seen the crutches?" This startled Nobu, who hurriedly scanned the shop. *Was it possible that Showa operatives, even Watanabe, had entered the shop during the commotion over Mag and removed the crutches with their valuable contents?* He panicked.

Running into the alley, he spotted one of the MPs who had accompanied them from the dock. "If you are looking for the handmade crutches, Mr. Yoshida, they are being watched in the room behind the shop." Nobu sat right down in the alley and wept with relief.

Mag had regained consciousness and the shot of morphine administered by Blaz seemed to have minimized the pain from the deep wound. Blaz asked, "Do you feel strong enough to return to the *Benevolence* this afternoon or would you prefer to spend a night here? Yoshidasan has offered a place for you to recuperate."

"No offence to Nobu, but it would probably be in the best interest of all of us to get those bloody swords back to the ship as soon as possible. Is our shore patrol escort still available?" asked Mag.

Blaz replied, "They are sill with us. They checked with their Shinagawa office right after you were wounded. They advised our friends to stay with us until we were on the launch headed for the *Benevolence*."

Mag drank the last cup of strong tea, ate some more rice cakes and said, "Let's hit the road."

The crowd that had gathered at the shop entrance early on in anticipation of a show was mostly still there. They clapped excitedly as a cumbersome figure in a wheel chair, carrying the most ornate sticks they had ever seen was rolled out of the shop. He said, "I had hoped to walk for a little way down your street on these, but a Showa Brotherhood Ronin changed my mind."

Ragnor pushed the chair, and Blaz walked beside the wounded veteran carrying two small packages. Some within the crowd might have guessed their content, it probably didn't matter. Two burly shore patrolmen walked behind with batons and side arms.

They were on the docks before the scheduled departure time of *Benevolence*'s liberty launch. Once they had made Mag comfortable, they all spent a good while examining the beautifully detailed work on the ornate sticks. It was still obvious that Blaz and Ragnor were more excited than the unflappable Magwitch, but there was no mistaking the pride in his eyes.

Once they had departed the dock at Shinagawa, Blaz pulled a roll of bills out of his pocket and handed then to the old cowboy. "Mr. Yoshida ask me to give these back to you. These represent their small investment in restocking your ranch. Now I quote, 'The sticks are yours to remember us by. May their graceful lines remind you of what is good in Japan and help you forget that which was not so good.' And finally he said, 'Mata yo, we will meet again.'"

Mag simply bowed his head, hoping to cover his emotions.

STRONG ARM

Late Saturday afternoon, Mag was relaxing with a fairly up to date *Country Gentleman*, when two strong-arm types in civilian clothes approached his bed on the *Benevolence*. "Are you Magwitch Russell?" the apparently senior one asked.

"Who the hell's asking?"

The senior man replied, "We are with the US Intelligence Service working with SCAP, and it might pay you to keep a civil tongue in your mouth."

"And what are you going to do if I don't, send me back to the Fukuoka Coal Mine?"

The senior man ignored the reference to the slave labor camp and responded, "The Supreme Commander is working within a very delicate political framework and wishes to minimize the effect of POW treatment on the American public. We have here a confidential document that declares that you will not discuss your treatment as a prisoner of war in Japan when you return home. Once you sign, we will give you a gratuity of three hundred dollars."

"Three hundred dollars for this mangled foot? Three hundred bucks for the TB, the malaria, the dysentery, and the intestinal parasites? How about for the lives of all my friends who have already succumbed to the brutality of these little yellow bastards? Get out of my sight you sickening maggots. Orderly!"

By this time, it seemed the whole ward had encircled the staging area. The intelligencers backed away cautiously. Boos and catcalls followed their lackluster withdrawal. When the orderly appeared, Mag demanded, "Report this to Captain Jones. These jackals have no business here."

OUTWARD BOUND

27 November 1945

The USS *Benevolence* sailed from Yokosuka. That evening, Ragnor telegraphed his brother in San Francisco:

> Jubal (stop) Magwitch departed on Benevolence today (stop) should arrive Port of Embarkation Piers 12 December (stop) try to meet him at pier (stop) otherwise probably transient at Fort Mason couple of days (stop) put shears in white sacks (stop) you and Mag each take one (stop) Ragnor.

The crossing to San Francisco took sixteen days. On the day of arrival, 12 December, Mag sent a telegram to Carvajal.

> Pastor (stop) sheep shears arrived safely (stop) the Skinner met us on the dock (stop) advise about shearing (stop) Merry Christmas (stop) Mag.

WHITE SACKS

Mag's mother and brother were on the pier, temporarily assigned to the *Benevolence*. They had been there for over two hours before disembarkation of any personnel began. Even then, it took a good while before a seaman pushing a wheelchair brought Mag to them. The home folks had barely welcomed the prodigal before another scarecrow showed up. "Mag, you old son of…" The voice trailed off, with the realization of who was standing there.

"It's all right Mom, just more crow bait from Bluewater. We have a bit of shear trading to do."

"Now Magwitch, don't you get into illegal horse trading before we even get you home."

"It's all right, Mother; he already knows I've warned the good people in Alliance to watch you so you would not steal the graveyard."

She was off in a huff, but like a mother hen, was back in a few moments.

Mag turned to Jubal Ragnvold. "Well old Skinner, did Ragnor send you any instructions or recommendations that we can ignore or change?"

"There was something about shears and white sacks?"

"Yeah, this younger generation, they like to talk in riddles and rhyme. Just before the ship left Yokosura, they brought two plain wood scabbards they called 'shirasaya.' 'Shira' means white, and 'saya' means scabbard, but in literal Jap, it means sack. They also mentioned that lacquered cases held moisture. We are supposed to wipe down the shears with a soft cotton cloth and talcum powder, then store them suspended horizontally in the plain wood cases."

All the while, mother hen was growing more agitated. "Magwitch, we need to be going. We want to get some supper and find our rooms before we get lost in this rabbit warren of a city."

"Now Mother, as post mistress, you must know there is no rushing Uncle Sam. The seaman has not yet returned with my gear. And I still have to check in at Fort Mason."

In due time, the seaman did return with Mag's luggage on a cart. He informed the impatient mother hen that he would escort them to the processing center on base. This seemed to smooth her feathers that Mag seemingly loved to ruffle. In any case, she turned to Jubal and asked, "Young man, would you like to go to supper with us?"

Processing at Fort Mason was tedious, but it gave the Russells time to catch up on the minutia of the social life and cattle business in Lino County. It also allowed Jubal to realize just how much ranch life along the continental divide resembled that in Lino County just to the west. He thought, *There seems to be something innate in that rugged existence that prepared men for survival, even on death marches and hell ships.*

The medic said, "Your mother sure has pull, somewhere. By all rights, with your medical conditions, we should send you directly to Letterman Hospital in the Presidio. However, I have orders cut for you to report to Bruns Army Hospital, Santa Fe, New Mexico, on or before 28 December 1945. That's a Saturday. Here is enough medication to control your malaria and painkillers for your foot, leg and chest. Be careful not to exceed directed dosages."

"Say, Doc, is there any way to trade these in for three bottles of Jack Daniels? I'm already addicted to it."

The medic just smiled and handed the bag to the mother.

TALCING THE TASHI

Following a great seafood dinner on Fisherman's Wharf, through which Mag complained that he would much rather have steak out of a Dutch oven, they drove to a hotel near the Presidio. Jubal and the brother brought the luggage into the small suite.

Mag was already ensconced in the highest padded chair, the ornate lacquered crutches propped nearby. From that vantage point, he directed activity. "Jube would you hand one of the crutches to me?" It was the right hand crutch that held the Masamune, Fiery Blade of the Enduring Comet. Mag grasped the upward, protruding portion of the back stick. This he rotated a half turn to the left then lifted it upward, revealing the bare sword hilt. That section of the crutch resembled a tsuka or hilt section of a saya. With a much-washed cotton handkerchief, he grasped the tang and drew the Fiery Blade from its crutch case and laid it on the bed. He motioned for the other crutch and with like procedure placed the Muramasa, Firstborn of the God of War, on the bed beside the Masamune.

"The shirasaya are in the long duffle. See which goes with which blade." Jubal pulled two light-colored, untreated wood cases from the canvas duffel. Each case was marked with Japanese characters, but since neither could read them. They simply matched them to blade lengths. Each case consisted of two parts, the saya or sack that would contain the blade. From the sack extended the tang, which would be covered by a hilt or tsuka section.

"Where did we put the talcum powder?" Mag asked his brother.

When he returned with the shaker can, Mag handed him two more soft cotton cloths. "Wipe down the blades, but be careful not to touch them with your hands. Check them for any fingerprints or signs of rust. Use the talc to wipe off any such marks."

During this process, both Jubal and the brother took opportunity to carefully examine the exquisite temper lines and texture of the highly polished steel. They even made copies of the chisel marks that recorded makers, dates, and names.

Now Mag asked for the camphor-wood boxes containing the sword furniture. He identified the first box as belonging with the Masamune by the gold pheasant inlaid on the iron tsuba. To double check, he opened the other box that contained an iron lace tsuba and a tsuka with teal green *ito*, wrappings. He handed the first box to Jubal, then the other to his brother to examine.

When they finished, Mag said to Jubal, "If it doesn't matter to you which blade you take, I would like to care for the 'Firstborn.' I kind of got attached to that story."

"Mag, I don't really care. They are both so beautiful that just being caretaker of either is quite an honor. However, if you could spare that duffel for me to conceal it in, it would be much appreciated."

Mag then cautioned that everything about the swords must be held in absolute secrecy, not just for the sake of the swords, but for their own safety as well.

As Jubal prepared to leave, he fought to control his emotions. "You know Mag, when you left Cabañatua for Bilibid, I never thought to see you again." He turned quickly to conceal his own emotions and thus failed to see the welling of tears around the old puncher's eyes.

As the brother drove Jubal back to Letterman Army General Hospital in the Presidio, they talked about Mag and his ranching prospects. They discussed caring for and hiding the swords. Most of all, the brother seemed concerned with confidentiality. "Mag has a great propensity for openness, and I fear he might tell the wrong person about the existence of these swords."

Lastly, they discussed the importance of keeping in touch.

There was no one to see Jubal, as he carried a long bag and small wooden box to his locker and secured them within using his own heavy-duty padlock.

SHOWA REARS ITS UGLY HEAD

1 December 1945

Back in Japan, Ragnor had learned to speak and understand a few words of Japanese. Reading was a completely different matter. Even with the simplified Romaji, syntax was still a problem. Like most Americans, though, he had long since learned his way through the black and gray markets as well as the "Floating World" of ancient Yedo. For the less initiated, those who lived through the economic rigors of wartime and occupied Japan, frequently referred to the gray market period as the "onion life," where in order to survive, many families stripped their personal belongings and heirlooms layer after layer as from an onion to sell on the gray market—not quite illegal but frowned upon by authorities. With the rowdy GIs, even the gracious Pleasure Quarter of old Yedo was taking on a new "wham bam" flavor.

The transport infrastructure, though improving, was slow to meet the demands of Japan's major metropolitan agglomeration. A black market of transport had sprung up near the numerous military motor pools. Jeep drivers routinely shuffled servicemen and sometimes even Japanese nationals to their destinations for a reasonable gratuity. Some routes were so popular that a potential rider could usually find a "black" taxi in thirty minutes or less.

Local taxis and rickshaws provided at best a sketchy service and often, the rickshaw peddler would require assistance from the passenger on the difficult uphill sectors.

Interurban service was improving, but riding the sporadic and ill-equipped metro system still required a brave heart, as well as a measure of gusto. Nevertheless, the dynamic duo of Carvajal and Ragnvold set off early that morning from Omori Station, bound for Kamakura. They failed to notice two nondescript men in peasant dress who boarded and remained at the back of the battered car.

Into a small duffel bag, Ragnor had packed purified water, C-rations, and bananas. For trade, they carried Milky Ways and a few packs of American cigarettes. Camels and Lucky Strikes were so valuable; they represented the big bills of Tokyo's monetary system and were saved for important trading in the resurgent urban areas.

Once in Kamakura, a few words of Japanese and a friendly smile got them to the Zen Temple, Zuisen-ji. Just inside the torii, the abbot and a groundskeeper were discussing the essential balance of water, stone, and plants in the formal but simple garden layout. Blaz very politely asked if it would be possible for them to listen to their discussion, since he and Ragnor were students of Zen culture, presently studying with Yoshida Nobu and the Johkai Priest of Sengaku-ji in Shinagawa. The name dropping worked. They soon learned that both knew some English. They appeared delighted to discuss a few of the simpler concepts of Zen Buddhism, as well as Japanese landscape gardening. But it was the great bronze Amida Buddha that they most wanted to talk about.

It was mentioned that Yoshida had briefly discussed the Amida Buddha and Pure Land tradition and suggested they visit Kamakura because of its great religious and historical significance. This was the opening the Abbot needed. "Let us walk to the Great One."

Looking up at the kindly face on the colossal statue inspired a mix of feelings somewhere between awe and reverence. The Abbot resumed, "The Great Amida Buddha of Kamakura is the largest cast bronze in Japan. It is nearly forty-four feet high and weighs ninety-three tons. It is the most significant representation of the Mahayana School of Buddhism. *Amidabha* means 'Infinite Light.' In a long ago incarnation, a *Bodhisattva*, one who postpones *Nirvana* in order to save others, made the forty-eight vows necessary to create a Buddha *Setra*. That Bodhisattva's name was Dharmakara, and the Setra he established was called 'The Pure Land.' Dharmakara was a being of great compassion who gave up a kingdom to become a simple monk. Now you must understand that the Pure Land is a place of infinite light, but it is not the final destination. It is like a waypoint often viewed as the easy path to Enlightenment. Enlightenment is the ultimate attainment which brings ultimate peace and frees one from the recurring cycles of birth and death."

The Abbot suggested that Blaz and Ragnor take time to leisurely view the shrine gardens, take in some of the nearby historical sights, then return to take tea with him at the temple.

As they left the shrine gardens by an obscure entrance,

they were accosted by two men with bamboo *kendo* fighting sticks. The first assailant, with a *migi-do* stroke to Ragnvold's right rib cage dropped him groaning to the ground. The other, with the threat of a *tsuki* to the neck, held Carvajal at bay and began an interrogation in Japanese and broken English. "Where have you taken the Hachiman Taro?" The bamboo drew back with threatening intent of a two-handed swing posture.

The question was never answered. A *kote* strike seemingly came out of nowhere, but it was precisely timed to catch the right arm of the assailant at full cock. Yoshida delivered the blow, but he could not be sure whether the arm was broken or the muscle so badly bruised as to be useless. At the same time, Nobu's younger companion, Nao, had knocked the other assailant senseless with a *hidari-men* to the left temple and drug him into thick foliage of the grounds. He quickly returned to aid Ragnor, who was still wreathing on the grass.

Nobu now holding two kendo bamboos, with less than tender jabs urged the injured man into the shaded copse, where his senseless companion lay sprawled.

It took a few minutes for Ragnor to gain his feet. Each breath inhaled felt like a tanto thrusting into his side. His medical training told him that several ribs had been broken. Slowly, very slowly, he struggled to where the others were concealed.

Nobu took a package from the inner pocket of his coat. Addressing Ragnor, he said, "Please forgive my using your gift before you receive it." From the paper, he drew an encased tanto. Then drawing the blade, he put the handsome saya back into the pocket. He walked to the assailant, now holding an obviously broken right arm with his left hand. With the very sharp point of a blade designed for the initial thrust into the guts of one committing seppuku, Nobu nicked the soft flesh next to the man's larynx and dangerously close to the carotid artery. "Now my friend, I will conduct the interrogation. Why have you followed these men to Kamakura?" No response. Nobu took a little deeper nick. A trickle of blood ran down the assailant's neck and under his shirt.

"My friend, we don't have all day and a trickle of blood from the neck is much less painful than ritual suicide, for which this blade was designed." He looked at Ragnor, still in obvious pain. Then he thought, *This process must be sped up.* He placed the tanto to the left and below the navel. The intent was obvious—assisted seppuku. Nobu, with quick motion, thrust the point through the coarse peasant clothing and at least an inch into the abdomen. The would-be assassin got the point.

"Wait." Nobu withdrew the bloodied weapon and wiped it on the assailant's coat.

"Well?"

"We came to find out the destination of the Sengaku-ji Temple swords once they reached America."

"And who sent you?"

The man hesitated. Nobu again moved the tanto toward the bleeding abdomen. The response was immediate. "The Showa Brotherhood."

Keeping the dagger pointed, Nobu asked, "How did they know the swords were gone?" This time there was no hesitation.

"We put pressure on the lacquer man who finished the crutches for the crippled American POW who smuggled them out of Shinagawa."

"Be warned, my friend, if ever I catch you in Shinagawa again, I will finish the job started today. I don't care how you do it, but get your unconscious friend out of here and when he is awake, give him the warning I gave you. I have many friends anxious to deal with hoodlums like you."

Progress towards the Abbot's residence was slow, so Yoshida sent his young friend ahead. Fortunately, Nobu was a friend of the Abbot and was sure that help would be proffered. Seeing the injured man, the Abbot brought out a gurney-like cot, on which Blaz helped Ragnor sit. Very carefully, the shirt was removed, but there was no way to remove the pullover undershirt without inflicting more pain. Blaz used scissors to cut it away, revealing an angry five-inch bruise the width of two fingers. Several small lacerations were still seeping blood. Then with his fingers, he carefully probed. He was able to detect slight separations on the forth and fifth ribs down, about six inches from the spinal column. These concerned him very much. Quick movement or another blow could force a broken rib end to puncture the lung. He poured a cup of water into a bowl and dumped in half a vial of tincture of iodine. With this, he swabbed the entire rib cage from armpits to navel. When this was dry, he took a two-inch wide roll of adhesive tape and starting near the bottom of the rib cage, firmly wrapped the injured man up to the armpits.

"How does that feel?" Blaz asked.

Ragnor slowly inhaled, completely filling his lungs. "Not too bad, if I don't move quickly."

"You had better get some rest now," Blaz said as he nodded to Nobu and the Abbot to help. They carefully laid him back and lifted his legs on to the cot.

Outside, Nobu briefly told the Abbot about the trouble with Showa and the Temple Swords. This reminded him of the injured men they had left behind in the woods. He turned to his associate. "Naosan, perhaps you should check on the ronin we left in the Amida garden shrubbery. Be most cautious, since we do not know what forces Showa might have in Kamakura. Remain completely out of sight."

Now they needed to consider their options. To ride public transport back to Shinagawa in time to catch the afternoon gig to the *Benevolence* was now impossible. Besides it was a long, "round the elbow" trip that would certainly do the battered Ragnor little good. Remaining overnight could put the Abbot in harm's way. The deciding factor seemed to be that the Yokosuka Fleet Landing was probably less than six miles away. Since the US Military was planning to build a hospital at Yokosuka and already had other facilities there, Blaz reasoned there must be a motor pool of some sort near by. Blaz and Ragnor would hire a rickshaw and head toward the landing. If a Jeep should come by, they would hail it for the rest of the trip.

As they waited for the assistant's return and to give Ragnor more time to recuperate, they discussed the unexpected turn of events. "How did you happen to come to Kamakura today of all days, and why were you carrying kendo sticks?" Blaz asked Nobu, halfway expecting he knew the answer.

"Well it's something like this. When we were discussing Kamakura recently, I had considered accompanying you. Unfortunately, no dates were mentioned, and I had no way of making contact. The alternative was to monitor the Asano Fleet Landing and hope to catch you there. However, Showa has recently stepped up its harassment of the Johkai's people. There are almost always strangers lurking around Sengaku-ji and the shop where you saw the Fiery Blade of the Enduring Comet.

"Because of their constant surveillance, the Johkai has insisted that my young friend accompany me. He is expert in Koryu Aikido, as well as kendo, which affords me considerable protection as you witnessed today.

"So we started watching the fleet landing each morning, hoping you would come that way and we might catch you there. The first morning, we noticed two individuals in peasant dress carrying kendo bamboos. These characters looked familiar, probably some of the Showa surveillance. It was also apparent they were looking for you. So my protector and I eased out of sight.

"When we came on subsequent mornings to check on your possible arrival, we carried our own kendos. We watched them follow you on to the train. They were so busy observing you, they were unaware that we boarded the next car. It is always easier to watch the watcher. The rest is history that you know."

Nobu's protector returned to report. "Both assailants are gone. They probably have associates here in Kamakura. I hope the Abbot will not be harmed."

Nobu looked at the Abbot, who responded, "There are, among our adherent worshipers, those who are willing to lend a helping hand. If necessary, our gardener will seek out their help. For now, it is best that you get the injured one back to the ship. I have enjoyed telling them about the Buddha of Infinite Light and the Pure Land."

As they entered the Abbot's washitsu, Ragnor was stirring. "How are you feeling?" asked Blaz. "Are you up to trying a run to the ship?" Ragnor merely nodded.

"Instead of returning via Shinagawa, Nobu and I concluded it would be much easier to return by way of the Yokosuka Fleet Landing, which is not more than six miles away."

In response, Ragnor started to sit up. Nobu and Blaz ran to his assistance. He was apparently still in shock.

The Abbot intervened. "There is hot water on the ro; let us brew some fresh tea. I have a variety that is supposed to be good for shock and light-headedness." As a concession to time, the Abbot forsook the elaborate tea ceremony.

The strong tea worked its magic. Ragnor began to feel better, so they made their way through the grounds of Zuisen-ji to a rickshaw stand suggested by the Abbot. Nobu selected two he thought would be able to make the entire trip if necessary. He turned to Blaz. "Do you have a couple of cartons of American cigarettes to exchange?" Blaz nodded.

Nobu spoke in some detail to the pullers in Japanese. Returning to Blaz, he explained, "They are willing to go the entire distance for a carton each. Should you catch a Jeep sooner, you might bargain for the difference, but I suggest you don't. "

With his back to the pullers so they were unable to observe his actions, Nobu took from an inner coat pocket two short tanto encased in red crackle saya. "These are to express the thanks of Sengaku-ji for your help in removing our national treasure swords. Both tanto are from the Shinto Period, between 1596 and 1780. Both blades are signed by Tadamitsu Awataguchi. The kashiae furniture is more recent but still old and authentic. The great advantage of these small weapons, especially for you, is concealability. Good-bye for now. Have a safe trip back to the ship." He turned and left so abruptly they had no chance to thank him.

They saw no Jeeps on the way to fleet landing. The pullers decidedly earned their full cartons.

It took some two weeks before Ragnor was again up to the long ride to Omori Dock.

INTERNAL
ESPIONAGE

7 December 1945

It was an anniversary of significance, but not to Watanabe. He battled a cold wind with a little sleet blowing through the Evergreen Cyprus and Sugi Cedars near the edge of the large Meiji Shrine. This dense, wooded area was ideal for convenient safe drops. And not too far away and adjacent to the Meiji Police Station was a dilapidated wooden sign that provided a convenient signal for the message drops. The chains had been twisted three times, which meant that Roku, Number Six had left a message.

For the past week, Watanabe SJ-1 had been watching the station for citizens who might be turning in weapons. He was especially watchful of anything that might include temple swords or other national treasures. He had rented cheap lodging nearby that allowed a partial view of the station entrance. So far it had been a dull fruitless effort. He hoped the Roku message might liven up the routine.

As he reached the drop, the driving sleet was turning into a gentle wet snow. He carefully removed the tinned message box from its snow-covered hiding place. Turning his back to the storm, he read, "Be at the Meiji Shrine Torii at noon, 8 December."

Good, that gives me time to get out of this storm.

December 8 was overcast, but the wind had settled. The torii was almost hidden among the sugi. SJ-1 could see no one at the gate, so he walked a short way toward the sanctuary before he saw Number Six seated on a small bench bundled in a well-worn long coat.

Neither spoke as Watanabe took a seat; nor did either glance at the other. Number Six merely dropped his mouth deeper into the collar of the old coat and whispered, "Our informant who works for Tokugawa Iemasa has learned that his employer plans to turn in fifteen swords to the Meiji Police Station soon. It would appear that the station will relinquish them to the American Occupational Forces at the earliest possible date. Therefore, I have arranged for two members from the SJ Cell to aid you.

"We know that there is in that collection a Masamune blade called *Honjo*. Some sword historians believe the name came from General Honjo Shigenaga who won it in a sixteenth century battle. It was designated a Kokuho, a national treasure, in 1939.

"In any case, take as many swords as possible, but make sure you have the Masamune Honjo. Many consider it among the best swords ever made. Its acquisition would confer great honor on us and help mitigate the deprecations laid upon us by the brotherhood because of our failure to obtain the Sengaku-ji Nippon-to. Such fault finding has made my life miserable. So I'm depending on you to help compensate by obtaining this other national treasure.

"From now on, there should always be two of you at the safe house observing events at the police station. This will allow ample time to rest, even while providing backup for any contingency. We have obtained a pair of walkie-talkies from the US Army black market. They must only be used to signal SJ-3 and SJ-4 that the weapons have been loaded on a Jeep and should arrive shortly at the agreed upon hijack point.

"Make no attempt on the swords while they are at the station. It will be safer and more likely to succeed if we can hijack the Jeep with the swords at a more secluded spot. We have observed the typical routes of the confiscation vehicles over the past few weeks. We think the best spot for hijacking is at an improvised canal crossing directly south of the Meiji Shrine Forest. There is a makeshift bridge on a blind curve, which might be partially dismantled in a short time. This should give us opportunity to get control of the shipment. SJ-3 and SJ-4 are already set up at that point and have been briefed on procedures. Your role will continue to be information transmittal."

OPERATION HIJACK

An informant having connections within the Meiji Police Station found Roku at the saki house where he waited each evening. "Mr. Six, I have learned of certain events that might be of interest to you."

Roku poured a glass of saki and proffered it to the man. He shook his head. "No, this should be worth two cartons of Lucky Strikes."

Roku demurred; two cartons of American cigarettes was a high price for simple intelligence, especially in such a high black market.

The man turned to leave.

Roku placed a hand on his arm and withdrew two cartons of Luckys from his commodity bag.

"The Meijiro Station has requested that American MPs make a pickup of weapons tomorrow. This pickup will include the Tokugawa Iemasa Collection."

The pleased Roku again proffered the saki, which was promptly accepted.

A short time later, Roku in peasant dress stopped by the safe house. "Honorable SJ-1, we have been blessed by the Kami. Tomorrow, the MP Jeep will make a scheduled stop at Meijiro to pickup the Tokugawa Collection. I want you to watch and make sure it happens, but you will not need to inform those at the bridge. Only if the pickup does not occur before noon will you call. I will answer the walkie-talkie. Your response will be a simple 'no.'

"I will ride to the bridge now to inform them of the change in plan. Nighttime traffic on that stretch of road is unlikely, so sabotaging the bridge should be relatively easy. With luck, no traffic will precede the Jeep, and the hijack will go as planned. I only hope SJ-3 and SJ-4 will be able to partially disassemble the bridge tonight."

In spite of time constraints, Roku remained long enough to explain the importance of the collection and expand on its significance. "Rumor has it that the Tokugawa Collection still includes a nippon-to, the so-called "Masamune, Honjo." Its importance historically is close to that of the Masamune or the Muramasa that we failed to get from the Sengaku-ji. The Honjo is in some ways the best known work of Masamune. During a sixteenth century battle, General Honjo Shigenaga was attacked by one Umanosuke, a noted collector of warrior heads. Umanosuke's stroke with the Masamune split the general's helmet, but Honjo survived to take the sword as prize. The great blade has a few small chips suffered in that fierce battle.

"It was already famous before it reached the hands of the Tokugawa Shogunate. It was passed down to Japan's last Shogun, Tokugawa Yoshinobo, and was designated a national treasure in 1939. Now the lily-livered scion of the greatest Shogunate, Tokugawa Iemasa, plans to give it up to the Americans and their demolition furnaces. Acquisition of this blade would help us save face after our failure with the Sengaku-ji nippon-to."

With no more ado, Roku straddled his bike and rode south in the darkness.

SHOWA SCORES

There was no local traffic on the makeshift road that skirted the Meiji Forest Reserve. The locals still used canals for most of their transport needs. Furthermore, Allied military traffic uses it only during daylight and that sparingly.

Thus SJ-3, SJ-4, and Roku had all night to unbolt and pull down the temporary structure. With block and tackle, they drug most of the girders away from the embankment except for one, which they purposefully dropped along the east side of the channel to act as a further deterrent.

They finished in the predawn chill and huddled in heavy blankets to await the result of their efforts.

$$\Delta$$

Sergeant Cody Bonville, 7th Cavalry, had been driving Jeeps in Tokyo's Chuo, the central area, for nearly four months now. That is, since the Allied Occupation of Japan began back in August. Things had not improved much. He simply came to know where the meager road system led and where the worst obstacles lay. SCAP had recently ordered the filling of some of the small canals crossing the Chuo in order to build more surface connections. Still, it was a maze of dead-ends and roundabout connectors.

SCAP orders to confiscate weapons had reshaped his driving routines into increasingly defined patterns. On Tuesday 11 December, he and Corporal Sax Rhoner drove past the old Kinza Gold Mint for a routine pickup from the Ginza Police Station. From there, the roadway became more complicated because of the nearby imperial palace grounds, where few canals had been cross-filled to allow surface traffic. Even so, they made reasonable time, reaching the Meijiro Police Station for the scheduled pickup. To their surprise, fifteen swords plus a couple of worn out Arisaka 99 rifles, a Type 14 Nambu auto pistol, and a Baby Nambu officer's arm were ready for pickup. Cody signed the Japanese voucher without really knowing what it detailed. They tossed the old rifles on the floor in the back of the Jeep with the Ginza junk. The swords received better care. Rhoner wondered why Bonville bothered to wrap them in heavy packing quilts, since they were bound for the furnaces anyway.

As they drove along the east side of the Meiji Shrine Forest, Bonville found a place to pull off the road. Cody had learned just enough about Japanese swords and swapped enough blades to naively consider himself a broker. Naturally he was smiling inside at the size of this haul.

With care, they unfurled the quilts. The first five swords showed strong similarities. The furniture on these appeared almost identical. The *Kagu Gato* Tsuba, rounded rectangles of iron appeared to have been cast in the same mold and electroplated with brass. The design was not unappealing, but such regularity suggested partial factory fabrication.

Cody pulled the bamboo pin, holding each handle in place, to examine the tangs for signatures and dates. Although he could not read the chisel marks, he knew the position of dates and signature of the makers. He soon realized the signatures were all the same, but the dates varied.

Had he been able to read the glyphs on the tachi-mei side, Cody would have learned that the smith's name was *Kunihiro*. On the katana-mei side, the first two glyphs on the five swords were the same. Their vocalization would have been "Showa," meaning "Bright Reign of Peace," referring to the ascension of Hirohito to the Imperial Throne, 25 December 1926. The remaining glyphs expressed the dates the blades were signed in terms of years and months after the ascension date. The secondary dates ranged from the twelfth to the eighteenth year of the Showa Era, thus coinciding with Japan's rising military power. Cody expressed annoyance. "These are all *Shin Gunto*, New Army Blades, but most GIs will probably care less."

The next sword they unwrapped was immediately distinctive. Its handle wrappings were scarlet. The kashira, butt cap, was a dragon in the clouds that appeared to have been fire gilded, probably over silver. The irregular tsuba, shaped like a closed fist, Cody recognized as a *Kobushi Gato*. But the real surprise came as he pulled the blade from its black lacquered saya. The nie temper line truly sparkled like stars of the Milky Way against the night sky.

Cody became very excited. "Sax, let's get going. I'd like to get back to the Chou early enough to drop the best of this haul in my storage unit before we turn in the remainder for the demolition furnaces."

Sax looked confused. "You have a storage unit?"

"Certainly," replied Cody. "There's good business in Jap souvenirs, especially swords. Furthermore, some GIs are becoming quite knowledgeable about Samurai traditions, sword fabrication, and legends. Something like this red handled job is apt to bring five or six hundred dollars from a serious connoisseur. We just need to study up about this particular blade."

"Who said anything about my participation?" asked Sax.

"Well whatever, but let's get on our way. We still have another pickup at Shibuya before heading back to the center. That will take us past the south point of the Meiji Shrine Forest, where canal crossings are meager and roads rough."

Cody maintained a relaxed expression, but he was concerned. *Looks like I made a mistake not feeling out Rhoner before spilling the beans.*

He decided a little conversation would be preferable to the dead silence. "SCAP has been filling canals in some sectors, but the crossing near the point of the Meiji Forest is a real hazard. Just pontoon struts overlain with wood planking."

No response.

Cody picked up speed. Rounding a sharp curve they were suddenly there. The abrupt canal banks were no longer mitigated by any structural approach. With four wheels locked, the lightweight Jeep sailed out over a ten-foot drop before nosing into the opposite bank. Both MPs slammed headfirst into the windshield. All went black.

Roku did not wait for the unloading of the weapons, but headed back to the washitsu that served as the observation point. He had quickly checked the haul and was sure the Honjo Masamune was there. To SJ-1, he ordered, "Clean out this place. Take away anything that might lend suspicion. Pay the landlord for everything owed and leave a few chocolate bars. Then find lodgings elsewhere, preferably in or near the Chou. It should be a place where you can move about unnoticed for several months. Once established, leave a signal at the sign. I will meet you near the safe drop the evening of the second day following." With that, Roku was gone.

Back at the hijack point, SJ-3 checked the MPs. Both were out cold, but a good beat was felt in their carotid arteries. Number 3 and 4 of the SJ cell went to work. They promptly burned the invoice from the Meijiro Station. Onto a handcart they quickly loaded all of the swords plus the Baby Nambu and moved them to a temporary secure spot until darkness could cover any further activity. From a distance, they would watch the scene, hopefully to ascertain the reaction of authorities. With satisfaction, they watched a heavy falling snow. By morning, all traces of their activity should be covered.

CHUO

Watanabe SJ-1 had been so occupied with carrying out the orders from Roku that he had not had time to convert much of his black market goods to currency. It took him nearly three days to obtain the going value for the cigarettes, chocolate, saki, and even rice of the preserved kind, so desirable to the Japanese pallet.

It would soon be six months since SJ-1 had become associated with the Showa Brotherhood. His profit in the black market had been quite lucrative. With the last round of trade, he had accumulated a bit more than 900 American dollars.

Near the Chuo, Watanabe rented a three-tatami room with extending mizuya, water room for tea preparation, and a *tokonoma*, the raised alcove for displaying decorative mementos. The three-tatami size was approximately fifteen by twenty-four feet; small, but his needs were simple. There was only one entrance so the host and guests would be obliged to use the same, but he expected few guests. It had an added benefit; a landlord who would look after his meager possessions.

One tatami had been cut to accommodate a small ro, or fire pit, that would provide fire for tea, preparation, and warmth during the cold months. His sleeping blankets would be rolled and stored in the mizuya during the day. In the tokonoma, he would display his father's Russian Campaign Medal of the Meiji Era year thirty-seven and his short tanto. It would be necessary to obtain a small camphor wood chest in which to conceal the Baby Nambu auto pistol. He would be relatively comfortable.

Late that afternoon, SJ-1 traveled back to Meijiro. He twisted the chains holding the dilapidated sign three times.

In the twilight of the following evening, Roku met SJ-1 near the safe drop. They walked slowly for some minutes to ensure no one was following. In a quiet voice, Roku spoke, "Did you find a place?"

"Yes," SJ-1 replied. "It's in the Chuo on the Kinza Gold Market side. It's only a three-tatami, but my needs are simple."

"How is your black market trading progressing?" asked Roku.

"Until we hijacked the swords from the American Jeep, there had scarce been time to dicker with my clients. However, in the three days following, my cache of US dollars has grown to over 900. Right now, I have no more goods to trade; however, I had not perceived my roll with the brotherhood as that of petty trader."

"It seems that success at the Meiji Forest has gone to your head," said Roku. "Perhaps it would be well to consider our failure with the Sengaku-ji nippon-to."

Roku then changed the subject abruptly. "Showa is now considering the need to recover national treasure swords on an international basis. They have selected you for a specialized program to attempt recovery of swords from North

America. We know you have had some training in the English language, as well as experience with American POWs. Now we want you to undergo intensive language training, as well as studies in American history and culture. You will also attend a *Koryu Ryu* martial arts school to expand your *bujutsu* methods until you are completely at home with *budo,* the martial way.

"Koryu is literally the old school of 'Fighting in the Spirit.' It was an outgrowth of the Haitore Edict of the Meiji Restoration of 1866 that banned the wearing of swords. Showa secretly sponsors a Shinto-Ryu that is near your washitsu. One of your instructors there is Nisei, who attended school in California and speaks American English fluently. He will be your personal language tutor as well. He will probably also be a member of the team Showa plans to send to North America. Your prime objectives will be the recovery of the swords, Firstborn of the God of War and the Fiery Blade of the Enduring Comet, which the Sengaku-ji slipped out from under our noses, as you remember."

CANAAN'S FAIR AND HAPPY LAND

July 1946

Jubal Ragnvold was finally considered well enough to go home. He got off the Santa Fe Chief at Thoreau, New Mexico. When his brother, Gungnir, failed to meet him at the station, Jubal figured he was probably at the post of noted Indian trader John Wetherill. It was only a couple of blocks away, so he carried his gear, a small bag of personal items, a wooden box tied in such a way that rope formed a handle, plus two awkward-looking, long canvas packages. He found Gungnir talking turquoise prices with a Navajo silversmith employed by the trader. Fortunately, the younger Ragnvold was about through, and they were soon on their way south in a beat-up ranch truck that had out lived World War II. It was good to be home, almost to Agua Azul, good old Bluewater. To Jubal it was Canaan's Fair and Happy Land.

Homecoming was not without its difficulties. At first, the wide open spaces of the ranch seemed lonely. His prison camp years had conditioned him to crowded spaces. For the most part, it had been fellow POWs; later, it was nurses and medical personnel. Now there was only family, a couple of hired hands, and an occasional visiting rancher or cattle buyer. Haying and roundup were always busier and frequently, they took on extra helpers as required.

Initially, he weighed only 130 pounds on a frame that once supported 170. The intestinal parasites were gone, but his digestive functions were still recovering. Altitude bothered his weak lungs and worked his heart noticeably. At first, a full day in the saddle, though highly enjoyable, was totally exhausting. However, as the weeks passed, gradually increasing workloads, his mother's nutritional meals, and clean air were working wonders. All the while, he was searching for a suitable place to sequester the nippon-to, which was never mentioned to his parents.

At last, he made his decision. On a cow trail, perhaps quarter of a mile above the home ranch, was a collapsed powder house where the Forest Service had once stored black powder used for blasting. Rumor had it that an inept powder monkey had accidentally set off an explosion that had lifted the reinforced concrete walls completely off their base and dropped them randomly, forming a concealed room completely covered with rubble. Jubal and Ragnor had discovered the room years ago when they were kids, building their "Butch Cassidy Hideout." At the time, they had tunneled under and found an opening through the eight-inch floor into a narrow space where one wall fell across another. The way he remembered, it was dry inside, even during the heavy cloudbursts of summer. He had almost forgotten its existence and doubted that Gungnir even knew of it.

Late in July, they finished putting up the third cutting of alfalfa. The parents decided the following morning would be a good opportunity for them to go to town for supplies. They asked Jubal to ride up to the summer range and check on the stock there. Gungnir probably had thoughts of business in town as well, but Jubal cut that short by asking him to ride along, because he would know the stock better.

Very early the next morning, as the parents drove north toward Thoreau, Jubal took the youngest brother into his confidence. "Gun, I need your help. Come over to the house. There's something I want to show you."

From his closet, Jubal took a long awkward package wrapped in a canvas duffle. He carefully untied the knotted bindings to reveal the plain, wood *saya* and a more elaborate, empty one. He then pulled the Fiery Blade of the Enduring Comet from its un-lacquered sack. He opened the camphor wood box to reveal the sword furniture. Gun, who was already a collector of artifacts and weapons, stood with slack jaw. He said nothing as Jubal related the history of the nippon-to and why it was currently in his possession.

"Now, Gun, it is imperative that this be kept secret. There is potential danger from the Showa Brotherhood involved with this blade. I don't want the burden of this knowledge ever dropped on our parents. Should anything happen to me, immediately contact both Ragnor and Magwitch Russell. Russell has a ranch on the Rio Lino, but gets his mail at Redondo. Find me a scrap of paper and I'll jot it down for you." Ragnor handed his brother a used envelope. On the back Jube wrote "Mag Russell, P.O. Box 31, Redondo, Arizona." However, under extreme circumstances, you may wish to load these things in the truck and drive directly to Mag's ranch."

Gun asked a few questions about care of the sword then broached the obvious. "Where do you plan to hide it?"

Precisely the opening Jubal was after. "You know the old powder house?" Gun nodded. "Have you ever looked around it?"

"Not really. Too good a place for rattlers."

So Jubal told him about the "Butch Cassidy Hideout." "Do you have a flashlight with good batteries?" Gun nodded.

On their way to the summer pasture, they stashed a shovel and the flashlight near the ruin of the powder house.

Dark was approaching as they came back by the powder house, but Jubal was anxious to check it out. Gun was right; it was a likely place for snakes. After clearing the area of rocks and rusting pieces of corrugated roofing, they started to dig for the tunnel entrance. But memory was unreliable. They would have to come back in daylight.

A few days later, following a series of heavy thunderstorms, Jubal and Gun returned to the powder house. In full daylight, they soon uncovered the tunnel dug years before. The upper six inches of soil were very moist, but the sloping surface had carried away excessive water. The tunnel and interior were totally dry. Surprisingly, they could almost stand upright inside the concrete room. The floor space was roughly four by eight feet. There was some loose concrete rubble that they used to chink the cracks. Later, they came back with water and red adobe clay with which to bind the hand placed rubble. The tunnel entrance was covered with cedar posts and rusted roof metal.

The following week, they returned with the sword and accoutrements. The blade, in its *shirasaya*, they suspended horizontally on hemp ropes. The box of sword furniture and lacquered saya wrapped in the canvas duffle were set on large chunk of concrete above floor level. This time, they placed the posts more carefully above the entrance. Over these were placed rocks and soil, sloping in such a way as to carry off excess precipitation. The next rainfall should obliterate any evidence of their activity. Being on their private property, there was slight chance of casual discovery.

TURTLE CIENAGA

Before the end of the Pleistocene, early man was already utilizing this favorable environment created by unfailing springs. These were fed by aquifers extending down the north slope of Mogollon Geanticline for twelve to fifteen miles before issuing from under the impervious basaltic cap, where it has been fractured by subsidence. Here in a broad sinkhole, a number of springs bubbled to the surface to form a lake within the adjacent cienagas. Even during times of drought, the springs yielded a permanent tributary to the Rio de Lino, one and a half miles to the east. Reliable water attracted the large mammals of the late Pleistocene, including the Arizona Mammoth and Royal Bison.

As a youth, Mag had picked up a number of spear points including Clovis, Sandia, and related long-stem Paleos. This suggested a mega-fauna hunting culture had utilized this water hole during the cool humid climates of some 8,000 years ago. Later, as climates turned dryer and the mega-fauna became scarce or extinct, the specialized hunting cultures gave way to hunters and gatherers who eked out an existence in increasingly marginal habitats.

Agriculture, or more accurately, horticulture, evolved slowly, following the domestication of maize, squash, and beans, and their spread northward out of the area that would become Mexico. Mogollon and Anasazi horticulturalists tended to concentrate in communities situated on larger tracts of arable soils. For them, the nearby Rio de Lino valley was the more obvious choice. Then, during the thirteenth century, a number of factors, probably including drought and decreasing length of growing seasons, seemed to have forced these Pueblo people out of the high country of the Rio de Lino drainage. However, they still performed rituals at ceremonial peaks and sacred springs in the mountains. Certain resources such as obsidian, quartz, and animal products were still collected from the high country. In fact, Mag's first recollection of seeing an Ashiwi was when a small group of priests came to collect turtles at the Cienaga for ceremonial purposes. If Mag had been a little less attracted to bronco ridding, chariot racing, or cattle raising and more like his older brother in scholastic bent, he probably would have been a paleontologist or archaeologist. But history does not reveal its alternatives.

By the 1860s, railroad construction was advancing across New Mexico and Arizona. Meanwhile, New Mexican sheepherders, *pastors*, had discovered the cienaga and often camped there. One of the short drainages feeding into the small basin is still called "Vigil Run."

Completion of the Atlantic and Pacific Railroad in 1878 would be paid for with federal land grants in millions of acres that usually ignored prior claims by small holders. These vast grants would forever alter land patents across these territories and set the stage for overgrazing and soil erosion. In 1886, Atlantic and Pacific sold one million acres of arid lands in Northern Arizona to the Aztec Land and

Cattle Company, a consortium of investors from Texas and New York, and even a few Brits. They immediately trained in 33,000 head of mostly longhorn cattle from overgrazed Texas ranges. The checkerboard pattern of land grant sections allowed Aztec Land and Cattle Company, also known as the Hash Knife Outfit, to control much more range than they owned. Economic development in Lino County was greatly diminished by such federal policies, which not only devastated natural productivity, but also increased criminal activities largely built around cattle rustling. The dregs of Tombstone to say nothing of Lincoln County, New Mexico, and all of Texas flocked into Lino County, which was long on cattle and short of law enforcement.

Perhaps one glimmer of progress out of the Hash Knife morass came from its southernmost outlier, the S-S Ranch that broke away from the general operations through the finesse of two British investors, H. Smith and M. Stevens. They set up their headquarters near the edge of Turtle Cienaga. A basalt rock house was constructed above the entrance of a lava tube that ran some eighty feet back under the malpais cliffs and into another well-concealed sinkhole behind the structure. They had found the exit opening only after following the lava tube into a sizeable room. At the far end, a small shaft of light betrayed a second opening. It was barely large enough for a man to crawl through and well concealed among large malpais boulders on the outside. The large room had once been an Ashiwi ceremonial chamber, but Smith and Stevens either failed to notice the ceremonial objects or were only interested in the lava tube, as an escape passage, should their break with the Hash Knife result in open warfare.

They closed the opening with two sizeable boulders and chinked the cracks with smaller rocks. Two saddles with rifle scabbards were placed near by. Across these, they laid two rifles, a Winchester Mode 1873 Trapper Carbine chambering a 44–40 cartridge, and a high powered Model 1885 single shot plains rifle in 45–90. Ammo for each was contained in leather pouches.

The sinkhole outside the escape passage was just large enough for two horses, but it did have a small spring, and they could cut enough meadow hay to keep the mounts fed. At the entrance below the house, they always kept a coal oil lantern, lucifers, and extra fuel.

Just into the tube, from the house side, they constructed a deadfall, in case of close pursuit. Above the gable roof of the house, they build a copula, from which a 360-degree vantage was possible. Only one problem remained; they were too busy looking after the livestock to ever look out of the copula.

Even so, luck was with them. Sheriff Commodore Owens was putting so much pressure on the Hash Knife rustlers that they didn't have time for a range war with the S-S, so Smith and Stevens prospered. They sold out in the late 1890s. Smith was tired of life on the frontier and went back to merry old England. Stevens felt it was becoming too calm in Lino County and took his share to purchase a ranch at Horse Springs, Frisco County, New Mexico. "Better lion and bear hunting you know. After all, a one-armed man needs a little excitement in his life."

Henry Cavendish purchased the S-S outfit and used the Turtle Cienaga as part of his winter range. Here, the spring roundup and branding would occur before moving his herds to leased summer ranges, high up on the Fort Apache Reservation. After Cavendish was killed in a shootout over a range dispute, John Russell, Magwitch's father bought the old S-S Ranch from the Cavendish widow circa 1917. This acquisition worked out well, since it tied in with other Russell properties, especially the later purchase of the Lux Soap Ranch to the north, run by his older brother.

When Mag returned from his long imprisonment in the Philippines and Japan, the family agreed that this would be Mag's ranch. He would be expected to pay it off in ten annual payments, due after shipping each fall. This was according to the best land economic theory of the time. "Land is worth ten times its annual return."

A young man, Paco Rubi, was hired to help Mag at the ranch and take care of it when it was necessary for the veteran to go to Santa Fe for medical care. Mag tried his "looking for sheep" salute on Paco, who merely laughed and ignored the intended insult. They soon became friends, and Mag grew to trust him with ranching operations, as well as confiding in him with the matter of the national treasure sword. Paco reminded Mag of his friend Blaz Carvajal, who had since returned to Albuquerque, where he was working on a pre-med degree at the university while pulling weekend duty at Bruns Army Hospital in Santa Fe. This was still just rumor to Mag, since he had not seen the "Sheepherder" on his recent visit.

It was now early summer 1946. At Turtle Cienaga, elevation nearly 6,000 feet, temperatures were pleasant, although there was always a danger of heat stroke if one didn't drink enough water in that rarified atmosphere.

Spring roundup had fallen completely to Paco, but once the herd was in the holding pasture, Mag could help with the branding. Branding had been quite uncomfortable with the unwieldy cast. Fortunately on his last trip to Bruns, they had fitted him out with a walking cast that was still heavy, but more maneuverable. He could now work from horseback. It was just the getting on or off that posed problems. Fortunately, the loading chute at the main corral served its named purpose. Mag would hobble up and sit on the end. Paco would lead Jupiter, his favorite pony, alongside, so Mag could swing his right leg across the cantle and ease into the saddle. Paco would then force the foot part of the cast into the left stirrup. Everything would be all right, unless Mag had to dismount out on the range. Then it would usually require finding a near vertical arroyo bank to work from.

The new cast was obviously more helpful as they got into the restoration of the old rock house. It was a real labor of love. Mag had always enjoyed camping at the cienaga, but now replacing broken windows and repairing the fireplace would make the place more comfortable when the snows fell and the winds of spring raged. But there was the stock to consider. Sheds were in need of repair, as well as the barn roof. The latter he left to Paco, since the steep gable was more than he could maneuver with the cast.

He was surprised at the size of his breeding herd. All during the war, his father and older brother managed his cows well. They had retained all the heifer calves suitable for breeding. If the market was right, they sold off some of the yearling steers to buy purebred Hereford bulls from the White Mountain Hereford Ranch. He came home to find 120 young breeding cows and six purebred bulls. If the beef market held this year, by shipping time, he could sell off enough yearling steers and older cows to make the first payment on "his ranch," pay taxes and Paco's wages, buy groceries, and retain enough for drinking expenses and maybe a down payment on a new truck. There would be no addition to the nest egg this year. To be sure, there was the back pay from four years of war and imprisonment that he had promised himself to use for the purchase of breeding stock. However, his father and brother had shown such generosity in the management of his small herd during his long years as a POW that his range capacity was fully stocked. So his frugal mindset determined that the nest egg bank account could only be used to buy more farm or ranch property. He would have it to provide leverage with First National for more favorable loan terms. And should he become serious about a little courtship, there might be a slight cushion.

He thought, *Oh for the serenity of a Jap coalmine where there were no decisions to be made.*

CLOSE SESAME

June 1930

Spring roundup and branding were over. The cattle had been moved to the high mountain pastures. It was a month until the Fourth of July rodeo, so John Russell put Mag to work cleaning up the old rock house; that was when he could pry the young man away from chariot construction. In the beginning, that young man considered it a form of punishment, but progression produced stimulus. It was apparent that Cavendish had never used the structure. Evidence of the British owners was everywhere. Books were abundant, most behind wooden doors that had protected them from rats during the interim, and since the roof was still good, there had been no water damage. Mag was soon engrossed in Rudyard Kipling and Omar Khayyam. He memorized all thirty-two lines of Kipling's poem, *If* and at least half the couplets of Khayyam's *Rubaiyat*. Both poets would serve him well in the difficult years to come.

As he cleared out debris, he noticed that some of the floor planks in the north room appeared to be loose. On closer examination, he discovered that three of the foot wide boards had never been nailed down. Spike heads showed on the upper sides where the planks lay on the floor joists, but the spikes had been cut off so they wouldn't reach the joists below. Over the years, the wood continued to shrink and warp slightly so that someone walking on them might notice. Mag quickly moved the three, six-foot sections. Below, he discovered it opened into a lava tube nearly big enough for him to stand upright.

His father was riding fence and his brother repairing corrals. This would give him time to explore his find undisturbed. He quickly lit the coal oil lantern and descended into the recess. The initial tube was fairly uniform, smoothed by flowing lava. Then it opened up into a large chamber formed by magma escaping from a sizeable pocket. The tunnel's collapse when the basalt was still molten, perhaps 10,000 years ago. That fall out had created a chamber loaded with alcoves, shelves, and hidden storage places. Near the center, ashes covered a fire pit, behind which a slab of malpais would seem to have deflected smoke toward the far end, away from the tube entrance. This puzzled Mag. So he took his dim light to the far end, looking for some kind of smoke hole. To his surprise, two old-style saddles with brass horns lay on a rock shelf just above floor level. In the scabbard of one was a short carbine. In the other was an obviously high-powered rifle. *Looks like the English Gents ran off without their popguns,* he mused. Above the saddles, carefully placed stones closed what might once have been an opening. He would check the outside later.

But his discoveries were only beginning. Some of the large niches contained polychrome ceramic vessels depicting Kokkos, Masked Dancing Gods. Fetishes, carved from turquoise, white Zuni stone, and Catlinite sacred pipestone were found in select spots. He found two full-sized bows and a dozen arrows tipped with obsidian and white quartz points. The wood in these were in a state of perfect preservation. Even the fugitive-color decorations remained vivid. There were also miniature wooden weapons, crooks, and prayer plumes. Most, he left untouched until his father could see them, but he took one bow and one arrow tipped with a gorgeous white point out with him to examine in the light of day, after centuries of darkness. Back in the north room, he replaced the planks and muttered, "Close Sesame."

OPEN SESAME

Late July 1946

It was a rainy afternoon when Mag and Paco entered the north room of the old rock house. Then Mag showed his eager helper the noted weapon. With a clean, soft cotton cloth, he pulled the naked blade from the shirasaya and handed Paco another cloth so he could hold it. Then he opened the camphor wood box containing the sword furniture and placed it on the bed recently brought into the north room.

With Paco still holding the blade, Mag wiped dust and lint from each piece as he fitted them over the tang. First the habaki copper sleeve was slid all the way to *mune-machi* notch where the tang meets the blade proper. This was followed in succession by fuchi spacers, the tsuba guard, more fuchi spacers, the handle of wood covered with the same of giant ray skin beautifully wrapped with silk tsuka-ito, and terminating with the cast bronze pommel. With the handle in place, Mag secured it with a mekugi bamboo peg extending through handle and tang. After Paco had a chance to hold and examine the total system, the process was reversed and Mag carefully wiped each piece of furniture as it was placed back in the box that was closed and tied with sisal twine. Then he wiped the blade, dusted it with fine talc, and wiped it again before placing it back in the untreated wood saya.

Mag then slid the bed away from the wall and removed the unsecured floor planks, at the same time saying, "Open sesame." With the cave opening exposed, Paco lit the white gas lantern and stepped down into the entrance. Favoring his gimpy leg, it took Mag more time to reach the cave floor. They then began preparing the cave as the hiding place for the temple sword. They carefully checked the mortared rock masonry connecting the solid rock of the lava tube opening to the planks and joists of the floor above. The cave appeared to still be sealed from rats, snakes, and other critters. Satisfied of its security, they turned their attention to finding the best place to suspend the *saya* in which the sword would be secured.

Mag then handed Paco the camphor box, the ornate saya, and then the sword in its moisture-repellant untreated saya. Paco with the light, the box, and ornate saya, followed by Mag with the blade in the plain *saya* made their way into the large room. On the left side, they suspended heavy sisal cords with spliced loops, into which they secured the saya in such a way as to have the cutting edge of the blade downward. The accessories were placed on an eye-level ledge just behind.

Back in the north room, they replaced the planks and secured them to the floor joists with just enough rusty nails to give them an aged appearance. They replaced the heavy metal bed, so the legs of the headboard rested on the plank nearest the wall. They hung a thin pry-bar with other household tools behind the kitchen door, just in case they needed immediate access to the sword cave.

Outside, they decided to check the small sinkhole where the S-S owners had once hidden their horses in case of Hash Knife reprisals. The plugged opening looked innocuous enough, but Paco noticed a large boulder near the top of the cliff that might be pried loose to provide an impenetrable barrier.

It was now late afternoon. The sun had dropped below a sky full of black thunderheads and cast a warm golden glow over the plateau country. Mag sat on a malpais boulder enjoying the ambience while Paco went for a crowbar. They worked the bar into a crack between the boulder and the solid cliff face. Slowly, a few inches at a time, they pried it from its bed. Each small gain was secured by dropping rocks into the crevice. At last, they needed a fulcrum for the big leverage. With both men on the end of the five-foot steel bar, the boulder teetered at the edge then dropped to the right, lodging between great boulders at the cliff face. In essence, they slammed shut a three-ton outer-door, now completely covering the masonry plug put there by Smith and Stevens over three-quarters of a century ago.

COLT

21 December 1946

Mag found a notice in his Redondo Post Office that there was a package for him. The return address on the heavy, shoebox-sized parcel was Ramon Marcos, General Delivery, Baguio, Philippines. Mag was puzzled. He knew no one by the name of Marcos, nor did he know anyone in Baguio. He hurriedly ripped open the package. A Colt 1911 A1, .45 caliber semiautomatic pistol, standard army issue, fell onto the counter. It looked intriguingly familiar, but then they all looked alike. A brief note lay inside.

> *"My brother asked that I send this to you with his thanks. He carried it through the entire Philippine Resistance. It was given to him by a peasant family near the route of the Bataan Death March with a message something like, 'Give these to the Resistencia por Martar Japos.' He found your name scratched under the right hand grip. At the end of the war, I helped liberate the Cabañatua No. 1 POW Camp. During that time, I came to know Jubal Ragnvold. I told him about the "Magwitch Russell 45." To my surprise, he knew you;*

but thought you were transported to Japan in 1943. Two months ago, he wrote saying that you had survived and that I could send the Colt to this address. In addition, my brother still has the Springfield Model 1914 Rifle that the same peasant family gave to him. If you would like it, we would be pleased to send it as well. My brother is so busy with Philippine politics that he asked me to take care of this for him.

> *With appreciation,*
> *Ramon Marcos."*

Mag scribbled a quick note thanking Ramon and his brother for their thoughtfulness. He also said he would be most appreciative of the second weapon. Mag reasoned, *After all, how many POWs would be able to say they had the very same weapons that were issued to them at the beginning of the war?* Mag checked the postage on his package and put in enough American dollars to cover five times the postage on the package just received. He even splurged and sent the note airmail before leaving the post office.

CORBAN

26 March 1948

In 1948 the *Paschal* Full Moon fell on April 2. In biblical times this would have been the beginning of the Jewish New Year, the first day of the month of Abib, which opens with the full moon nearest the vernal equinox. In this way the Hebrew calendar accommodated the differences between lunar and solar years.

In Exodus 12:2, the Lord told Moses, "This month shall be unto you the beginning of months: it shall be the first month of the year to you." Accordingly, the observance of Pasch, the Jewish Feast of Passover, occurred on the fourteenth day of Abib. The coincidental occurrence of the Christian crucifixion and resurrection around the lunar timeframe of Pasch would create a constant shifting of Easter on the Julian and Gregorian solar calendars used by most Christians. Rome and Alexandria, two great centers of early Christianity, would compound the disagreement. Blaz Carvajal might have been surprised, had he known the Good Friday of 26 March 1948 that he was now celebrating with 195 fellow survivors of the Bataan Death March would not be celebrated by Orthodox Christians until 2 May 1948.

Fortunately, such calendrical confusion did not detract from the straightforward faith of Carvajal, as he watched with pride the gathering of all but two of the 198 surviving members of New Mexico Artillery Battalion. He considered each man his personal friend. And though he would never admit it, the survival of many of these valiant individuals was due to his efforts and those of Magwitch Russell, who was without doubt his closest friend on earth.

It was a mix of pride and humility that filled the soul of Carvajal as he stood in the designated parking area east of Santa Cruz, New Mexico, on that Good Friday. This was the starting point of the Promesa. As cars and trucks filled the fallow field reserved for the POW pilgrims to park, he could almost determine which of the ex-POWs had gone back to their agrarian roots, versus those who opted for greater monetary rewards, by the type of vehicles they were driving. He was still anxious that his blasphemous friend, Mag, might renege.

With grateful relief, he watched a somewhat battered truck pull into the field. In the cab were Mag and his friend, Yates, from Socorro. The two bruisers nearly smothered Blaz as he came to the truck to welcome them. Mag then pulled from the truck a pair of custom-made crutches of deep cherry color, wrapped with black silk. "I plan to use these for the last hundred yards of our pilgrimage," Mag informed his friends. Blaz held out his hand, into which Mag placed the left crutch, which had once concealed one of the nippon-to that Mag had smuggled out of Japan almost three years ago.

"I had nearly forgotten how beautiful your sticks were," said Blaz.

"Yeah," said Yates. "I'll probably end up carrying Mag and those damned crutches both, before we get to the *Sanctuario*." So went the banter from the lighthearted, sacred pedestrians. Yet beneath it all, there was a sense of thanksgiving to be among those who had survived.

True to his word, Mag used his crutches to negotiate the final hundred yards. He even gathered a small sample of the sacred earth to take back home. No one knows how many buckets of sacred soil left the Sanctuario that day, or even if the number of pilgrims set a record. The important factor resided within the hearts of those sacred pedestrians who thought enough of the Virgin, of Blaz, and of each other to fulfill the *corban*. The overwhelming fulfillment of Blaz Carvajal's sacred *promesa* that day would serve him well for a lifetime.

Δ

Mag did not forget about his saddle blankets. As the pilgrims dispersed following Holy Week, Mag and Yates went back into Chimayo in search of an ancient weaver named Joselito. They found him in a small adobe still at his loom, even though his eyesight was obviously failing. Mag called out, "Joselito, you old thread puller, how have you been?"

The old one thought a moment, and then asked, "Is that you, Magwitch? You ornery son of a…" But he was too courteous to apply the rhyming closure. He stood and hugged the burley loudmouth. "I've been wondering when you would be needing saddle blankets?"

Mag explained how the war had interrupted his thriving horse-trading business. But in this sanitized version, he did not include the fact that a judge's order had forced him into the New Mexico National Guard, which resulted in four years as a prisoner of war. Still, Mag was astounded that Joselito would remember his voice after many years

The old man hobbled to a shelf of rolled saddle blankets and spread several for their perusal. Even the sardonic Yates was impressed with the quality of weaving and the symmetrical designs executed in mostly organic dyes formulated by the weaver himself. He purchased five to take back to Socorro. Mag found seven to his liking. He also bought two large rugs for the house at Turtle Cienaga. All in all, it was a good day for both the weaver and the cowboys.

RAGNOR'S RETURN

June 1949

Ragnor Ragnvold finished up his naval tour of duty and headed home to New Mexico. It was dry, as usual, for that time of year. Even so, it looked good to his long-wandering eyes. Still he was unable to settle in. Wide travels had engendered a wanderlust that was proving hard to break. He helped around the ranch for several weeks and was surprised how well Jubal had fit into the bucolic life there. *Give him a milkmaid for a wife, and he would certainly remain until he became the Ancient of Days, but I'll be moving on,* thought Ragnor.

He wrote a letter to Magwitch Russell, who responded immediately, asking him to visit Turtle Cienaga and help finish the chariot being prepared for the Fourth of July Rodeo in Vale Redondo. Ragnor borrowed a car and was on his way. Before nightfall, he was at Turtle Cienaga. Mag and Paco were cooking supper and had a monster steak set aside to throw in the frying pan when the traveler arrived. Sourdough biscuits were in the oven and a pot of gravy on the stove. Such was the hospitality at the Cienaga.

They spent the next several days aligning wheels, reinforcing the tongue, and painting the chariot as a garish Star Spangled Banner. Only then did Mag take Ragnor into the cave to view the Hachiman Taro. As Mag drew the sword from its shirasaya, the bright light of the white gas lantern was scattered in every direction. Ragnor was again enthralled with the beauty and power of such a weapon. Both were silent for some moments as they gazed at the workmanship and reveled in the sweep of history before their eyes.

On the Fourth of July, they loaded Mag's racing team into the truck bed and proceeded to tow the garish chariot to the rodeo grounds at Redondo. Ragnor and Paco made up the support team, harnessing the horses, hooking up the chariot, and wiping off any traces of dust before the grand entry, where contestants of every event would show off their Hollywood best before the dust, muck, and sweat of the arena conveyed the real nature of the contests in progress. Mag would liked to have been competing in the saddle bronco or bull riding, but a once broken back and crushed leg had left him so "stoved up" that such competition was no longer thinkable. But Paco, with the optimism of immortal youth, had paid entry fees for both bareback bronco and bull riding.

Mag made no concessions to pop culture. He wore rubber-soled work shoes that gave better footing in the chariot, well-worn Levi's for nonbinding comfort, a well-faded shirt with pearl snaps for convenient egress, and a dirty white Stetson with a two-inch wide sweat stain under the crown. It was patented Magwitch attire.

There were two other drivers in the chariot race, both of whom Mag had known all his life. All three drove like Lucifer himself. Each would cut competitors off in the tightest turn or think nothing of forcing a competitor's chariot to flip, nearly killing them. But when the race was over, each would have given one another the dirty shirt right off his back. Their meanest weapon was a chaw of Day's Work chewing tobacco, which they claimed kept down the dust in their mouths and throats. None would spit even close to anyone in normal life, but who said the chariot race was normal behavior?

More than one such race had been lost because of temporary blindness, having its root in a foot-long expectorate of brown lightning. There was a new rule this year: "No chewing tobacco allowed." The judges checked each entrant, confiscating two plugs of Day's Work and one of Mail Pouch—a new entrant in the event. Each driver was forced to drink a full cup of water as they waited at the starting line. Folks in Redondo would come to say that it was the cleanest race in forty years.

After drawing lots for position, three chariots pulled up in front of the judge's stand at 2:15. The starting line was freshly chalked. The drivers fought to control their high-strung teams. Over the public address system the judge iterated that the race would constitute four laps of the arena and anyone crossing the line before the starting gun would be automatically disqualified. He held up the pistol and fired the blank.

Three teams shot forward. The crack of whips was inaudible in the scream of resisting wood and metal. Mag was thrown sideways against a steel rail as his team maneuvered to cut in front of the inside vehicle. By sheer luck he was able to grasp the hemp loop tied to the chariot cab.

The race track was setup so that all turns were counterclockwise. Mag liked a clockwise track better since they allowed him to utilize the strength of his strong right arm in executing the right hand turns.

Approaching the final lap, Mag was behind by a horse's head, but he held the inside on the turn. Using his weight, he slipped the chariot sideways into that of his opponent, putting stress on both wheels. With a loud snap, the axel on the opposing vehicle broke clean, dropping the chariot body on to the ground. Mag veered off to the left crossing the finish line all alone, except for the cloud of dust. *Where was the mail pouch when one needed it?*

Paco placed second in bareback bronco riding, but an ignominious Brahma nearly threw him out of the chute, where he had to scramble like a sand crab to avoid a hoof or horn until the clown was able to distract the angry bull. It had been a glorious Fourth, but all voted to go home after Mag had a couple of beers at the Bar X Bar.

Three days later, Ragnor left for the Bluewater Ranch. His mind was made up. It seemed certain that he was better suited to be a medical doctor than a cattleman. *Let Jubal run the ranch, I'll follow Blaz and specialize in healing. My GI Bill will help me finish an undergrad premed and with my experience as a medic I should be a shoo-in for medical school.*

TROUBLE IN PARADISE

April 1951

The past few weeks had been tweaked with rumors that Allied occupation of Japan might soon be ending. Roku, the Number Six of the Showa Brotherhood, assembled the three-man team chosen to conduct temple sword recovery operations in North America. Watanabe SJ-1, once known as Watanabe Hattori, was selected as the team leader. He had been an operative for more than five years and was highly functional within the brotherhood network.

The second man would be known as "Eddie Wan" (real name Eddie Oshima). Eddie was "Kibei," meaning, born in the US but sent to Japan for a "superior education" following high school. Eddie was a senior at the University of Tokyo at the time of Yamamoto's attack on Pearl Harbor. He was immediately inducted into the IJA as an intelligence officer. His connections with his American parents were completely severed. At war's end, he was demobilized, without employment, and afraid to approach the American Embassy about his problems. So he was readily open to Showa's offer of financial help and a furtive way to get back to California. He considered himself the epitome of the Japanese adage, "The offset between good and evil controls the doorway of destiny."

The third man would be known as "Tule Minoru."

Roku spent considerable time briefing the three-man team preparing to leave for North America. "The political situation in Japan is changing rapidly. If the present provisional government remains in power, it is likely that greater protection will be afforded to Shinto Shrines and Buddhist Temples. From a pragmatic point of view, this means that temple swords will be given much greater protection by the central government. They will attempt to eliminate the international black market in art swords, so Showa will lose much of its revenue. Specifically for your team, it means recovery of the Sengaku-ji nippon-to, sent to the United States by the Johkai Priest and his associate Yoshida Nobu. We have promised these blades to very rich collectors through intermediaries in Abu Dubai. You must intercede before the swords can be returned to Shinagawa.

"At best, our information concerning the whereabouts of these swords is sketchy. The lacquer man who worked for Yoshida gave us three names that might provide leads. Blaz Carvajal is probably career army with a medical degree. He could be almost anywhere. He is unlikely to have either sword in his possession but probably would know the whereabouts of the other individuals. Ragnor Ragnvold has presumably returned to civilian status and may reside near Bluewater, New Mexico. Lastly, Magwitch Russell, the disabled former POW, whom they used to smuggle the swords out of Japan, might be the one most easily traced. He is likely a cattle rancher in the Southwest, possibly in Lino County, Arizona.

"Unfortunately, we will be unable to provide you with passports or visas. You will be smuggled into California on a Japanese freighter. Once in San Francisco, try to meld with the Japanese Americans who have recently started to return to the Bay Area in significant numbers. Their wartime relocation away from the coast and subsequent confiscation of properties has left many of them bitter. You may find some who would be sympathetic to your endeavors. But take care; many are still loyal citizens of the United States. Each of you speak English well enough to blend in with that group.

"It is estimated that more than 100,000 people of Japanese origin were forcibly relocated, so you have a sizable group with which to work. Some 19,000 of these internees were concentrated at Tule Lake in Siskiyou County, California, near the Oregon border. This is an area of cold, high desert. Little wonder it was the focal point of frustration and resentment by folks accustomed to the mild climate and rich farmlands of the central California coast.

"When the U.S. Government finally passed a law allowing internees to renounce their citizenship, only 5,589 chose to do so, but of these, 5,461 were from the Tule Lake Relocation Center. A like percentage of the 1,327 individuals actually repatriated to occupied Japan in the immediate post war period were from Tule. Showa has contacted a number of these, and a few have expressed a desire to work with us.

"Watanabe SJ-1 and Eddie, meet the third member of the team—Tule Minoru."

The three team members shook hands.

"Now, Tule, your knowledge and experience will be of great value, but it is a double-edged nippon-to. Forgive the pun, but it can cut both ways. There is always danger that someone from Sonoma or Tule Lake might recognize you, and remember that you renounced your American citizenship and were repatriated to Japan. If that person is still loyal to the United States, he or she might very well report you to the FBI or other agencies concerned with citizen affairs. I would suggest you stay away from returning internees. Perhaps you can concentrate your search on army hospitals, veteran affairs, and libraries. After all, you haven't seen some of your 'old buddies' since prewar days and would like to touch base again.

"Most of your contacts in the aforementioned areas will not be Asian. Even so, it might help to modify your appearance, grow a mustache, wear glasses, comb and cut your hair differently, even wear different style clothing.

"As for Watanabe and Eddie, you should try to integrate with the returnees. Learn about their goals, the aspirations for their children, even their hopes for America's future. Perhaps most importantly, pick up their stories about the injustices and places of concentration. Then when you go to Arizona and New Mexico for your real purpose, you can pass yourselves off as badly treated Nisei internees looking for a place to start over.

"It might also be beneficial for all of you to spend time in Chinatown. Pick up some of their culture and speech patterns. You could never pass for Chinese in San Francisco, but away from the coast, few Americans will be able to tell the difference. Passing as Chinese might open doors still closed to Japanese because of wartime propaganda.

"Showa has made arrangements with the first mate on the freighter, *Daihoshi Maru*, now in Yokohama Harbor taking on silk and Nortaki porcelain bound for Chinatown, San Francisco. You will be signed on as apprentice seamen. Once in Chinatown, Tule will know how to blend into the polyglot population there.

"The *Daihoshi Maru* is scheduled to sail Tuesday 10 April 1951. You have but three days to put your affairs in order before leaving.

"We have leased a facility here in Shinagawa for safe storage of a few high value possessions. It is under guard around-the-clock. Each of you has been assigned a steel locker in which to store such personal effects until you return. You should put your own heavy-duty padlocks on these. We don't anticipate that any of you will die in America, but if such should happen, it will be the responsibility of the others to secure the assistance of a Buddhist priest to help with the rituals; I suggest cremation.

"Lastly, and hopefully more pertinent, money transfer will be handled through a numbered account with the Bank of China office in Chinatown." Roku handed each of them an identification card, and on a separate slip, a coded number. Watanabe will normally take charge of withdrawals, but each of you will have access through your own identity card and coordinated number in case the unexpected should happen. There is presently 15,000 dollars American deposited there. Each of you will carry the dollars you have accumulated in your own trading activities. Once established, you should set up a post office box for routine correspondence."

YOKOHAMA

Watanabe SJ-1, with his two companions, caught the train at Omori Station adjacent to Shinagawa for the seventeen-mile journey to the harbor at Yokohama.

From the station, they made their way along the smelly dockside of the fishing fleet to the more cosmopolitan area serving a now booming international trade. As they traversed the waterfront, the pervasive odors had not decreased, just changed. It was uncertain what Watanabe had expected by way of an ocean-going freighter. The *Daihoshi Maru* was just plain ordinary. Far cleaner, dirtier, larger, smaller, prettier, and uglier vessels were docked all around her.

The first mate was busy with loading and directed a young cabin boy to show them the crew quarters where they would bunk. Watanabe threw his gear on a bottom rack and suggested the others take racks above. There was little of worth in their gear, but each was careful to conceal a four-pocket money belt under their baggy shirts. All pockets were on the front, so no telltale bulges would show at the sides or behind.

As the Showa team was settling into their quarters, the cabin boy silently slipped back in and reached his hand into Watanabe's gear. Unfortunately for the cabin boy, Watanabe took notice. Watanabe grabbed the boy by his shirt, lifted him up, and held him against the wall. He produced a tanto and held the tip to the boy's throat. "I have slaughtered many men for much less," said Watanabe. Lowering the boy back to the deck, He motioned for Tule to secure the boy and cover his mouth. Once Tule had done as instructed, Watanabe grabbed the boy by the wrist. "This is what thieves get." Then with a quick and vicious jab, Watanabe sunk the tanto into the boy's upturned palm. Tule's hand muffled the boy's screams. Watanabe produced a cloth to wipe his blade clean and said, "If you try any more tricks or tell anyone of what just happened, you will get much more than a warning." With that, he sheathed his tanto, grabbed the boy from Tule, and slung him out of the cabin.

Then Watanabe SJ-1 sat down on the bunk to think. Anger from within boiled up then subsided as he relished thoughts of the revenge he would take on the ex-POWs, Blaz Carvajal and Magwitch Russell. *Those skulking thieves, why did they have to pirate the nippon-to that rightly belonged to Showa. They deserve more than that nipcheese cabin boy got. Had they committed honorable suicide instead of accepting capture, we would already possess the Sengaku-ji Kokuho,* he thought.

$$\Delta$$

It was decided that since Showa had paid their fares, and the apprentice seaman status was more for cover than actual duty, they should find a saki house to honor their *saku sayonara*. When they returned late that night, Watanabe found his gear bag open and clothing scattered over the deck of the crew quarters. He thought, *That miserable cabin boy has been at it again.* Then he saw the burley seaman asleep on the rack where he had thrown his bag. Two affronts in one day were too much, but reason told him that injuring a working sailor like he had the cabin boy would likely get them thrown off the freighter. Showa's approbation frightened him more than any mortal combat. Unlike the Watanabe of the Shinagawa POW hospital, who shook with impotent fury as Hanare Masahiro easily controlled him with koryu. He thought to himself, *Now, I am the Master of koryu. I fight in the spirit. My years of training at the Chuo Otome Ryu have at long last come to fruition.*

Watanabe SJ-1, the new man of Showa, bent over the sailor sleeping in the bottom bunk. Grabbing the man by the shirt with both hands, he pulled him to his feet then slapped him roughly across the left side of the face with his open right hand. The sailor pulled back a fist to strike. Watanabe jabbed the rigid fingers of that same right hand into the man's Adam's apple, simultaneously releasing the grip with his left, letting the man fall back against the metal supports. As the sailor gasped for air, Watanabe nudged him with his toe. "You will pick up my clothes, roll them, and place them back in my bag. Then we will talk about this."

The man continued his violent breathing. So Watanabe nudged a bit harder. The increased urgency seemed to generate a more amenable response. Not looking at the raptor-beaked attacker, the injured sailor picked up the pieces of the meager wardrobe, rolled them neatly, and placed them in the canvas bag.

"That's better," was the Watanabe response. "Now find a clean futon cover and make up my bed. Then find yourself another rack, and we will talk about this in a couple of days."

By this time, everyone in the crew quarter was wide awake, but no one appeared upset about the incident. It was obvious that Watanabe had picked on the top bullyboy, and no one appeared to regret the incident. The ex-top-dog was beginning to catch his breath and went for the clean cover that he threw on the futon where he had been sleeping.

Oh, the shortness of human memory, thought Watanabe as he stood staring at the man, a look of total disbelief spreading across his raptor face. *So much for fighting in the spirit.* In anger he shoved the heavier man against the steel bunks. Holding him there as he drew the short tanto from his waist-band. With the razor-sharp weapon he sliced the soft flesh below the left side of the ribcage.

"*Baka*, what is your name? Or has your brain failed to communicate with your larynx."

"Sorry, Takaisan, Mr. Tall-one, my name is Sato." His cracking voice now had a more conciliatory note, and the "reflective one" began immediately to remove the futon cover and replace it with the clean one.

"That's better. We may yet grow to understand one another." There was a collective twitter, but the crew quickly settled down knowing tomorrow would be a long day. Heavy ship traffic always made for slow going out of Tokyo Wan and Uraga Suido. Relief would come only after they reached Izu Shichito and began an open sea routine.

CHINATOWN

The Pacific crossing took twenty days. The first two days were tolerable. They steamed to the northeast in order to take advantage of the Japan Current feeding into the high latitude arc of the North Pacific Gyre. As they approached the latitude of Sendai, where the planned route would swing directly east, they were caught in the teeth of an unseasonable gale, blowing head-on, creating heavy rollers where the bottom of the atmosphere encountered the eastward trend of the gyre. The next three days had the feel of an eternity for Watanabe and his companions. The seasoned sailors merely laughed at their agony and advised rice crackers. On the evening of the third day, Sato came into the crew quarters carrying a pot of heavy chai, strong green tea, and three tin cups. He ordered the stricken landlubbers to "sit up and drink." Watanabe cursed him and tried to lie back down, but nausea was overwhelming, and he grabbed the barf bucket and retched violently. It helped. But the smiling Sato forced the cup back into his hand with the order, "Drink!" Now the flail was in the other hand, but Sato used it with reason. The thick tea had a gentle, soothing effect.

With sincere gratitude, Watanabe spoke, "Arigato. I owe you one." The gale continued for another day and a half, but the stricken three had recovered enough to almost enjoy the ride. By the second evening, following administration of the thick tea, the weather had calmed enough that the *Show-atachi* (Showa group) scrubbed the crew quarters they had so befouled. They showered as long as permissible under maritime constrictions; then washed the filth and stench from the clothing and futon covers so badly abused over the past few days.

Feeling much better, Watanabe took the next opportunity to make things right with Sato. With most of the crew present, Watanabe pointed to the contested bottom rack and said, "All right Satosan, the bunk is all yours. After your version of the tea ceremony, which I would not quite consider chakai, its effect surpassed that of any I have ever experienced. I surrender all claims to your bottom bunk. At the same time, I acknowledge your authority as lead man for the crew." He then bowed deeply to Sato.

For the remainder of the voyage, Watanabe participated in all sailing activities, watching every move of the crew, but with special attention given to the duties of the lead man.

In late April, they sailed through the Golden Gate and docked at the San Francisco cargo facility. Watanabe helped with the entire docking operation, even as Sato explained, "This was the original settlement of San Francisco then called Yerba Buena. The cargo facility is really Clark's Point. From here, California Rancheros once lightered their cattle hides and tallow to Yankee clipper ships anchored in the bay. Now I must truly sympathize with those sailors after having endured what you and your mates did to our quarters."

Watanabe's response was a wan smile.

The *Daihoshi Maru* was fully docked by early afternoon, and much of the crew had already gone ashore. The Showatachi would wait for the cover of darkness before they ventured up into Chinatown. With time to think about contingencies, Watanabe thought, *It might someday be useful to have seaman's papers.*

"Satosan, do you think the first mate would consider issuing seaman's papers to me?"

"Well, it certainly wouldn't hurt to ask."

They hurried to the quarterdeck where the skipper and first mate were filling out a final manifest for the port authority. As they entered, the first mate held up his hand for them to stop while a few final adjustments were made to the document. Then he motioned them up to the table. "What can I do for you?"

Sato made the initial approach. "Watanabe thinks it might be useful to have seaman's papers and since you control personal matters for the ship, I said we should ask you."

The first mate turned to Watanabe and asked him a number of procedural questions. Then he asked Sato, "What is your evaluation of this man's ability to perform a seaman's duties?"

When Sato gave an affirmative response, the First Mate turned to Watanabe "I can only give you provisional papers now. However, when the ship returns to Japan, I will fill out the proper forms, have them authenticated, and send them to whatever address you designate in the United States. What name shall I make them out to?"

Problems raised their ugly heads. Still, he considered his life beyond Showa. "Make them out to Watanabe Hattori. I will be renting a postal box here in San Francisco. Would it be possible to send an address to you as soon as I obtain one?"

The first mate nodded and proceeded to fill out the provisional papers. He also filled out apprentice seaman identification documents to get the Showa group through passport control for short-term liberty. Watanabe was concerned about the remaining problem. "How do you account to the port authority and passport control for three seamen not returning from shore leave and presumed departure for Japan?"

"Not to worry," replied the first mate. "Sato and his crew have been through this routine before. Your problem is how to obtain identification documents, in case you should be stopped by local authorities. Driver's licenses are the best and about the only form of identification used in the United States. Do all of you drive?" Three heads nodded confirmation. "Good, Sato will give you the address of a dealer in Chinatown who can provide you with top quality documents, for a price. Don't forget these Americans drive on the wrong side of the road. Shiawa or as they say here, good luck."

It was a dark, foggy night when the Showa three, accompanied by Sato and four Japanese seamen, passed through the port authority and customs. They crossed the Embarcadero near Powell Street, where they caught the cable car up to Chinatown. At Pacific Avenue, they left the cable and Sato gave them a walking tour. He pointed out the best greasy spoons, cheap rentals, and the shop where they could obtain fake drivers licenses.

Finally Watanabe asked, "Is there a place where we can get good Japanese food and decent saki?" Sato led the way to a small eating house, explaining that, "These folks are Chinese, but they will serve boiled rice with sashimi and most importantly, they import a good *amakuchi* saki.

There was scarcely room for all of them in the tiny establishment, but the proprietor cheerfully rearranged the accommodations. They were soon consuming raw fish and sticky rice flavored with an occasional sip of the pale, sweet amakuchi, brewed only in the winter. When it came time to pay, Watanabe pulled out American dollars and said to Sato, "This is our thanks to you and your crew for all your help."

SONOMA

During the last few days of April and into May 1951, the Showatachi lived in the cheap lodgings Sato had pointed out in Chinatown. They obtained fake driver licenses and began integrating themselves into the polyglot society of coastal California. Tule Minoru was able to get a custodian job at Letterman Army Hospital in the Presidio. There, he carefully cultivated the attention of Chiyo Sakamoto, a lithesome young Nisei clerk who worked in the records division. Her careful search of military medical records turned up two items of potential interest. First was the record of "Jubal Ragnvold, former POW in Japanese occupied Philippines, treated for malaria and intestinal parasites then released—home address Box 16, Rural Route 1, Bluewater, New Mexico." Second was a transfer record for "Magwitch Russell to Bruns Army Hospital, Santa Fe, New Mexico." There was no home address. Tule made careful note of these facts.

Meanwhile, Watanabe and Eddie had decided San Francisco was just too impersonal for any real help, so they moved north to Sonoma. Here, they hired out as day laborers in the vineyards and truck farms. They were soon gaining experience driving farm vehicles and picking up American vernacular. Even more valuable was their contact with Nesei wartime internees, from whom they learned much about the intricacies and foibles of American society. Even the nuances so difficult for the Japanese mind were taking on a degree of familiarity. Sonoma was a pleasant place, and they were beginning to feel at home in the Japanese-American community there. Unfortunately, the nippon-to temple swords were probably 1,400 miles away.

Their next move was to ask Kit Nakaya, a Nisei auto mechanic, to find an inexpensive half-ton truck. A couple of days later, Kit informed them that he had found a 1946 six-cylinder Chevy pickup that they could purchase for $325. They agreed on the price with the stipulation that for another ten dollars, he would take care of title transfer and licensing, at their cost of course. Two days later, they were the proud owners of an American vehicle.

Back in San Francisco, they discussed the necessary tactical changes that faced them. It was decided Eddie would remain in Chinatown. He would manage money transfer matters. He would also keep the phone and the small rental so the other two could contact him immediately, if necessary. He would continue to search libraries and other information sources. He even went with Tule to Letterman Hospital to see if there was a chance of replacing him in the custodial job.

Watanabe and Tule Minoru, the now abbreviated Show-atachi, would leave immediately for New Mexico in the truck. They made up bedrolls in canvas tarps and acquired a large waterproof box with hinged lid and lockable hasp that they bolted to the truck bed. They even hung canvas water bags, American style, from stakes along the pickup bed, where they had placed their few personal things and some food items. They scrounged up a number of glass bottles once used for vinegar or apple juice. These they filled with water and stood them up in pasteboard boxes, anticipating the desert crossing they knew lay ahead of them.

The adventure didn't really begin until they merged into the traffic feeding onto the San Francisco-Oakland Bay Bridge. Watanabe was certainly glad that Tule was driving; at last, his American experience was paying off. The trip south through the San Joaquin portion of the Great Valley of California was an absolute revelation. Never had he seen so much agricultural land.

At Bakersfield, their route turned east. Here, the Tehachapi Mountains formed the eastern boundary of the San Joaquin. Now, they were entering the western edge of the Mojave Desert. The southern San Joaquin had seemed desolate, but this was unimaginable to Watanabe. His concept of desert was just a generic description from a Japanese geography textbook. They stopped to gas in Barstow and from the service station heard the now familiar strains of "Get Your Kicks on Route 66."

It was a long crossing that now lay ahead of them, but just perhaps they realized they were lucky it was May rather than July or August. The final crossing into New Mexico became a glorious red letter day. A few miles east of historic Fort Wingate, but a little short of the Continental Divide, they found tire tracks leading into the cedars. It was just after sunset, but the long day of driving was catching up with them. It took a while for the twilight glow to fade, but full darkness came on with an astral display beyond anything either man had before seen. There was something about the rarified atmosphere along the divide on a moonless night that made the stars seem twice as large.

SAN RAFAEL

They crossed the Continental Divide and moved on into Thoreau. The next turnoff was Bluewater. They didn't have a firm lead on Ragnor Ragnvold, but this Jubal character had to be some kind of a relative. They drove into the village and then followed what seemed to be the only other road out. South of town about two miles, they started seeing post boxes along side of the road. Some were marked with a number only, but most were labeled RFD 1, plus a number and frequently a family name. In most cases, a house was visible nearby. Otherwise, rutted tracks led into the distance with no house or other buildings visible. These seemed to serve more distant domiciles, probably cattle ranches. Finally, they found number 16 with the name Ragnvold painted below. "Yatta, we did it," exclaimed Tule.

A quick perusal of the surroundings revealed no buildings. The area was quite secluded. Tracks led south from the gravel road along a gentle, grassy ridge disappearing in the foothills of a distant mountain range. Near the post box, the area was more wooded. North of the road, cedars and junipers provided extensive cover. Numerous tracks led into the woods, where locals cut fuel. It would provide adequate cover from which to observe postal deliveries. But for now, they needed to move on. The gravel road led on to the southeast, where it joined Route 66 again. About ten miles further along, they saw a sign indicating the road to San Rafael. On a hunch, they turned off.

It was a truly pastoral setting. Broad watered meadows supported a variety of livestock. The village was scattered at random over the valley. Even though it had been settled before Victorio's raids in the 1880s, there was no vestige of plaza-style defensive fortifications. If such had ever existed, they had long since washed away. Each adobe homestead seemed to have its own dooryard garden and a larger field of corn. Nearby were corrals and sheds for cattle, sheep, and probably a horse or two. Around the house and corrals, there were usually small groves of alamos, providing the leafy green shade of summer. In the midst of this verdure stood a cruciform, adobe church surrounded by its Campo Santo. A small mercado with an attached cantina and service station stood nearby.

They were entranced. Tule drove slowly through the village all the way to the far end. On the way back, they explored the narrow side lanes leading to other properties. East of the Mercado, perhaps a quarter of a mile, a "For Rent" sign caught Watanabe's eye. He looked at Tule. Without a word, he nodded and pulled the truck over.

They walked into the yard peering in windows and examining buildings. The small four-room adobe stood near the road. Two large silver maples shaded the south windows from the afternoon sun. Twenty yards south of the house was the well, equipped with a windmill and elevated tank, from which gravity flow carried water to the house and animal troughs in the corral area, located in a small grove of alamos. Beyond this, a field of maize showed about four inches of new green.

By this time a young companero had joined them. "Buenos dias, senors. My name is Vicente, may I help you?"

Tule nodded at the sign. "Is it furnished, and how much are you asking?"

"Si, it is furnished. My father says that we must get forty-five dollars a month, but that includes a garden spot and a weekly turn of water for irrigation. A fair deal, eh no? We also sell eggs, butter, milk, meat, and vegetables in season."

Tule turned to Watanabe, as if questioning the value.

Vicente immediately added, "It even has an indoor bathroom and a refrigerator."

They smiled at the young man's eagerness and agreed to rent the house. They walked with him to the landlord's dwelling. Opening the screen door, the landlord introduced himself. "I'm Flavio Zavala, and I see you have already met my son, Vicente."

After paying the agreed upon two months rent and obtaining the keys, they remained another thirty minutes stocking up with eggs, milk, butter, and even a dozen tortillas. The lady of the house threw in a bunch of radishes and multiplier onions, which were the only vegetables currently in season.

They moved in their gear and buried most of their money in a steel box, deep under the floor tiles and three feet of adobe clay for fire protection. Only then did they build a fire in the wood range in order to cook their first Nihon-Mexican meal with tea.

Later, the landlord came down to explain that the water heating system was dependent upon the wood range. "A pipe from the hot water tank runs through the range firebox. As the water in the pipe heats up, it circulates into the hot water tank, from which the pressure of gravity flow carries it to the sink and bathtub. There is enough cedar firewood behind the house to last a couple of months, but you might want to throw the two-man crosscut saw and axe in the back of your truck. Then when you are exploring the countryside and run across good pieces of dry cedar or juniper, you can add to your fuel stock."

Flavio then took them outside and showed them how to use the saw and axe properly.

It can't be said that they looked forward to obtaining their own winter wood supply. However, the thought of becoming proficient in the use of saw and axe was more of a challenge than a burden. At times, when they were not going to monitor the Ragnvold mailbox, they would ask Vicente to accompany them in their exploring. It was he who introduced them to the ice caves, the string of volcanoes, El Moro, and finally Towa Yallane and Halona Itiwanna.

They finished the weekend enjoying their fresh food, strolling along the ditch banks and observing Zavala's various animals.

THE MAILBOX

By Monday morning, it was all business. They left San Rafael at 6:00 a.m., so as to be at their lookout point before the RFD man was likely to arrive. They parked the truck across the road, hidden well back in the woods. Close to the road, they found cover in the heavy foliage of a red cedar, where branches extending all the way to the ground hid them completely from the sight of anyone passing on the road.

Their wait turned out to be a long one. It was well past 1:00 p.m. before the delivery occurred. Then as agreed upon, Tule ran quickly across the road, sorted through the letters for anything with Jubal or Ragnor's name. They repeated this routine until Saturday. Nothing for either appeared. However, a delivery pattern was emerging. Apparently delivery occurred only on Mondays, Wednesdays, and Fridays, sometime after noon. Through that first week, they had waited to see when someone would come for the Ragnvold mail. On Monday and Wednesday, it was after 5:00 p.m., but on Friday, it was after dark. Tule voiced their reasoning: "This late pickup must have been circumstantial. Nonetheless, these observations will make our job easier in the future."

More weeks of watching turned up nothing. Then on the third week of July, information began to flow. On Monday 16

July 1951, the RFD driver dropped off Ragnvold mail at 1:20 p.m. As soon as the truck was out of sight, Tule dashed across and found two letters of possible interest. The remaining mail he carefully returned to the box. Then they drove home to San Rafael, all the while anticipating with savor what the letters might reveal.

Once home, they lit a small fire, just enough to boil water in the bottom of a flat pan, over which they were able to steam open both letters. The first letter was addressed to Jubal Ragnvold. The return address was: Magwitch Russell, P.O. Box 31, Redondo, Arizona. Watanabe made a quick note of the correspondent's address. The letter made mention of the "safety of the shears." This the readers passed off as inconsequential. Then there was an item that grabbed their attention. "Somehow I've lost Ragnor's address. Would you be so kind as to send it along? Hope things are going well in Bluewater. Sincerely, Mag."

Watanabe turned to Tule, "If Ragnor is not living at the Bluewater Ranch we may need to adjust our surveillance to accommodate the change."

The second letter was also addressed to Jubal. Its return address was: Ragnor Ragnvold, 478, Constitution Avenue, Albuquerque, New Mexico. The letter inside was all about his efforts toward reinstatement at the university, consolidating his GI benefits, and the new job at the university hospital. Near the end, he made a curious statement. "Be sure to look after the shears and stay in contact with Magwitch."

Watanabe voiced the question in both their minds. "Did you notice anything odd in those two letters?"

Tule thought a bit and replied, "Why are they so concerned about shears?"

"Exactly," replied Watanabe. "Is it their oblique way of referring to the temple swords? If so, we must be close to our objectives. This confirms that our surveillance might need adjustments to accommodate Ragnor. What would you recommend?"

"I believe we have concentrated our efforts so closely around the Ragnvold part of the equation that we are missing something. Perhaps it is time that we make a visit to Lino County and check out the Magwitch factor. If need be, we can check on Ragnor and Albuquerque later." Watanabe nodded.

They carefully refolded the letters and sealed the envelopes with mucilage that had been purchased for that very purpose. But they would wait until Wednesday to replace the letters in the RFD box. They didn't want the delivery person questioning why two letters were left behind from the previous delivery.

The truck was loaded with their camping gear, food, and water. They stopped by the landlady's to let her know they going camping but also to augment their food stocks with two dozen tortillas, ten sweet corn roasting ears, and two pounds of cured cheese, plus a jar of fresh cheese curd. They left San Rafael at mid-morning, leaving enough time to conceal the truck before the scheduled mail delivery.

It was 1:30 p.m. when the mail arrived. When the truck was out of sight, Tule sprinted across the road, checked the delivery and added the two letters to the box. It was still early afternoon, so there was ample time to get to Witch Wells and find a good campsite before dark. However, they would have to wait to explore the nearby canyon the Anglos called "Hard Scrabble," but the Ashiwi referred to as "Hantlipinkia, Place of the Stealing."

LINO COUNTY

When Francisco Vasquez de Coronado led his army across this land in 1540, he was captivated by expanses of wild Blue Flax. He named the principle stream, "Rio de Lino." Future settlers would call their political entity "Flax County," but the official name would retain the Spanish usage "Lino County," after the river's name. The first village that Watanabe and Tule came to was Lino County Seat."

On the east side of town they crossed a small stream. The sign on the bridge identified it as the Rio de Lino. As they crossed into the settlement Tule pulled over. "We need directions to the Magwitch ranch," he said.

Watanabe replied, "It would be foolish to let anyone know why we are here. The roadmap shows only two paved roads leading out of County Seat. I suggest we drive out a few miles on each of these and look for signs that might identify his place. If by chance we should see workers along the way, I should be able to tell if he is among them. Our spotting scope will help with this."

Not fully convinced, Tule put the truck in gear and pulled into the sparse west-bound traffic. A few handmade signs identified ranches or owners, but none pinpointed Magwitch Russell or Turtle Cienaga. They checked out several ranchers putting up hay or working cattle. Even with the scope, the Bird saw no one that looked like the gaunt hulking Mag. Some fifteen miles out the discouraged Tule turned the truck around and headed back. In town they took the southern road, performing a similar surveillance. This time Tule had checked the odometer, at fifteen miles exactly he swung the truck around. "We've got to have instructions," he said. "Besides we are getting low on gas." Tule turned into the Richfield service station. To the attendant he said, "Please fill it up. And can you tell us how to find Turtle Cienaga?"

The Mexican fellow who pumped the gas replied, "It's on the road south of town, leading toward Redondo, probably sixteen or seventeen miles. There is a sign near the turnoff that reads 'Mag Russell, Turtle Cienaga Ranch Tule mentally kicked himself for stopping too soon. He paid the attendant, and they were soon on the road which pointed them toward a long rim of mountains well to the south. Near the eastern edge of this expanse but sitting apart from the main chain was a distinctive blue mountain made up of several rounded peaks. Near the western edge and sitting at the top of this long expanse, the pointed peaks of its apex were also visible. The country through which they drove was now clad in a blue-green verdure the local cowboys called "blue gamma." The lushness was evidence of heavy summer rains.

A sign outside the right-of-way fence read, "Mag Russell, Turtle Cienaga Ranch." An arrow pointed west. They could see the copula top of the ranch house, a large barn, and other out buildings; closer to the cienaga was a grove of alamos. But no adequate cover appeared nearby.

A couple of miles to the south, they could see the large expanse of a broken lava flow and cinder cones that might offer more concealment. A few gates broke the expanse of the right-of-way fence. But the first promising one came where the road transected a large coulee. Here, a gravel off-ramp would cover their exit tracks. They followed the tracks into the malpais, where huge blocks of basalt provided ample cover for their truck. They grabbed a water jug, some lunch, a spotting scope, and binoculars, then headed to the north edge of the flow, from which they could observe the Magwitch ranch headquarters.

There seemed to be no human activity at the ranch. They waited until well after dark and were just about ready to hit the sack when they saw lights turn off the main road into the ranch. Watanabe grabbed the spotting scope and trained it on the house. Saddles were hung over the high rails above the truck bed. Obviously, the riding stock had been left elsewhere. Two men got out of the truck and went into the house.

Watanabe and Tule watched until all lights were extinguished. Then they went back to their camp near the coulee. They would need to be back at the observation post well before daybreak. It was decided that if the cowboys left early the next day, they would slip down to the house and check things out.

It was still too dark to make out the buildings with the naked eye when S J and Tule resumed their observation. However, the light-gathering spotting scope made objects quite discernable. Lights were already showing in the ranch house. Shortly, two men climbed into the truck, drove to the road, and turned south toward the mountains.

The observers hid the spotting scope and binoculars. Grabbing two small packs containing food, water, and a small revolver Tule had purchased in Thoreau, they headed north into their three-mile hike. As they drew near the buildings, they took cover behind a small cedar. From this vantage, most of the domicile could be seen. They watched for probably half an hour. Nothing large moved, except the horses grazing in the cienaga. They slipped around to the back of the house, as it related to the access road. The main entry was on the east, so they took care to limit exposure as much as possible to anyone who might be approaching from the south or east. Watanabe stood on the west side until Tule could check the door. It was unlocked so Tule gave a soft birdcall.

Inside, they took turns watching from an east window while the other searched. The most obvious artifacts were Mag's lacquered, deep cherry colored crutches with tsuka ito bindings. Watanabe carefully removed the tsuka covers, just in case Mag had been stupid enough to leave the blades in their transport saya. Once it was determined that the swords were not in the crutches, they made a thorough search of the house. They felt under every cover, every mattress, and lifted each rug looking for trap doors. But every plank appeared solid, and the spike heads in the planks under bedstead in the north room appeared normal. The old trick of Smith and Stevens now held good. Their search of the cupola revealed only a broad view of the road and a 360-degree sweep of the surrounding countryside. Watanabe would like to have stomped the beautiful crutches to pieces, as they represented his failure at Sengaku-ji. But fortunately for Mag, the Showa need for secrecy controlled that urge.

The searchers checked everything inside again to make sure there was no hint of their visit. Near the front step, Tule had placed a small cedar branch. This he used to sweep out any traces of their movement until they were well into the sward on the ridge beyond the house.

They were back in camp well before sunset. They were famished and decided to prepare a celebratory feast before leaving for San Rafael after dark that very night. They took out the axe, hunted up a few dead branches in the scattered cedars, and began to hone their skills of Mexican-American camp cooking. They kindled a fire with the twigs and smaller branches they could break by hand. They quickly learned that cutting the large, hard cedar branches with a semi-sharp axe was not child's play. Using a ploy often exercised by Dutch-oven cooks, they laid the heavy pieces across the small fire and continued to add more fuel to the center blaze.

They had borrowed ovens from the Zavala's who wisely threw in ganchos for lifting the ovens from the fire by their heavy wire handles. Their mentor had suggested taking the axe and shovel. Then specifically, he added, "Turn the ovens upside down over the fire to sterilize and heat them up before starting to cook." Flavio had handed them a coffee can one quarter full of beef tallow for frying tortillas. He also offered an admonition: "Go easy on the grease, just enough to add a little crispness and prevent burning without making them soggy. Slice a little cheese and lay it on the tortillas to melt, but don't turn them over, unless you want burnt cheese. For the roasting ears, dig a shallow hole next to the fire and lay in a couple of ears. Place hot coals on them and turn them occasionally, until you think they are done. Camping is a marvelous appetizer. You will eat things around a campfire you would not touch at home. As my Anglo friends would say, only half in jest, 'Burnt on the outside, raw in the middle, just like Mom's home cooking, ain't it good.'" After that discourse, they had been more anxious than ever to get on the road.

Meanwhile, at the camp in the coulee, the Japanese, would-be cowboy cooks were struggling. Stoking the fire, tending the pots, and turning the roasting ears kept them busy. But like old Flavio had hinted, they had never tasted anything so good.

In the twilight, they put out the fire and drove almost to the road, where they would wait until full dark. Tule drove and Watanabe took care of the gate. There appeared to be no traffic on the road. With the coming of darkness, they drove north. As they approached the Turtle Cienaga Ranch sign, they could see a light in the distant window of the house they had been in a few hours earlier. Just at the sign, a car coming from the north turned sharply into the ranch. Watanabe and Tule laughed easily at the urgency of the driver. After all, they were on their way home, home to San Rafael. They might have been more concerned had they known the driver's connection or purpose.

AVISO

The automobile the Showatachi saw turning into Turtle Cienaga that Friday evening was driven by Alvaro Rubi, Paco's kinsman. He switched off the lights and ran up to the door, knocked, and ran in.

"Well come on in," said Magwitch.

"What's wrong?" quizzed the more serious Paco.

"I wanted to come last night, but between fixing flat tires and pulling stuck people out of the blue clay hills I didn't get off work until midnight. I had to work again today but rushed out here as soon as possible. Now Mag you old skinflint, if you had had a telephone, I could have called you when you got back from the mountain last night."

"So what's the big push, amigo?" asked Mag, as he poured Alvaro a hot cup of coffee and shoved a pan of sourdough biscuits in his direction.

Alvaro tried to talk while juggling a hot biscuit, scalding coffee, and pulling up a chair. Finally, the words came gushing out. "Yesterday, I pumped gas for two Japs in a '46 Chevy Pickup with California plates. I wouldn't have thought much about it; except old eagle beak asked about Turtle Cienaga. Then I got suspicious and thought I'd drive out that evening, but never made it."

Mag interrupted, "Was eagle beak taller than the typical Jap?"

"Come to think of it, he was quite a bit taller than the driver. He also had a funny dry scar across one cheek."

This seemed to confirm what Mag was thinking. "It appears that the Showa Brotherhood has finally found us, but it took them nearly six years. Paco, look over the house; see if there are any signs they might have been here."

The first thing Paco checked was the planking in the north room. The head of the bed still rested on the plank nearest the wall. The bedding may have been moved a little, but who pays any attention to such things? He tested the tsuka covers on the crutch saya. They seemed a little loose, but it was nothing definitive. "There is nothing I can put my finger on. Unfortunately, everything seems suspicious. Probably the power of suggestion."

Alvaro was becoming antsy. "What the hell? Is there any place around here where they could hide out and watch the place unobserved?"

Mag immediately thought of the broken lava flow south of the cienaga. He grabbed an old Model 12 twelve-gauge off its pegs on the fireplace chimney, handed it to Alvaro, together with a box of shells. "Paco, get the flashlights. There are two Winchester 30–30s in the truck. Alvaro, do you have an extra light?"

When he nodded, Mag said, "We'll take the ranch truck. Paco, you ride shotgun in order to get the gates." Mag threw cinders twenty yards as he gunned the old truck out of the driveway. In no time, they were pulling off the road into the access for the big coulee. Alvaro saw them first; tire tracks turning left across the main ruts were clearly visible in the soil softened by recent rains. Mag stopped right in the main access, so as to block or slow down any escape attempt. He flipped off the headlights and shoved the keys into his Levi's. He cautioned them to leave the flashlights off to avoid being sitting ducks. The truck doors were left akimbo, but each man brought out his weapon, readied for action. It took a bit for their eyes to accommodate the low light levels.

Then they spread out, following the tracks as best they could. Finally, Mag pulled up at what appeared to have been a campsite. Using his light, he pointed out that the same set of incoming tire tracks had turned around and gone out. Dirt had been thrown on the fire. He placed his hand on the covering soil. It was still faintly warm.

"Well boys, it appears that we've just missed them, but we best keep it low until we check the track pattern near the truck, in case they were just moving camp further up the coulee." The pattern around the truck confirmed their disappointing conclusion, "The Japs have made their getaway."

As they came up out of the coulee onto the main road, Mag didn't slow down; if anything, he shoved the throttle closer to the floorboard. "Alvaro, would you mind a fast trip into County Seat before we take you back to your truck? Just in case our Showa friends should stop for some reason."

Alvaro's reply was immaterial; Mag's heavy foot was already pushing the old truck at an unsafe speed. Both passengers were holding on for dear life. It had become the fastest, longest seventeen-mile ride of their lives, but it was to no avail. The town was already rolling up its street. The Bucket of Blood Saloon was the only open business and no green '46 Chevy graced its parking lot. If the Japanese had come this way, which was likely, they were seemingly long gone. Alvaro took a slip of paper from his pocket and handed it to Mag. On it was written, "1947 Chevy pickup truck, green, California plates, 5F18 81."

SHOWATACHI RETURN

As the men of Showa drove north along the gravel road between the Lino County Seat and Witch Wells, they tried to evaluate the events of the past two days. Watanabe said, "This trip was profitable in that we know for certain of Magwitch's culpability and how to find him. The continuing downside is, we did not find out the exact location of either sword. Second positive factor, we know that Ragnor Ragnvold is now in Albuquerque. Downside, we don't know the degree of his present involvement. Third positive, we have ready access to postal communication with Jubal Ragnvold, who appears to be involved with sword sequestering, assuming our interpretation of 'caring for the shears' is correct. Downside, we have no way of tapping telephone conversations. So Tule, where does that leave us?"

"To me, it seems we have really only two alternatives, plus an outside consideration we must always keep in the back of our minds. First, we know Ragnor's address in Albuquerque. We could find him there and put pressure on him to divulge the location or locations of the swords. Unfortunately, this is not really a viable course of action, considering we have no real way to apply pressure. At present, it seems that we have only one alternative, to keep reading the Ragnvold mail until we discover better leads. Now the outside consideration—there is a possibility that Magwitch might have had suspicions of our visit to his place. It is unfortunate that we had to inquire about Turtle Cienaga from the service station attendant."

By this time, they were at Witch Wells. They decided to go through Halona Itiwanna and save twenty miles over the longer route through Thoreau and Bluewater. By midnight, they were back home in San Rafael.

$$\Delta$$

Before noon, Watanabe and Tule were back at their observation point on Bluewater RFD Route 1. It was a pleasant morning. The scrub jays flitted in and out of the junipers. They took turns sleeping under the concealing foliage of the large, red cedar as they waited for the RFD driver. Once the delivery was made, Tule grabbed the only letter addressed to Jubal Ragnvold and whispered, "*Ma deyo*," as he hurried past the red cedar on his way to the Chevy truck hidden further back in the elfin forest.

In the evening of the same day the Showa operatives returned to their observation of RFD Box 16, Mag and Paco drove to the telephone central in Redondo. After a number of attempts, the operator made the phone connection with Jubal at the Ragnvold Ranch. Mag took the connection in the sound retardant booth. Paco had been instructed to watch the operator to make sure she did not open the line with her key once the conversation was in progress. Paco, with the boldness of youth, sat right down in front of Mrs. Chappel. She was most annoyed but did not touch the key. However, she did consider charging Magwitch double toll for the insult.

"Hello, Skinner, how are things in lively old Agua Azul? Anything questionable happening in your neck of the woods?" Mag's low gruff voice was instantly recognizable.

"Well, hello Mag, when did you buy out Mountain Bell?"

"Now don't be a wise-guy, Jubal. I think we've got a serious problem on our hands. A couple of days ago, two Nips came through Lino County Seat. It appears that one of them is probably an ex-POW guard that Ragnor called the 'Brutal Bird,' real name something like Watanabe. These yahoos spent a couple of days checking out my place at Turtle Cienaga while we were working cattle on the mountain. They came in by way of Witch Wells and probably left the same way. You should warn Ragnor immediately of the danger and tell him to get a hold of Carvajal as well. I think the sheep herder is still in Albuquerque."

The disquieting news fairly shook Jubal. "Thanks for the warning, Mag. We'll try to be more watchful. I have been concerned about the security of our postal system; the last letter from you took several days longer to be delivered than your previous correspondence. Perhaps it was coincidental, but I am doubtful.

"Incidentally, Ragnor will be coming August 18. If that isn't too long to wait, why don't you come over for that weekend? We'll have a Dutch oven cookout, and I'll guarantee you will not need to lift one oven or one shovel-full of hot coals. You and I will sit on our duffs and let ranch hands and younger brothers do the grunt work. We will only peer into the ovens when someone else lifts the lids so we can check on the proper gold tone for the biscuits.

"Just one last thing, don't say anything about the 'shears' around my parents. Rag and I decided it would be better that they didn't know, less worry."

Mag's reply was a little uncertain. "You place me between a malpais and an obsidian point. I need to come so the three of us, and if possible, Blaz Carvajal can talk over what to do—that's the malpais. The point pressing into my side is Paco, my right arm, and left leg. He is very capable and can handle any problems with the ranch and cattle, but I would feel heavy guilt leaving him alone with the possibility of those Nip operatives prowling around the countryside."

Mag continued, "The eighteenth should be fine. Just let me see if there is a possibility of hiring someone to help Paco out without him feeling a loss of my confidence. So see what you can do about Blaz, and I will work on the Paco impasse. I'll call you in a few days. Adios."

As they drove from Redondo back to the ranch, Mag broached the subject. "I need to go to Bluewater to check out some problems with Jubal and Ragnor. But there are so many projects hanging fire between now and shipping time that I hate to leave. Probably the most pressing is the need to replace that section of fence in the southwest pasture we discussed last week. It needs to be finished before we bring the cattle off the mountain in October. If I can hire Lazaro Madrill to come out and help you, could the two of you replace that section while I am in Bluewater?"

"Caramba, Mag, I can replace that line by myself and save you having to hire old Laz."

"That may be so Paco, but pulling barbed wire can be tricky. I'd hate for a strand of wire to snap and catch you up with no one to help. I would feel much easier if someone were here to assist," Mag replied. After dark that night, they again drove to Redondo. This time, he didn't care if Mrs. Chappel opened her key.

PIONEER DAY

24 July 1951

It was Pioneer Day. An anxious Jubal spent the morning waiting for a toll line operator to place a call to Ragnor in Albuquerque. The operator finally reached him in the staff lounge of the university hospital. He was lunching with Blaz Carvajal, MD, when an attendant asked if he would take a call on the nearby staff phone. He excused himself and crossed to the wall-hung pay phone.

"Yes?"

"What have you been doing?" asked Jubal. "I've been trying to reach you all morning."

"Sorry, I've been helping Dr. Carvajal with a rather long medical procedure. So what's the big deal?"

"Mag called to say that Showa operatives, including one named 'Watanabe,' had been checking out his ranch. He thinks they might be working out of New Mexico, since they came into Lino County Seat via Witch Wells Road. His opinion is that we still have a little buffer since they failed to find his set of 'shears.' However, he is contemplating a different hiding spot."

Jubal continued, "I hope you are still coming to the ranch on August 18. I have invited Mag for that weekend. He also said it would be good to invite Carvajal if you could get hold of him that quickly. But that doesn't seem to be a problem."

Here, Ragnor cut in. "The problem might be whether he can reschedule his appointments in time; that's only a little over three weeks, you know. I will do my best, however."

$$\Delta$$

Finally, Mag decided to go car shopping. In some ways, he was a real conservative. He hated to spend hard-earned money on frills, even though he had put money in the bank to purchase an automobile at least four years ago. Now events were prying open his tight fist. He sent Paco shopping for groceries, barbed wire, and rifle ammo. He got out in front of the Chevy dealer. His druthers would have been a sporty coupe. But the thought of a certain little widow in the county seat with a couple of kids allowed the deep pragmatism of his mind to control such rashness. He asked Rob, the salesman, to look at the four-door sedans. They looked at the '51 models. Mag either rebelled at the colors or the prices.

Rob, in desperation, finally said, "Mag, I have just the car for you. It belonged to the proverbial, 'little old lady from Pasadena.' It's a 1950 Model. Clean as a whistle with only a few miles. I'll let you have it for only 1,500 dollars."

Mag hemmed and hawed.

"All right Mag, 1,400 dollars, but I want you to know you are taking the crusts right out of my children's mouths."

In response, Mag dug into his pocket and pulled out a quarter and handed it to Rob saying, "I feel bad. Here, run over to Will's market and get some bread for those youngsters."

They both laughed and walked inside, where Mag wrote out a check for 1,400 dollars and said to Rob, "This of course means a lube job, oil change, and a tank full of gas. I'll be back in about an hour to pick it up."

Mag walked three blocks up the street to the farm supply store where Paco had just loaded the second spool of barbed wire. Mag called to him, "Have them throw on eight bags of cottonseed cake. We just as well get some on hand before the winter snows hit."

They drove by the Madrill adobe, where Mag negotiated for some day labor with Lazaro. Paco would pick him up that morning. Room and board would be included with his wages. Mag now felt much better about the upcoming trip to Bluewater.

SWORD
PROTECTION
SOCIETY

Mag left Turtle Cienaga early Friday morning. At first, the comfort of the sedan felt odd compared to the stiff springs and shock-absorber-less wonder he called "the ranch truck." However, he was becoming accustomed to its comfort. Mag thought, *This might become addictive. I'll probably have to give it up, after all, I can't afford another addiction; the Jack Daniels already costs me too much.*

At Witch Wells, he considered going through Halona Itiwanna but decided he would rather try the new wheels on Route 66. He arrived at the Ragnvold Bluewater Ranch a bit after noon.

Somewhat after Mag arrived at Bluewater, Ragnor finished his duties at the university hospital and picked up Blaz Carvajal. They made a hurried trip to the home ranch. On the open ground behind the big house, several cooking fires had been burning long enough to produce deep beds of orange-red coals. In spite of Jube's promise that he and Mag would do nothing more than observe the progress of cooking, both were scurrying around with ganchos and shovels, keeping ovens and coals in juxtaposition.

After a hearty dinner of prime rib steaks, sourdough biscuits, and thick white gravy, the four contrivers in the sword sequestration scheme walked leisurely away from the main group that was still enjoying the repast. When out of earshot, Jubal opened the discussion. "Since I spoke to any of you, a new bit of intelligence has surfaced. One of our cowboys mentioned that a couple of Nisei Japanese are living in San Rafael. Now most of us wouldn't know a Nesei from Hirohito himself. But from Blaz's description of Watanabe, it should be easy enough to check out if someone can get a look at him. However, it should be someone whom he would not recognize; since the three of you are known to him by sight. I suggest that we bring Gungnir, the youngest Ragnvold son, into the scheme. Then he and I will drive to San Rafael tomorrow and see if we can get a lead on the Bird.

"Meanwhile, Mag, what do you think our next step should be?"

"Unfortunately, Jubal, I don't really know. It appears that the Showa Brotherhood has established at least one cell in America, and it seems to have ferreted out our whereabouts and connections to the temple swords. It is also quite likely that other cells exist, perhaps even working with Watanabe, or at least capable of assisting him as necessary. The other side of the coin lies with what is happening to and in Japan. There is much talk that the US is negotiating a new treaty that will probably withdraw Allied Occupational Forces. The question then becomes, what will the incoming government's position be regarding cultural treasures like the nippon-to? Perhaps Blaz can tell us more about that? What have you heard from Yoshida?"

"The last I heard from Nobu was probably three months ago. He was optimistic that, if the Provisional Government remains in power, Shinto and Buddhist shrines are likely to be afforded more protection, and it should soon be safe for them to bring the nippon-to back to Japan. As soon as I get back to Albuquerque, I'll send a cable requesting his instructions"

At this point, Ragnor entered the conversation. "I agree that Jubal and Gun should go to San Rafael soon and check on Watanabe. But whatever the results of their findings, we should hang tight until Blaz hears back from Nobu. My main concern is for Mag and the Hachiman Taro. Do you think it's safe for a few weeks more, or would you prefer to change its hiding place immediately?"

Mag thought a bit then replied, "If Nobu gives us an answer before time to ship and bring the cattle off the Mountain, Paco and I can probably keep a pretty close watch. After that, I suspect it will need to be moved. So until then, let's just hang on. However, no more confidential postal correspondence, and take care even in phone chatter. No more talk about shears. After all, we have become the 'Unofficial Sword Protection Society of Sengaku-ji.'"

Gungnir Ragnvold, youngest of the three Ragnvold brothers, also showed up at the ranch, a little late for the festive meal, but there was plenty of steak and biscuits. Someone even warmed up a little gravy. Gun had recently finished the course work for a MA in Prehistoric Cultural Ecology at the University of New Mexico. The Southwest Region of the USFS had hired him to conduct research on prehistoric sites in the Cibola and Apache National Forests. This fieldwork he planned to incorporate into his thesis. But Gun was always ready for a little extracurricular adventure.

When Gun had finished eating, Ragnor brought him over to where the Unofficial Sword Protection Society was still in conference. Ragnor introduced Gun to Mag and Blaz then explained, "Gun is somewhat familiar with Jap swords and what we are trying to do. He actually helped Jubal sequester the Fiery Blade of the Enduring Comet."

Ragnor then explained how Mag had found out about the Showa Brotherhood spying at the Turtle Cienaga Ranch and why he suspected they were probably surveilling the Ragnvold Ranch as well. Then he explained the big connection. "When Alvaro Rubi came out to Mag's ranch to warn them of the Jap inquiry, Mag's first thought was, *Could this possibly be Watanabe that gave Blaz and the POWs at Shinagawa such a difficult time?* When Mag described the height and bird-like beak of that Ainu warrior, Alvaro immediately confirmed the probable connection, Mag called to warn Jubal the next day. Although Mag didn't mention it, he would know the man well. Watanabe stabbed him under the left shoulder the day that he pirated the nippon-to out of Shinagawa."

"The rumor of Japs, possibly illegal operatives, in San Rafael came to us only yesterday. One of our ranch hands returned from a visit to his folks. He casually mentioned to Jubal that some Nisei farmers were interested in buying farmland in San Rafael. They have rented a house from Flavio Zavala about a quarter of a mile east of the Catholic Church. Since you and Jubal are the ones that Watanabe is less likely to recognize, we're asking that you check it out."

Gungnir turned to Jubal. "What about it, big brother?"

"Does eight in the morning sound about right?"

Fifteen minutes more discussing details for Gun's benefit plus suggested operational procedures, and the Unofficial Committee for the Preservation of Sengaku-ji Temple Swords broke up and joined the others around the dying embers. Darkness had settled all along the New Mexico Continental Divide. Intense stars stared out of the black velvet of night.

$$\Delta$$

"Drowsiness shall clothe a man with rags." Jubal quoted *Proverbs* as he pulled Gun out of the rack. "Must be on our way little brother, to visit San Rafael; Home of the Archangel." Gun grumbled, but slowly rose to his feet. They decided to take the ranch truck. It was less conspicuous than Gun's flashy Ford coupe. Within twenty-five minutes, they pulled into San Rafael. They turned left into the lane south of the church and soon spotted the '46 Chevy truck, but no apparent human activity

"Looks like the Japs may soon be wearing rags," said Gun. Jubal merely smiled in reply and handed him the spotting scope case to open. Beyond the mother ditch on the east side of the valley was a gentle rise of land that provided a general view of the village. Jubal drove north until he found a clear view of the rental house, then he turned the truck to face the valley. The powerful scope brought the house and truck up so close they could read the figures on the license plate. They hunkered down to wait. Meanwhile, they drank Delaware Punch and chewed Walnettos.

Sometime later, two men came out of the adobe and began to hoe in the garden patch near the house. "Looks like Showa is making their operatives forage for their sustenance," Gun offered.

"More likely the inborn nature of an Ainu peasant's need to be near the soil," said Jubal. "Did you see the snout on the tall dude?"

"Sure did. Do you reckon we should go down and lean on them a bit?" Gun asked.

"Probably not, it would be best if they don't know we are on to them yet. Jubal started the truck and they were on the way back to Blue Water.

FALCON ZAVALA

Sunday evening, the "Unofficial Sword Protection Society" came together briefly to discuss events in San Rafael. "Perhaps we should notify the FBI office in Albuquerque about these aliens," said Jubal.

To which the pragmatic Blaz responded, "Just what are you going to accuse the Nips of? Unfortunately, we know nothing about the legality of their status. For now, it might be prudent to leave governmental bureaucracies out of the picture."

Mag seemed to agree. "Someone listening to us might think the Yellow Peril was about to over-run us. Surely we can hold our own against two puny Japs until Blaz gets some response back from Yoshida."

Early Monday morning, 28 August, Blaz composed a cable to Yoshida Nobu.

"Watanabe in US (stop) knows general location of Nippon-to (stop) is restitution to Japan now feasible (stop) will find new place to sequester if needed (stop) advise (stop) Blaz."

Shortly afterward, Blaz visited the regional FBI office. He asked to speak with an agent. He was soon in the office of Special Agent Falcon Zavala. He related their suspicion of mail tampering and the visit of Jubal and Gungnir to San Rafael and asked, "Is there any possible way to check on the immigrant status of one Watanabe Hattori?"

Special Agent Zavala pondered a moment and then shook his head, "If Watanabe is in this country illegally or under an assumed name, it is doubtful that either customs or passport control would have any record. However, I will check it out. Perhaps more immediately, we should consider the possibility of mail fraud or tampering. Would you call your friend Jubal Ragnvold and set up a time for me to meet with him at the ranch? It should be a confidential visit, so I will drive an unmarked vehicle. You might also suggest we set it up as though I am seeking employment.

A few days later, a telegraph delivery boy found Dr. Carvajal at the university hospital and delivered Yoshida's cabled response.

"Japan politics unsettled but look promising (stop) plan to come to US soon (stop) possibly 17 Sept (stop) if feasible will bring back blades (stop) Nao will assist (stop) can you meet us in San Fran or an alternative city (stop) somewhat nearer than NM (stop) perhaps Salt Lake or Las Vegas (stop) advise (stop) Nobu."

Blaz saw Ragnor in the staff lounge a little later and recounted the talk with Special Agent Zavala. Then he showed him the cablegram. When Ragnor finished reading,

Blaz said, "Why don't you come by my place this evening so we can discuss both factors and consider our options? Then we'll call Jubal. If he agrees with us and with Zavala's suggestion, perhaps we can persuade him to go to Turtle Cienaga afterward to talk with Mag, since he doesn't have a phone."

That evening, Blaz and Ragnor discussed the pros and cons of Zavala's suggestion and Nobu's cablegram. Then they called Jubal, who readily accepted the FBI proposal. However he noted, "The timing of Yoshida's arrival might be tricky for both Mag and me, too close to fall roundup and shipping. We might need to enlist Gungnir's help if Nobu and Nao have already booked passage to San Francisco."

Ragnor clarified a couple of points. "If we obtain some firm dates from Yoshida, I'll work on Gun. He seems to have the most flexible schedule of any of us at present. However, your scheduled operation dates appears to be the most crucial factor. Once your time is firmed up, I will try to work around both your schedule and Yoshida's. We need those dates as soon as possible."

FALCO PEREGRINUS

A day later, Agent Falcon Zavala arrived at the Ragnvold Ranch in a grungy old Ford and asked to speak with Jubal. Falcon was dressed in well-worn jeans, khaki work shirt, and dusty ranch boots. He looked like he was ready to fix a mile of fence by himself. As they checked out sheds and corrals, Jubal explained, "The Showa operatives whom Gungnir and I dropped in on at San Rafael seem to have been definitely reconnoitering our area. As I was driving west from San Rafael to Bluewater the other day, I met them headed toward San Rafael. They were probably a half-mile east of our RFD box. The timing was too neat to be coincidence. My guess was they were still checking our mailbox. So Ragnor suggested a little counter-espionage. The plan was that he would write a letter to me saying something about Yoshida's coming, but make the dates sometime in October or November. Normally mail from Albuquerque to our box takes two days. So if Ragnor posted a letter today, Monday 10 September, I should receive it on Wednesday the twelfth.

"Ragnor then suggested sending one of my ranch hands down to recon the RFD box about an hour before delivery time on the scheduled days for the next several days. Looks like you are that hand, just tailor-made for the job. Perhaps we should look over the area before it gets too close to their set up time. Do you have a spotting scope and a rifle, just in case?" The rest of the thought remained implied.

After they scouted the area for suitable concealment, Jubal suggested they go back to the house and round up some early lunch.

THE KIBEI TURNS

In mid-August 1951, Eddie Wan, the Showa operative based in San Francisco, made a return visit to Sonoma. He loved the vineyards and truck farming of the wine country that reminded him so much of his youth in Santa Rosa, where his parents grew sweet corn and strawberries. Eddie rented a room in town for a few days. It was close by the accommodations he and Watanabe used earlier that year. It was also just a few blocks from the auto repair and gas station run by Kit Nakaya, who had helped them buy the old Chevy truck now in New Mexico.

Eddie needed to talk with an American-born Japanese. There were many questions and problems in his mind. His own American childhood seemed so long ago he could scarcely remember it. It was like his life began with his enrollment at the University of Tokyo in 1939 and was consumed by the awful war years of privation, starvation, and firebombing. .

Kit was busy with a costumer, so Eddie merely asked, "Can I buy you dinner this evening?"

Kit replied, "Sure, meet me here at six thirty. My dining habits are like the 'suppertime' of an American farmer."

When Eddie returned that evening, he was surprised to find a scrubbed and polished Nesei gentleman in a natty sport jacket standing at the front of the station. Even the mechanic's grease had been dug from under his fingernails. The clean apparition spoke with an America accent, no trace of *kokugo* in his speech: "What kind of food are you in the mood for?"

This caught Eddie completely off guard. He had expected Kit would have a Japanese greasy spoon nearby. Eddie said, "Anything but chop suey or chow mein."

"There's a sushi restaurant across town, but if you'd rather have your fish warm, they will do that as well."

They ordered, and then Kit said, "Now my friend, what can I do for you? Is the truck not running properly or what?"

Eddie responded quickly, "No, no, so far as I know its fine. It's in New Mexico with Watanabe and Tule, but I'm still working in San Francisco. However, my problems are more personal, and I need some outside input. As you know, I am *Kibei*, born in America but educated in Japan. My parents sacrificed greatly to send me to Japan to go to university. They thought I would learn more in a well-structured program. That was in 1938 when I was seventeen years old.

"As long as Japan was preoccupied with its military and looting efforts in China, beginning in July 1937 and lasting until December 1941, I was left to my studies. I was a senior at the University of Tokyo when the Pacific War broke out, and all of a sudden my knowledge of English language and American culture were of great interest to the militaristic regime. I was conscripted into the Japanese army and after basic training was transferred directly to the Kempeitai, Counterintelligence Division. My primary duty was to ferret out disloyalty among expatriate Japanese returning from North America. Just why they thought I would be more trustworthy than others with similar backgrounds, I didn't know.

"Perhaps they felt that the horror stories they fed me about the treatment of my parents by the US War Relocation Authority would make me feel anger and the need for retribution, which it did. Haruzo Naoji, the information officer of my unit, said that sources in America had learned that authorities, using the Alien Enemies Act of January 1942, had forcibly removed my parents from their home in Santa Rosa. This was apparently justified under the military exclusion, because their home was within a hundred miles of the Pacific Coast. Furthermore, he emphasized the US military believed that all Japanese immigrants would remain loyal to the emperor and would aid and abet the impending invasion of North America. My parents would have been doubly suspect, having sent me to attend university in Japan.

"Their assets were frozen: a home, farmland, a truck, and bank accounts. They said my mother was sent to Mazanar, California, but my father, who was considered a troublemaker, was sent to an isolation center at Dalton Wells near Moab, Utah. The Kempeitai allowed that some of this group was used for live bayonet practice by American troops. The implication was that my father was so treated and probably died as the result. I was so angry that I asked to be transferred to the social censorship group, TOKKO (Thought Police), so I could serve the Inassimilable Emperor to the best of my ability. I took to heart the wartime Japanese adage: 'luxury is the enemy.'

"I became a devotee of Radio Zero and faithfully listened to Tokyo Rose, whichever one she happened to be. But most significantly, I bought into the militarist doctrine. In this cause, I became a successful interrogator, prying out the most condemning secrets from returning expatriates. Sometimes such secrets led to sequestered wealth, which was usually diverted to the needs of wartime Japan. Surprising to me, most of this wealth was the result of looting and extortion directly connected with the Golden Lily."

"Wow," exclaimed Kit. "You left me sitting beside the road way back there. I have never even heard of the Golden Lily, or the Kempeitai for that matter."

Eddie took a long time to explain the extent and subterfuge of wartime economics and the role looting played in financing such. He even attempted to relate how such theories might pertain to epic battle philosophies such as *Tennozan.*

As they dined and well into the night thereafter, Eddie belabored the concept of Tennozan for Kit: "In 1582, a pivotal battle was fought in Yamazaki, Kyoto Prefecture. Its legendary impact on the unification of Japan as a national state has come to signify a near mythic force beyond the control of mankind, even powerful Samurai warriors. During this conflict, the forces of an upstart turncoat, Mitsuhide, crossed the river seeking to occupy Tenno Hill. Heavy arquebus volleys drove them back, and Mitsuhide was killed."

"Over time the name of the battle became *Tennozan no tatakei*, the Battle of Emperor Hill. The ultimate victor was Hideyoshi Toyotomi. It was he who recovered the lands of Nobunaga Oda, who had been forced to commit seppuku by the unfaithful Samurai retainer Mitsuhide Akechi.

"It was Hideyoshi who became the great unifier in the drive to create a national state on the home islands. And Tennozan had taken on the aura of a person's or a people's epic struggle to attained a perceived rightful outcome. Sometimes, it took the form of a penultima. For example, following early military successes in East Asia and the Pacific, Japan realized that she could not sustain a prolonged war against the military-industrial power of the United States and her allies. At some point, that realization caused many Japanese, probably including the imperial family, to hope for and perhaps even pray for a Tennozan epic battle that would consolidate their territorial gains. Once it was realized that this was not going to happen, they began to abbreviate their ambitions, hoping that a lesser Tennozan would serve to convince the United States to allow them to retain certain occupied territories, most notably the Philippines. Faith in such an outcome was perhaps the reason for dumping much of the Golden Lily loot there. But that faith was groundless and by the time realization was crystallized, it was too late to remove it to the homeland.

"Later, in the closing months of World War II, any optimists that might remain in Japan prayed for a Tennozan that would shift the military advantage back to Japan long enough to avoid an unconditional surrender. Perhaps this is the reason that the bloodiest and most brutal battles in the Pacific were fought at Okinawa and the Ryukyus. Even in our postwar timeframe, the term 'Tennozan' is often linked with the Battle for Okinawa.

"For me, 'Eddie Oshima,' there is a longing for my own Tennozan, albeit a battle of the mind needed to resolve my conflicting loyalties between America and Nihon.

"You know Kit, I'm not sure at what point I became disillusioned with the Kempeitai, but there has always been this driving need to find out what became of my parents. I come to you because you are my only contact with the Nisei reality of my youth."

Kit released a heavy sigh and slowly spoke. "In spite of many mistakes the Americans have made, I am still an American through and through. The system, and by this I probably mean the constitutional government, is bigger than the individuals who try to run it. I have never lived in Japan; in fact, I have never even been there, but my parents, who emigrated from the mainland and lived through the wartime abuses in the United States, would never consider going back.

"I would suggest we try to find out if your parents are still alive and go from that point. There is an informal network among Japanese Americans set up to reunite families separated by internment and war. This group is also trying to establish reparations for properties confiscated at the time of concentration. I know an old gentleman here in Sonoma, who is the main contact person for the grape country. Perhaps he can provide some leads for us. I'll call him early on and see if he can see us soon."

The following evening, Kit Nakaya and Eddie Wan met with Awajiumi. When Kit introduced Eddie Wan, Mr. Awajiumi's first response was, "What is your real name? Wan is not a Japanese name. If we are going to find your parents, we will need their real names."

"My apologies, Awajiumisan; when the Showa Brotherhood sent me here, they gave me the pseudonym 'Wan.' They thought it would be more useful while working in

Chinatown. My real name is Eddie Oshima. My father is Oshima Kuro, and my mother is Oshima Sayuri."

"That's better," responded Awajiumi. "Now where did your parents live before the internment?"

Eddie replied, "I was born in Santa Rosa, and they were still living there at the time of our last correspondence. That would have been in 1941, before Pearl Harbor and the outbreak of the Pacific War. I was enrolled at the University of Tokyo at that time. Since coming back to California, I have checked the Santa Rosa area but could find no Oshimas there."

"Well, our network is probably more comprehensive. Give me a few days to make some phone calls and touch base with the right people; then I will get back to you. Can I reach you through Kishi? Forgive me; I should have said 'Kit.' It is hard for me to be totally American. That's going to have to be up to your generation, the Nisei of the Promised Land."

"Contact through Kit would be great. So I'll bug him," said Eddie.

It was probably a week later when Awajiumi called Kit. "Tell our Kibei friend that I'm pretty sure we have found his parents. They are with a group of internees who have leased ground in the Sweetwater Valley near San Diego to grow strawberries and sweet corn. They seem to be all right. There is only one phone for the entire group of probably thirty people, and I have no idea how long he might have to wait when he calls, but he should call late in the evening. You know how Japanese peasants like to work."

A tearful reunion via Ma Bell followed that first call. Eddie promised the folks that he would come to San Diego just as soon as he could straighten out a few matters with the immigration people and the FBI. He asked Kit to look for an auto he could purchase, thanked him profusely, and caught the Greyhound to San Francisco.

On Saturday 15 September 1951, Eddie returned to his room in Chinatown. There was correspondence to answer, and his landlord said the telephone had on occasions sounded like it would ring off the hook. He was barely back in his room when the phone began to ring again. Eddie lifted the receiver, "Where the hell have you been? We have been trying to get you for the last week." It was the harsh voice of Watanabe.

"Sorry, I had to go up to Sonoma and check on a few things. So what do you need?"

"We have just learned that Yoshida will be coming to the United States very soon, and there will be a transfer of nippon-to shortly. We are going to need a faster auto, so wire money for us immediately. Send at least 4,000 dollars US for a car and to cover the expenses of tracking these *gaijin* interlopers. Send the funds to the Western Union in Gallup, New Mexico. For security reasons, we are moving our base of operations."

Eddie replied, "The bank is now closed, so there is no chance of wiring the money before Monday morning."

When the Bank of China opened at nine o'clock the next morning, Eddie was waiting at the door. He withdrew 4,000 dollars to wire to Gallop. He also withdrew another 4,000 for his own automobile and expenses. It was this second action that lent definition to his Tennozan. The epic battle within his mind seemed to have reached absolute resolution. He knew assuredly that his full loyalty lay with the land where he was born and not with his Kibei years in a faltering and oppressive society.

From the express office, Eddie made his way by cable car and bus to the San Francisco Federal Bureau of Investigation Headquarters. In a few minutes, he was ushered into the office of Special Agent Sam Branin. Eddie introduced himself and explained, "I am Kibei, which means that I was born in the United States but was sent to Japan to go to university. During my senior year at the University of Tokyo, I was conscripted into the Imperial Japanese Army. After the war, I was unemployed and totally unsure of my citizenship status. I was starving on the streets of Tokyo but afraid to approach the US Consulate. Six years later, I was getting by but still had no adequate job. When the Showa Brotherhood recruited me for a special mission to America, it was my chance to get home, so I took it. Now I'm asking for your help and offering you information in return."

Agent Branin pondered the points that Eddie had made, then observed, "Since you are native born, there should be no question as to citizenship. Your service in the IJA and membership in Showa will have to be considered separately. Nevertheless, your freewill approach to us should weigh considerably in your favor. Have you contacted your parents since you arrived?"

"About a week ago, I learned that they were still alive, and I was able to speak with them by phone. They thought I was dead, and I thought they were dead also. That was our first contact since before Pearl Harbor in 1941. Once we finish with the problem here, my hope is to go to San Diego and see them."

"All right, Eddie, let's get on with it. I will need all the information you can provide about the other members of Showa who came with you and your purpose in the United States. Why don't we start with the Showa mission?"

"It seems that Showa started out with a mission to save some of Japan's most valuable cultural treasurers, nippon-to art swords that were destined for the smelting furnaces of Macarthur's shortsighted disarmament policy, but early on that altruism turned to greed, as they realized how much potential profit resided in the temple swords. They had lined up buyers for two such swords owned by the Buddhist Temple Sengaku-ji in Shinagawa. Rumor was that a buyer or buyers, through a contact in Abu Dubai, were offering more than a million dollars American for each blade. The Johkai Priest of Sengaku-ji and his assistant, Yoshida Nobu, with the aid of three Americans, were able to get the swords out of Japan under the very noses of the brotherhood. Two of the Americans were members of the medical corps, American Occupational Forces. One of these was a former POW, who was asked to remain behind and help with the medical and psychological needs of his fellow POWs. The third man, who actually smuggled the swords out of Japan in December 1945, was a badly injured POW and close friend of the POW who remained to help with the evacuation.

"The objective of the Johkai and Yoshida was to sequester the swords outside Japan until the political climate there made it safe to restore such national treasures, called Kokuho, to their rightful places.

"Then just this year, with the talk of withdrawing occupational forces and returning the government to the Japanese, Showa decided it needed to act swiftly before the temple swords could be returned to Sengaku-ji, where they would receive the full protection of the national government."

Agent Branin then asked, "How desperate are your associates, and do you feel that the individuals who helped sequester the swords might be in danger? There is certainly the possibility of assigning a surveillance team to track their activities."

Eddie was surprised at how quickly things had moved. He felt the need for caution in the answers he would supply. "As to the desperation of my former associates, I can only offer some details of their background. Watanabe was a guard at the Shinagawa POW hospital, where the prisoners referred to him as the 'Brutal Bird.' He holds a Black Belt in the Koryu School of martial arts. He was once on the list to be tried for war crimes, before Macarthur changed all that.

"Tule Minoru is the second agent involved. 'Minoru' is probably his actual family name, but his given name is really 'Tsuji.' He was interned at the Tule Lake, California Relocation Center in May 1942. Late in the war, the United States passed a law making it possible for internees to renounce their US citizenship; Tule was one who did so. He was repatriated to Japan. I think that was early in 1946."

Branin finished scratching notes on his yellow pad, then asked, "What are the names and addresses of those involved in the sword removal?"

Eddie replied, "Blaz Carvajal is the ex-POW who remained in Japan to aid his fellow POWs. He is probably now an army doctor living in Albuquerque. The second occupational force medic was Ragnor Ragnvold, who may also reside in Albuquerque. The third man, Magwitch Russell, is a rancher in Lino County, Arizona. In addition to these three, Ragnor's brother, Jubal Ragnvold, may have helped sequester the swords and might be in danger. He resides at the Ragnvold Ranch near Bluewater, New Mexico."

Agent Branin ask a few more questions to help clarify his notes then told Eddie, "Stick around while I call the FBI in Albuquerque. I will probably need your help to clarify some of the details."

APPREHENSIVE SHOWATACHI

22 September 1951

Watanabe and Tule pulled their truck into the usual hiding place at exactly 12:25. They could not have noticed that eyes as dark as their own observed the truck turn off the road and thread its way through the elfin forest until it was out of sight in the bushy cedars. Nor did they realize those same eyes aided by optical enhancement were watching their progress to concealment within the large red cedar.

The RFD delivery occurred at 1:13 p.m. As soon as the post truck was out of sight, a short Oriental darted out of concealment, crossed the road, and rapidly sorted the contents of the box. He shoved a single letter into his shirt pocket and replaced the remaining pieces. Within a few moments, the green Chevy truck pulled out of the cedars and headed down the road toward San Rafael.

The envelope was addressed to Jubal Ragnvold, with a return address to Ragnor.

Once in the adobe, they quickly built a fire in the range and prepared to steam open the cover. With the letter open in hand, they became increasingly excited. In essence, the cause was the following: "Received a cable-gram from Yoshida informing us that he has booked passage and should be in San Francisco about 9 November 1951. He has asked us to meet him there or some other predetermined city with the paraphernalia. We must make plans and firm up arrangements very soon. Any suggestions you might have will be appreciated, Ragnor." The Showatachi made careful notes, got out the mucilage bottle, and resealed the envelope.

On Friday 24 September, Falcon Zavala was at his covert early on. The Showatachi were punctual as expected. They assumed their cover in the great red cedar. As soon as the delivery truck had passed from sight, the short one darted across the road, sorted the mail, and stuck a couple of envelopes in one pocket. He then pulled an envelope from another pocket and laid it on the top of mail inside the box.

When they were out of sight on the road to San Rafael, Falcon walked down to the box, took the top piece, and placed it in his shirt pocket. The remaining mail he carried loosely in his hand until he reached the grungy old Ford and drove back to the Ragnvold Home Ranch. He gave the stack to Jubal, and then pulled the letter from his pocket and said, "Look what was on top of the pile."

Jubal ripped it open, read it quickly then handed it to Falcon. "Guess this confirms our suspicions?"

"It would seem so," replied Falcon.

"Looks like I need get back to Albuquerque and do some networking. In fact, it is urgent enough that I should leave as soon as I can throw my gear in the clunker. But I'll keep you informed, by phone of course. It appears that too many gentlemen are now reading other gentlemen's mail."

AGENT TO AGENT

After Agent Branin explained the purpose of his call to the Albuquerque Bureau phone operator, she excitedly exclaimed, "Special Agent Falcon Zavala has just returned from a surveillance operation near Bluewater. It involved two Japanese operatives and postal theft. I'm sure he will want to talk with you. I will ring his office."

After introducing himself, Agent Branin explained why he had called, then relayed the information that Eddie Oshima had provided. When he had finished, he asked, "What do you think?"

Zavala replied, "It looks to be a perfect match." When he had explained the mail surveillance at the Ragnvold Ranch RFD Box, he asked, "Do we have cause enough to set up a full-blown surveillance and sting operation? After all, they are illegal aliens conducting illicit operations in our country."

Branin replied, "Certainly. You should start the setup from your end, and I will clear it through the regional office. Then I will bring two more agents to help with the operation. Oh, one other problem, what should I do with Oshima?"

"Perhaps you should bring him along. He may be able to supply additional useful information. But if he should prove to be a problem, we can toss him in the hoosegow here. One final consideration, I feel that it would be more effective if we can keep the planned surveillance a secret from the Americans involved, for as long as possible."

THE SHOWATACHI MOVE

What a night of sleep. Watanabe was thoroughly at peace in San Rafael, but he knew it was time to move on. He roused Tule, and then put water on to heat for tea. He removed the front stove lid and placed the heavy cast iron skillet directly above the blazing cedar to heat. He removed tortillas, queso, and huevos from the coil-top Frigidaire. It would be a sumptuous breakfast. He was becoming a connoisseur of Southwest Mexican cuisine. Deep down, there was an underlying sense of loss. This would be his last meal in the adobe home, where he had felt more contentment than any other place he had ever lived. They ate slowly savoring every bite, then sipping the strongly sweetened black tea.

They dug up the money box, loaded their few belongings into the truck and drove north toward Route 66. They constantly turned the dial on the little radio, but "Get Your Kicks on Route 66," just wasn't priority for any disc jockey that morning. A few miles south of Blue Water, they pulled off the road to change a flat tire. Just as they got the spare on and threw the flat in the back, an old farm truck stopped in front, blocking their way.

Δ

It was a few days after agent Zavalla had uncovered proof of mail tampering that Jubal and Gun happened upon the green Chevy truck along the Blue Water road. "Should we stop and lean on some operatives now?" ask Gun. Jubal immediately wheeled the farm truck to block their exit. The brothers jumped out and ran to confront the Showatachi.

Tule and Watanabe were out of the Chevy immediately. Tule grabbed a kendo bamboo from the truck, striking Jubal with a migi-men to the left temple, dropping him like a sack of oats. Meanwhile the brutal Watanabe had subdued Gun and pulled him into the cedars with the intent of interrogating him concerning the sword coverts. To Tule he bellowed. "Get that idiot out of sight."

He turned his attention to the younger Ragnvold. "Well my friend, now we learn where you have hidden the swords." With the back of his hand he slapped Gun across the face. The blow felt like it had been delivered with a cudgel. Gun was no wimp, but this was no after school fight. He struggled to turn over. Watanabe let him turn, then grabbing Gun's hair in his left hand, he drew the iron hard fingers of his right across the throat. The younger Ragnvold knew exactly what he meant. Still his struggles were in vain.

Meanwhile, Jubal, who was an older but smarter fighter, had recovered from the *migi-men* and broke loose from Tule. Jube knew the shotgun behind the truck seat was their only hope against the martial art of Watanabe. He broke for the truck, not realizing that the other opponent was closer than he.

The yell from Tule caused the Brutal Bird to drop Gun and tackle Jube.

Realizing Jubal was probably the better informed one, they used their belts to bind his hands and feet, carried him to the truck and tossed him in. With Watanabe watching their prisoner, Tule drove to the nearest unused road and followed it into the woods. In a secluded spot they jerked Jube out and after a few substantial kicks the Bird began the interrogation. "Now you miserable lackey, where have you hidden the swords, that rightly belong to Showa?"

The silent form received another boot. Watanabe continued, "Are both swords hidden together?" By now multiple broken ribs made it nearly impossible for Jube to breath. He thought, *The concealment of two swords, even kokuho, can't be worth a broken rib through my lung, There's still a chance we can protect the swords even if these ronin know.* "

Jube could barely whisper. "One sword is at Ragnvold ranch the other at Turtle Cienaga." He blacked out from shock and pain.

The Showatachi knew most of what they needed. *Best be on the road before the brother rounds up some law enforcement.*

Within the hour Gungnir and a deputy sheriff found Jubal and headed for the Gallup hospital. Their course would not have been altered, even if they had known the Showatachi was thirty minutes ahead on the same road.

CALL FOR REINFORCEMENTS

In Gallop, they rented a room in Mexican town; then walked back to the business district to find the Western Union. With money in hand, they hurried along auto row to see what was available. At first, they were set on a new vehicle, but along the way, they became infatuated with a 1950 Hudson Hornet with a two-toned paint job; it looked fast and powerful. For 1,300 dollars plus title transfer, they considered it a bargain. Each was anxious to drive it first. So the salesman flipped a coin, and Tule drove it off the lot.

They drove to the outskirts of town and practiced driving the newly acquired power machine. When they had found their confidence, they drove back into town. They negotiated with their landlord to rent a rundown adobe shed. There, they parked the old truck out of sight, behind heavy plank doors. The casual passerby would never know of its existence.

With the logistics of pursuit largely taken care of, Watanabe decided they needed to make plans on how to proceed. "Tule, you have had more dealings with Americans than I. How should we proceed from this point? Our biggest obstacle is lack of knowledge of the exact locations where the Kokuho are sequestered. Furthermore, our information from the postal box seems to have dried up or has been deliberately planted. So talk to me."

Tule replied, "I agree, information flow is still our dilemma. We must discover where the swords are hidden and take them directly from their coverts, or we will be forced to wait until Magwitch and the Ragnvolds remove them in order to return them to Yoshida. In the latter case, it seems we would have to watch both ranches constantly and at the same time. Perhaps we are spread too thin. I would suggest it is now time to call that phone number Roku gave you in case of extreme emergencies. We need reinforcements, immediately!"

As they walked toward the business district, they decided it might be more prudent to try a cablegram first. That way they would be less likely to catch Roku at an inopportune time. It would also give him time to consider options. A phone conversation could always be used as a follow-up. With these considerations in mind, they stopped at the Western Union. Watanabe tried to word the cable as succinctly and innocuously as possible.

> "Roku (stop) can't keep up with all our friends (stop) Yoshida due to arrive in near future (stop) gifts will be moved soon (stop) gifts appear to be in separate locations (stop) need help with observation and acquisition (stop) a second team would simplify problem (stop) advise (stop) signed Watanabe."

Watanabe told the operator where to deliver the return cable. Then they stopped by a market to stock up on travel rations and liquids, in case they needed to act swiftly. They also purchased another handgun, a .45 caliber semiautomatic, with several boxes of cartridges. Once home, they spent the day fashioning weighted kendo sticks from lengths of bamboo found behind the furniture store.

In early evening, a Western Union delivery boy, pumping hard against the gravel and ruts of Mexican town, finally handed a copy of a cablegram to Tule, who was in the front yard still working on his kendo.

> "Watanabe and Tule (stop) will send second team now working Salt Lake City (stop) they have auto (stop) wait for them in front of Western Union day after tomorrow (stop) important to obtain gifts before Yoshida arrives (stop) Roku."

They waited across the street from the Western Union most of the morning on the second day. Finally, a rather ragged-looking sedan parked directly in front. Two men got out and looked around. When they spotted the Hudson and those within, they nonchalantly crossed the street. Watanabe spoke, "Mattemashita, we've been waiting for you. Get in your car and follow us out of town, where it will be safe to talk." North of town on the Navajo Reservation, they pulled off the asphalt into a secluded area. Watanabe, obviously the senior man, took charge introducing himself and Tule. The new men responded with their names, Showa Ichiban and Showa Saku, obviously the artistry or Roku.

"For convenience, we will just use Ichiban and Saku, said Watanabe.

When he learned the new team had a spotting scope and adequate supplies, he focused on the tactical objectives ahead. "Since we lack information on possible rendezvous or hand-off arrangements with Yoshida, it will be necessary to play it by ear." He turned to Ichiban and said, "You and Tule will watch the Magwitch Ranch for any indication of sword removal. Your responsibility is to follow whatever vehicle might be used in transport. Most likely, it will not be their old farm truck. In any case, you will be absolutely responsible for that sector. Meanwhile, Saku and I will take responsibility for activities at the Ragnvold Ranch."

With a few more words of instruction and caution, Watanabe put Tule and Ichiban on the road to Turtle Cienaga. Then he and Saku drove past the Gallup lodgings to pick up a few needed items before hitting the road to Bluewater. They were wary about parking near the RFD box, so they pulled into another cedar thicket a bit further along. Then on foot, they followed the wooded cover, southward up the ridge toward the ranch buildings, stopping frequently to check their position, as well as looking for the optimal surveillance point. Finally, they selected a spot a little southwest of the house that commanded a good view of the access road from the north as well as the canyon leading upward to the southwest into the Ashiwi Mountains. Here they settled in and took turns watching and napping.

Meanwhile in Lino County, Tule and Ichiban were just approaching Lino County Seat. Tule said, "It's less than twenty miles to Turtle Cienaga. As we draw closer, it will be necessary to watch for a spot to hide the auto and have cover for our surveillance. It should be on this side of the ranch and the west side of the road, hopefully not too inaccessible."

They could not yet see the ranch when Tule suggested turning off on a rutted range road. It led over a low malpais covered ridge and into a broad volcanic sink, perhaps half a mile in diameter and forty or fifty feet lower than the surrounding plateau. Ichiban found a small clump of cedars where he parked. They grabbed the scope, some water, food, and blankets, and then headed south to the crater rim, where hopefully they would be able to watch the ranch and its access. As they settled in to watch, Tule warned Ichiban to keep the scope lens out of the sun to prevent it from acting as a signal mirror that might reveal their position. They each scanned the broad panorama before them. They then settled into a routine of watch and nap. Through the remaining daylight, the only activity at the ranch seemed to be Mag and his hired man Paco repairing fences. With darkness, the vigil became more boring. Finally about 10:00 p.m. when Tule was just about to doze off, he saw the lights of an auto pull up near Mag's house. As the car turned to park, Tule noted a distinctive violet glow from the taillights. With the powerful light gathering capabilities of the spotting scope, he could tell that it was a 1948 Ford coupe. One man got out and went in the house. Perhaps an hour later, two men came out. One was carrying a small wooden casket and a longer scarcely discernable object. A second man carried what appeared to be a long white stick. *It's the shirasaya!* thought Tule. He quietly shook Ichiban. "They are loading the sword now." Ichiban looked through the scope as the shirasaya was handed into the car. The Ford pulled away, but the house lights continued to burn.

Tule and Ichiban hurried as quickly as possible to their car. Once on the road, they drove rapidly until they were able to discern the violet glow of those lynx-eye taillights in the distance ahead of them."

Δ

Back at the Ragnvold Ranch, Watanabe and Saku were experiencing their own excitement. Near twilight, a strange car they took to be a Plymouth drove past the ranch house, then as far as it could go up the canyon toward the southwest. Two men got out with shovel and flashlights and walked another half mile before they disappeared behind a pile of rubble on the canyon slope. Perhaps thirty minutes later, they reappeared with the shovel, flashlights, a small wooden box, a long canvas wrapped object, and similar-length white stick.

"The shirasaya," exclaimed Watanabe. He was so excited he almost forgot to let Saku observe through the scope. They grabbed their gear and hurried down the long ridge to where the Hudson was parked. Those in the Plymouth must have lingered at the ranch, since Watanabe and Saku were in their car waiting well before the Plymouth pulled out of the ranch and onto the Bluewater road. Still, they waited until the sword-carriers had time to get through town and on their way north, before pulling out to give chase.

In the meantime, the Ford coupe was making good time over the sandy road between County Seat and Witch Wells. Ichiban, driving the ragged sedan, was having a hard time maintaining the pace. They were probably eight minutes behind when the lead car turned east on Route 66. However, they caught sight of the lynx-eye taillights before reaching Gallup, easily following the Ford's turn onto the Shiprock Road. A little north of Gallup, the Ford pulled up at the Little Bear Trading Post. Ichiban and Tule quickly pulled over, not wanting to compromise their surveillance. They waited well back in the shadows.

Tule turned to the new man. "Do you think this might be a rendezvous?"

Ichiban replied, "Seems likely, so we'd better hope the other Showa see us in time to pull up. Fortunately, the other blade runners will not recognize this car, but Saku should spot us immediately."

RENDEZVOUS

It must have been an hour before the Plymouth pulled up and stopped on the far side of the Ford. The occupants of the two cars conversed briefly; then three of them walked into the lighted trading post. The fourth man remained, ostensibly to guard the nippon-to. Fortunately, Watanabe and Saku, who had been tailing the Plymouth with the Hudson Hornet, saw that Tule and Ichiban had pulled off well back in the shadows and they were able to swerve in behind. What they didn't see was a fifth auto pull off, even further back.

When the Showatachi could not ascertain any movement by the guard, they thought it was an opportune time to make an attempt on the swords. The four Showatachi moved stealthily toward the parked transport cars. At their near approach, Blaz Carvajal leaned from the open window to blow a shrill warning on a police whistle. From the post burst Magwitch Russell and the Ragnvold brothers Gun and Ragnor with newly purchased shotguns, blasting birdshot over the heads of the scurrying Showatachi. Mag jumped in the Plymouth with Blaz, and they dug out. The Ragnvolds followed in the Ford to provide a rear guard.

The Showatachi now followed at a respectable distance. Still further back in the fifth car, Special Agents Zavala and Branin joked about the shotgun barrage and their fear that the "Sword Protection Society" would not be able to care for itself. Still, they knew that a serious showdown was apt to occur, and they must be prepared. Even so, the road that lay ahead would be longer and more tiring than they had anticipated.

By the time they reached Cortez, Colorado, it was essential that they obtain gasoline. Blaz pulled the Plymouth into a modestly lit service station. Gungnir pulled the Ford along the other side of the pumps. Magwitch and Ragnor jumped out and ran into the shadows behind the cars and the station. They held that defensive position, while the attendant filled both cars. Apparently, the Showatachi had become more wary and had given up a sizeable buffer.

As the Showatachi waited at a safe distance behind the fueling operation, they held a brief operational conference. Watanabe said, "It appears that the gaijin have hedged their risk by transporting the nippon-to in separate vehicles. Obviously, we will have to divide our efforts if we are to obtain both swords.

"However, it now appears that the most likely place for them to rendezvous with Yoshida will be in Utah. Do you know of a good spot for us to meet after our attempt on the swords, whether we get them or not?"

Ichiban responded, "There's a secluded spot called 'Rock Canyon' in the southern Wasatch Range that Saku and I have used on occasion. It would be a good place to 'hole up' for a few hours or perhaps even a day or so. Both Saku and I know how to find it."

Saku then said, "Spanish Fork Canyon below Soldier Summit would provide a long lonely stretch of road with excellent spots for hijackings."

Watanabe again exerted his leadership. "Tule and Ichiban you will now take the Hornet. Somewhere just beyond Soldier Summit, you should pass the Ford so as to be in position to take out the Plymouth, which is now the lead vehicle. Saku and I will follow in the old sedan and care for the Ford with the violet taillights. In the first action, we will take out the second car, like Sergeant Alvin York's strategy in a turkey hunt. Once you see our lights disappear, take out the Plymouth at the first suitable spot. Afterward, we will meet in Rock Canyon, which both Ichiban and Saku know."

When the Sword Protection Group moved on, the Showa filled up at the same station. Much later, as they pulled through Soldier's Summit in the wee morning hours, Gun Ragnvold was surprised when a powerful Hudson Horned zipped around them and pulled in behind the Plymouth. He said to Ragnor, "It looks like the Nips are going to make their move. So be ready for anything." They were scarcely past the summit when a second big sedan pulled around and fell in behind the Hornet.

"What the hell is going on?"

HIJACK

"Better back off a bit," Ragnor said. A scarce eight miles had been covered when Gun slowed for a nasty curve. A ragged sedan pulled alongside and, with a sharp swerve, knocked the Ford over the embankment. Gun fought for control. The coupe didn't roll, but with the abrupt stop at the bottom, his head struck the steering wheel. He blacked out.

In his groggy recovery, Gun was shouting for Ragnor. There was no answer. He felt for the shotgun. It was gone. The only response was from a surly, cracking voice: "Get out of the car." He continued to fumble for a weapon, *any kind of weapon*. He felt a sharp nip in his left arm. He lunged outward. Then he felt the cutting tear of the tanto deep into his shoulder. He looked upward into a cruel, buzzard-like face of a tall Japanese-Ainu that he already knew too well; then blacked completely out.

Further down Spanish Fork Canyon, three other vehicles were choreographing their own ballet. The FBI surveillance car had backed off a bit to enjoy the *pas de deux*, before it became necessary to turn the action into a *pas de trois*. Then suddenly the heavy Hornet pulled in front of the Plymouth and decelerated rapidly. Blaz jammed the brake petal to the floorboard but still slammed into the rear bumper of the Hornet. Just as swiftly, the FBI car pulled in front blocking all movement. Mag stepped out and leveled his shotgun right at Tule's face. This action was followed by Agent Zavala's disarming of Ichiban. While the agents were cuffing the assailants, the Ford coupe sped around and was soon out of sight down the canyon below.

In the speeding Ford, Watanabe turned to Saku and said, "You will need to tell me how to find Rock Canyon. We must lie low somewhere and wait for Tule and Ichiban to come to us. We can only hope they are able to get away from the mess they're in and bring the other nippon-to."

The roads through Utah County were a frustrating maze of city streets, farm lanes, and ninety-degree turns. Watanabe was becoming increasingly agitated with Saku's attempts at navigation. Finally, they were on Canyon Road, and the younger man was relieved when he recognized the rocky entrance leading up into the rugged Wasatch Mountains. They followed a questionable road not really designed for passenger cars. Tires crunched over sharp rocks. Axels clumped down on granite boulders. It seemed the oil pan was constantly dragging. They wondered if any oil could possibly remain in the system. Finally, the little Ford could make it no further. At that point, others had also seemed to fail. To their relief, someone had cleared rocks and brush from a spot large enough to turn around in. Here, Watanabe backed into the turnaround and stopped.

He slipped out of the driver's seat, pulled it forward, and yanked the wounded Gungnir out of the back, throwing him onto the rocky road. Gun groaned in pain, but didn't seem to gain consciousness. The Brutal Bird then kicked him hard in the ribs and turned immediately to search for the temple swords. *Nothing in the back seat*, he thought. He yanked the keys from the ignition and opened the trunk. There were tools, food, water, and blankets, but no shirasaya containing a Muramasa blade. No Hachiman Taro. No Firstborn of the God of War. He kicked the unconscious Gungnir again. "We've been duped," he shouted at Saku. "Let's get out of this canyon before we become trapped. I have enough cash to get us to San Francisco. I'll call Eddie and tell him to make arrangements for transport to Japan. Tule and Ichiban will have to take care of themselves."

The false dawn was just a faint grayness above the canyon as they climbed into the Ford and started down the rugged declivity. Gun was left behind, bent backward across the edge of a sharp boulder.

Back in Spanish Fork Canyon, two separate dramas had been unfolding. Tule and Ichiban, in handcuffs and shackles, were forced into the back seat of the surveillance car. There, Tule was re-cuffed to the leg shackles of Ichiban. It would be uncomfortable, but it would keep them both out of mischief. It was decided the prisoners would be taken to the FBI office in Salt Lake City. There, the agents could set up an all points manhunt for the other illegals and their probable hostages.

Fortunately, both nippon-to were in the Carvajal Plymouth. He would follow Magwitch in the Hornet. The FBI vehicle, with the cuffed and restrained illegals, would follow behind Carvajal to act as rearguard. Mag would keep the shotgun, in case of another hijack attempt. It was assumed that the Ragnvolds were prisoners and probably hostages of Watanabe and Saku because of the way the Ford shot around them as they made the arrest early on.

Meanwhile, just a few miles up the canyon behind them, Ragnor Ragnvold had finally succeeded in loosening the cords that bound his hands and feet. He was deathly cold and continued to shiver involuntarily as he stood beside the dark roadway. Several vehicles passed him, afraid of the rumpled stranger standing in the darkness. Finally, a state trooper coming from Helper pulled over. Even though the trooper was warm, he turned up the heat for the shaking Ragnor, while extracting his story. Once he had the description and license number of the Ford, he called the dispatcher to issue an alert.

On the road further north, beyond Utah Valley, Watanabe and Saku saw the airport exit sign pointing west from Highway 91. Once they had their tickets, Watanabe attempted to call Eddie from a pay phone. The number rang and rang. Finally he hung up in disgust. "Where's that Gypsy gone now?"

While Special Agent Branin drove, Zavala monitored police radio frequencies. Thus, he was able to obtain the frequency of the Utah State Troopers and talk with the dispatcher from whom he learned that the alert for the Ford had already been called in by a trooper who now had Ragnor with him. There was apparently no word on the whereabouts of Gun. The dispatcher also provided Zavala with the FBI frequency, where he could initiate the master manhunt. Just as the three cars arrived at the FBI, word was received that the Ford had been found in the Salt Lake Airport parking. From the terminal ticket sales, the FBI quickly learned that two Japanese men had boarded an early morning flight to San Francisco on United Airlines. With flight number and arrival time, Agent Branin notified his office to pick up the wanted aliens. Still, they had no knowledge of Gun Ragnvold's whereabouts or condition.

GUNGNIR, SWAYING SWORD OF ODIN

21 September 1951

The phone rang in Deseret Athilstan's room at ten minutes of eight Friday morning. At first, she was irritated. She had planned to skip breakfast and run to her 9:00 a.m. lecture. But by the time she answered, she was almost civil and somewhat reconciled to the imposition. She thought, *I needed to be up anyway.*

"And, good morning to you." The authoritative male voice on the line startled her. "This is Captain Huck Snow, Bonneville Police Department. We have a Gungnir Ragnvold here, who has given us your name as a local reference. He gave his residence as Bluewater, New Mexico. However, he was found on Canyon Road early this morning by a local farmer who brought him to Valley Hospital unconscious and with a serious injury to his shoulder. He seems unwilling or unable to tell us much about what happened to him. Perhaps the shock and sedation are still affecting him. If I send a car for you, would you be willing to help us?"

By this time, Deseret was shaking so much she could scarcely hold the phone or answer the question. Finally, she blurted out, "I guess so." A roommate, hearing most of the conversation and without imposing her own questions, hurried Dessie into the shower and helped her dress. The police car was waiting before they were finished. And she declined the pastry offered as she went out the door.

The hospital staff had moved Gun into an empty room where Officer Snow was sitting quietly reading a detective magazine. Gun appeared to doze fitfully. Snow put down his magazine. "Thank you for coming. I believe he will feel more at ease with you here. I will leave you to talk privately. But I will be outside the door, so when you think he is ready to help us find the perpetrator, call me."

Dessie approached the bed. She gently touched his outstretched hand and said, "Gun, can you hear me?" His bloodshot eyes opened, and he took her hand.

"Thanks for coming. I've had a rough night, and much of it is still unclear in my mind. Have you heard from Ragnor? We were traveling together last night when something happened in Spanish Fork Canyon. For some reason, I can't figure it all out."

She shook her head and took his hand again, saying, "You were probably unconscious for much of the time and in shock even when conscious. Why don't we ask Officer Snow to help us sort things out?" Gun slowly nodded his head.

When Snow came in, Gun said, "I'm sorry that I can't provide you with a coherent narrative. My last clear memory was that my brother and I, along with two friends in a separate car, were bringing two Shinto Temple Swords of great value to Yoshida Nobu in Salt Lake for their return to the Shinagawa Temple, Sengaku-ji. These swords are well known to the international black market. Rumor has it that the Showa Brotherhood has been offered a cool million dollars for each of these."

Officer Snow gave a low whistle.

Δ

Little by little, the Bonneville Police were accumulating enough details to formulate a cogent story. Snow returned to his office, where he placed a number of calls. The first was to the Department of Public Safety. "This is Captain Snow, Bonneville Police. We have an injured man by the name of Gungnir Ragnvold in Valley Hospital. He was in an incident in Spanish Fork Canyon last night, but we can't seem to tie him in with much. I figured you would be the closest thing to a command central of information flow and might be able to clue us in."

"Yes indeed," replied the dispatcher. "We have been looking for a Gungnir Ragnvold. But it would save time if you spoke directly with the Salt Lake Office of the FBI. Ask for Special Agent Zavala or Branin. You might also tell Mr. Ragnvold we found his Ford in the airport parking. It has some big dings but appears to be drivable. We should be able to get it to him in a day or so. Thanks for the info."

Snow was immediately on the line to the FBI. There he was connected to Falcon Zavala, to whom he relayed the pertinent information about Gun. This included the injured man's concern about the swords. "Thank you, Captain Snow.

We have been greatly concerned about Gun Ragnvold. The attempted hijacks were the work of a Japanese secret brotherhood called 'Showatachi.' It is a brutal group, and we feared he might have been executed. For young Ragnvold's peace of mind, tell him his brother is fine and that we have both swords. The mix-up may have occurred during the first hijack attempt at the Little Bear's Market in Gallup. There his brother Ragnor and Blaz Carvajal placed both swords in Carvajal's car. Ragnor must have forgotten to tell him."

Snow related the good news to Gun.

OSEI FUKKO, RESTORATION

From their room in Hotel Utah, Yoshida Nobu and his assistant, Nao, looked down upon a temple structure, different in design from any they had ever before seen. No torii marked its entrance, although a high wall surrounded it together with its companion structures. Most notable was a great oval structure, roofed by an elliptical dome. They might have gazed longer into that singular compound had they not been anticipating a most important phone call. Still, it was mid-afternoon before the phone finally rang.

"Hai," Yoshida spoke into the handset.

"Yoshidasan, this is Blaz Carvajal. How are you? And how was your trip?"

"Well my friend, the trip was fine until I learned about your trouble with the Showatachi. I hope Ragnor and his brothers recover all right. It was disheartening to learn that Jubal was still in the Gallup Hospital with such serious injuries that he could not be with us. Have they found his younger brother yet?"

Blaz replied, "Yes thankfully. Gun is in a hospital in Bonneville and seems to be doing well."

"I am greatly relieved," said Nobu. "I have brought so much trouble upon my American friends that it is difficult to face you. All the same, let me be the first from Nihon to offer my congratulations to you on attaining your doctorate of medicine. Hello, Doctor Blaz Carvajal e Mendizaval."

Blaz replied, "I thank you Nobu, but how in the world did you remember the complexity of all those syllabic sequences and make them sound almost human?"

"Ah, my friend, you forget that I am a would-be linguist, and no language on Earth suffers more from convoluted syllables than Kokugo, which is my native tongue."

"You can forget the syllables for now. We have much sharper instruments to deliver. We should be at the hotel in less than fifteen minutes. I suggest we meet in your room for security reasons. In addition to Ragnor, Magwitch, and myself there will be two special agents of the FBI, but don't worry, they are quite unlike the old Kempeitai. Their main purpose, since mitigating the attempted sting by the Show-atachi, is to get you and those national treasures back on a ship to Japan."

It was a solemn but pleasurable reunion. Yoshida Nobu bowed deeply to each of the five. Each in turn attempted some degree of obeisance, but only Blaz and Ragnor managed the deep salaams of their revered mentor. Nobu said, "My friends, I must borrow a term from Tenno Meiji, the so-called Emperor of the Restoration, 'Osei Fukko.' For we who serve the Lord Buddha at Senguku-ji, this will be an even more 'glorious restoration.'"

Blaz and Ragnor, with considerable nostalgia, recalled their days of enlightenment under the firm but gentle guidance of Yoshida Nobu at the Spring Hill Temple of Lord

Gautama Siddhartha, the Supreme Buddha and Surpassing Being of Enlightenment.

But Mag was more interested in talking about how they slipped two national treasure swords out of Shinagawa right under the noses of Showa in the beautifully carved crutches that now adorned the walls of Turtle Cienaga Ranch. But most joyful were Nobu and his assistant Nao when they took the ancient blades from their shirasaya and realized they were still in perfect condition. No corrosion marred their sublime finishes.

Only then did the "Unofficial Sword Protection Society" relate in detail the happenings of the previous night and the details of sword sequestration five years ago, as well as the efforts of the Showa Brotherhood to obtain the Nippon-to over the past several months. Then Mag realized that they had failed to mention Gungnir's contribution and the fact that he had been seriously injured and was in the hospital in Bonneville. When they were fully briefed concerning Gun's condition, Nobu expressed his gratitude.

"My friends," he said. "We owe all of you so very much." He took from his case four sheets of exquisitely textured rice straw paper on which Japanese characters in broad-brush stroke calligraphy spelled out a citation from Japanese Prime Minister Yoshida Shigeru. From the top sheet, Nobu read:

FOR EXTRAORDINARY SERVICES RENDERED
ON BEHALF OF JAPANESE PEOPLE

IN THE PRESERVATION OF TWO
NATIONAL TREASURES—

THE MASAMUNE NIPPON-TO, FIERY
BLADE OF THE ENDURING COMET

AND THE MURAMASA NIPPON-TO,
FIRSTBORN OF THE GOD OF WAR,

I, YOSHIDA, SHIGERU, PRIME MINISTER
OF JAPAN DO OFFER THIS ENCOMIUM.

IT IS WITH HEART FELT GRATITUDE THAT WE
OFFER THIS TOKEN OF ACKNOWLEDGEMENT

OF YOUR SINGLE PURPOSE VALOR AND INGENUITY
IN THE FACE OF CONTINUED ADVERSITY

TO THE END OF THEIR SAFE RETURN
TO THE SHINAGAWA, SENGAKU-JI.

Nobu checked each to be sure he handed it to the correct recipient. To Ragnor, he handed a second for his brother Jubal and said, "Sorry I don't have one for the third Ragnvold, but it will be sent as soon as we return to Japan.

"Now for all of you, including Jubal and Gungnir, whom I look forward to meeting, please reserve the first three weeks of April 1952. During that time, all Imperial decorations will be awarded. The five of you will be honored on that occasion. You will be the guests of Japan. We will arrange all your transportation and other accommodations. And as a special tribute to Magwitch, Blaz, and Jubal, who spent brutal years in POW camps, all of you are invited to visit historical and tragic sites in the Philippines as well. Start planning your calendar forth-with."

At this point, Special Agent Falcon Zavala cut in. "As the rest of you discussed topics only peripherally meaningful to Branin and me, we have decided to make a few suggestions from the edge. If Mr. Yoshida and Nao are amenable, we would be happy to babysit the swords for a while, probably take them to the FBI office here, so Blaz, Magwitch, and Ragnor can take Nobu and Nao for a drive through the Wasatch Mountains and out to the Great Salt Lake, perhaps have dinner at Saltair. Meanwhile, we will put pressure on local law enforcement to speed up the sale of the confiscated Hudson Hornet and move Gun's Ford coupe from the airport to Bonneville.

"Then on Monday morning, Agent Branin and I will drive Nobu, Nao, and the temple swords to San Francisco and put them on the ship ourselves. We will even arrange with the purser or the captain himself, if necessary, to provide extreme security for the swords until they reach Japan, where the Prime Minister's office can take over that function. It is doubtful that even Showa would be bold enough to challenge the central government there at this time."

ARIGATO MATA YO

Jugatsu 1941

By the end of October, Gungnir had stored his fully restored and overhauled 1948 cranberry red Ford coupe in a shed along the east side of the Ragnvold Ranch barn at Bluewater, New Mexico. He drove a smooth running, if battered, Ford pickup truck for his archaeological surveys of cultural sites along the Continental Divide and Colorado Plateau for the University of New Mexico.

His brother, Ragnor, drove a two-toned 1950 Hudson Hornet, confiscated from Watanabe Hattori by the Utah State Highway Patrol. His was the only bid. Ragnor is currently working on a medical degree at Johns Hopkins University.

Watanabe was extradited to Japan and is now serving time in the Sugamo prison, where Tojo Hideki was held until he was hung as Japan's number one war criminal, 23 December 1948. Tule Minoru was sent back to Japan but seems to have slipped through the cracks. Best guess would be that he is back in the States, running some kind of Ponzi scheme.

As for Eddie Oshima, the Kibei interrogator, he resides in the Sweetwater Valley near San Diego and is well on his way to becoming a millionaire grower of sweet corn and strawberries. Seems he had to perform some kind of social service like telling kids about the evils of being an interrogator for the Japanese.

ZUIHO-SHO, ORDER OF THE SACRED TREASURES

March 1952

The "Unofficial Sword Protection Society," plus three wives, left the San Francisco port of embarkation, sailed through the Golden Gate, and took the great-circle route across the widest reaches of the Pacific Ocean. The Philippine Islands were their initial objective. Magwitch and Blaz had first embarked upon this same roadway through the sea more than a decade earlier. On 6 January 1941, the 200th Coast Artillery, New Mexico National Guard was inducted into the US Army. On 10 September 1941, they sailed through the Golden Gate on their way to Manila to help defend the Philippines. Jubal Ragnvold followed them shortly, only to end up on Corregidor Island instead of defending the Bataan Peninsula. For all three, it would become the longest four years in their young lives.

As their liner docked at North Harbor, Manila, it seemed like one hundred years had elapsed since the three warriors first viewed this skyline in November 1941. In many respects, they were old men. But their lives had been and were still full.

That afternoon they took a harbor cruise. The guide pointed out the spot where the cruiser Tenno Maru had been scuttled by orders of the Golden Lily in an attempt to conceal the looted treasure in four hundred feet of water. The guide assured them that Ferdinand Marcos either recovered or would recover that golden hoard. But the real gold mined that afternoon was the treasure of memories shared by Jubal Ragnvold as he recounted the defense of Corregidor to deny the Jap use of Manila Harbor until 6 May 1942, twenty-one bloody days after the fall of Bataan. Nor did he fail to grind on that latter point to the consternation of Mag and Blaz.

But the next day belonged to the sheepherder and his blasphemous friend who was always looking for the sheep that Blaz was supposedly herding. As the driver followed the route of the Bataan Death March from Mariveles through Pilar to San Fernando and Cabañatua, it was in some ways a repeat of the living hell they had gone through, but in no way would they have been willing to forgo the profundity of that abyss. For some reason, there was a deep reluctance to leave; yet their schedule forced the issue.

Three days later, they were in Tokyo. Their guide had taken them through the Fujimi-Yari, that is, the Fuji View Keep. This was the most distinctive tower or castle keep remaining from medieval Japan. To their surprise, a southwest breeze off the Inland Sea had cleared out enough of the urban air pollution to allow them a view of the distant sacred mountain. From there, they negotiated their way northward across the Imperial Gardens to the Kyuden, where a crowd was gathering for the presentation of *Jugun Kisho*, military service medals, and Order of Merit, also known as the Paulownia Sun.

Prime Minister Yoshida Shigeru stood on a slightly raised platform in order to place an Order of Sacred Treasures, Third Class, with Grand Cordon around the necks of Magwitch Russell and Blaz Carvajal. Blaz understood most of what the prime minister said as he conferred the medals. "It gives me profound pleasure to bestow upon each of you the Order of Sacred Treasures for your heroic efforts in saving two of our most sacred Kokuho, national treasures of Japan. The symbolism portrayed on each medal is derived from so-called 'Imperial Treasures.' First of these treasures is the *yata,* or mirror that is represented by the central blue stone bearing an eight-pointed star. Second is *yasakani,* the jewel, represented by fifteen red enamel dots. Third is the sword, even the emperor's personal sword, represented by sixteen white enamel rays."

Suddenly, Blaz realized the Imperial Treasures represented on the medals just received were parallel to the classes of votive offerings given to Shinto Temples. The values of which had been explained so carefully to them by Yoshida Nobu back in 1945. "The mirror represents the reflection of our true selves, the quality built into our own lives. The sword represents power, the power of purification. The jewel represents warmth, the effulgence, and fecundity of Amaterasu, the Sun Goddess herself."

As the ceremonies continued Yoshida Nobu was asked to make the presentations to the other three. They also received the Order of Sacred Treasures, Third Class. However, Jubal's was with the Grand Cordon. Ragnor and

Gungnir received the same medals pinned directly to their jackets. Blaz watched Ragnor as Nobu read the representations of the Imperial Treasures. The glimmer in Ragnor's eyes and the smile upon his lips convinced Blaz that his friend had understood what Nobu had voiced. Then Nobu explained that those receiving the Grand Cordons were so honored because of their internment as POWs in Japanese camps.

At the conclusion of the presentations, Nobu caught Magwitch and handed him a package. "For you Mag, who bore the brunt of getting the nippon-to out of Japan, as well as your efforts in sequestering the Hachiman Taro. This ancient tanto is but a small token from the Sengaku-ji of Shinagawa. It is a mate to those given to Blaz and Ragnor before they left Japan back in 1946. In case we are unable to talk again, they know the details concerning its design and maker. Thank you so much for your generous help. The Johkai Priest sends his thanks as well. In fact, he selected the piece himself."

Tough, old Magwitch lowered his eyes to conceal the tears. He whispered, "Arigato, mata yo. Thank you, we shall meet again."

BIBLIOGRAPHY

"What Is Amida Buddha?" Dr. Nobuo Haneda. No date http://www.livingdharma.org/Living.Dharma. Articles/WhatIsAmida-Haneda.html

Rank Structure and Insignia of the Imperial Japanese Army War II Era," J. Stevens, This Homepage, Copyright 1997, Isiu Island Provisional Infantry A Division of the Military History Education Association,http://patriot.net/~jstevens/Isiu-Island/ranks.html

Bronowski, Jacob. 1973, *The Ascent of Man*, Boston: Little, Brown and Company. (Shinto ritual and sword metallurgy, pp. 131–133)

Christie, Manson & Woods International Inc., 502 Park Ave., NY 10022, *Important Japanese Swords, Sword Furniture and Works of Art*, Auction Catalogue, November 5, 1982, (illus. tsuba hand guards pp. 8–79, menuki pp.124–127, tang inscriptions pp. 132–183)

Conlan, Thomas D. *Weapons and Fighting Techniques of the Samurai Warrior* 1200–1877 *A D*, New York: Metro Books, 2008, (Kendo pp.14–17, 66–71)

"Masamune & His School," Meito Kansho, no date, www.jp-sword.com/files/masamune/masamune.html

"Muramasa," Ratti, Oscar and Adele Westbrook (1991). Secrets of the Samurai: The Martial Arts of Feudal Japan, Tuttle Publishing, p.236. ISBN 0–804–81684–0, Undated 4 January 2011. http://www.en.wikipedia.org/wiki/Muramasa

Feifer, George. 1992, *Tennozan the Battle of Okinawa and the Atomic Bomb,* New York, Ticknor and Fields

Flake, Lester W. 1981, *The Remnant*, Mesa, AZ: Limited private printing. (Defense of the Philippines in World War II, Bataan Death March, Hell Ships and American POW's in Japan)

"The 47 Ronin," compiled by F.W.S., no date, http://www.samurai-archives.com/ronin.html

Fox, Steve. 1994, "Sacred Pedestrians: The Many Faces of Southwest Pilgrimage," *Journal of the Southwest*, Vol. 36, No.1 (Spring)

Golden, Arthur. *Memoirs of a Geisha*, New York: Vintage Press, 2005

Hawley, W. M. "The Japanese Sword: A Basic Guide to Collectors," pp. 258–273, *Guns of the World*, NY: Bonanza Books, 1977

Huang, Joseph. "Japan's Destiny–Yet To Be Fulfilled," http://www.hope-of-israel.org/japdest.htm (The Master Race, "The Japanese people were created on the islands of Japan, and are a superior race supporting an unbroken dynasty for all ages— quote from *Through Japanese Eyes, p.* 16)

"Jinga Shinto, Shinto Priesthood," jinja.jp/English/s-4b.htm (Johkai)

"Jomon Period in Japan," nbz.or.jp/eng/prehistoric.htm (Jomon and Yoyoi)

"Kokka Shinto," thefreedictionary.com/Kokka Shinto (State Shinto)

Nappen, Louis P., "Famous Blades that Never Existed," K*nives* 2007, Northfield, IL: DBI Books Inc. (Gungnir, Odin's Sword p. 8)

"Nippon-to," michionline.org/resources/Glossary

Seagrave, Peggy and Sterling 1999, *Yamato Dynasty: The Secret History of Japan's Imperial Family*, NY, Broadway Books, 1999 (Golden Lily)

Sotheby Parke Bernet Inc., 1334 York Avenue, NY 10021, *Important Japanese Swords, Fittings and Armour*, Auction Catalogue Tuesday, May 5, 1981

Storry, Richard. *The Way of the Samurai*, NY Galley Press, 1978

"Sukashi Tetsu Tsuba," shibuiswords.com/BITsuba1.htm

Tadako Keen. "Translation of the tang inscriptions from the author's Shin Gunto," 1976 (used the terms: *katana*-m*ei* [side closest to the body] on which the era and date were carved, and *tachi-mei* [side away from the body] which held the signature of the sword smith. Auction houses sometimes use the terms: "face" and "reverse" in the same sequence.)

Tanner, Hans (ed.) *Guns of the World*, NY Bonanza Books, 1972 (illus. Arisaka Type 99 Rifle, Nambu Type 14 Automatic Pistol and Baby Nambu pp. 186, 262)

"Tokyo Record, 1943," Quote from *Through Japanese Eyes* p. 16

"Tsuba Gallery," shibuiswords.com/tsuba.htm

"Type 94 and Type 98 Shin-gunto Tsuba/Seppa," stinger-scott.com/Export25.htm

|LIVE

listen|imagine|view|experience

AUDIO BOOK DOWNLOAD INCLUDED WITH THIS BOOK!

In your hands you hold a complete digital entertainment package. Besides purchasing the paper version of this book, this book includes a free download of the audio version of this book. Simply use the code listed below when visiting our website. Once downloaded to your computer, you can listen to the book through your computer's speakers, burn it to an audio CD or save the file to your portable music device (such as Apple's popular iPod) and listen on the go!

How to get your free audio book digital download:

1. Visit www.tatepublishing.com and click on the e|LIVE logo on the home page.
2. Enter the following coupon code:
   9a52-49b4-9aa4-29e4-660f-a1cd-3bef-0fc4
3. Download the audio book from your e|LIVE digital locker and begin enjoying your new digital entertainment package today!